Cult of
the Vampyr

K. R. Rubin

Nancy—
These guys
give a whole
new meaning
to the word
"Shredder"

KR Rubin

PublishAmerica
Baltimore

ISBN: 1-60672-690-0
PUBLISHED BY PUBLISHAMERICA, LLLP
www.publishamerica.com
Baltimore

Printed in the United States of America

Dedicated to my mother Kathi, for teaching me the love of writing, as the best way to tell your story.

Cult of the Vampyr

Ben Ruden, after graduating from State University, returns to his hometown to start a new life, in a new job. Upon purchasing an old church as a home, he is abruptly awakened to commotion in his new neighborhood that is just the beginning of events that will change his life forever. Ben discovers that several teenagers are disappearing, all under the same mysterious circumstances. Out of sheer curiosity, Ben decides to look deeper into this phenomenon. He quickly learns of a long defunct Cult, which has recently been reformed. Ben and a small band of townsfolk called "The Nine" may be Haven Hills or even humankind's last line of defense against "The Final Harvest."

By Kevin R Rubin

Cult of
the Vampyr

Prelude
The Legend Ontolli

It is three years after the British laid their arms down against the colonials from America, due to their overwhelming defeat at Yorktown. Since England's defeat, fog has seemed thicker and rain appears to come more often and stay longer.

The legend begins one foggy summer's eve, in a small England town, located off an old, now-weathered, unused pier. The awe-inspiring sight of the Queen Mothers majestic ships that used to dock here are but distant memories. The fleet is down to a handful of spice trader ships that, although in major disrepair, are still sea-worthy. As we make our way off the pier, we start to travel down a street consisting of fieldstone roadways. Lanterns hanging off the sides of the many little shops and homes are barely enough to illuminate the craggy outlines of the store fronts, all the while reflecting in the many puddles peppering this ancient roadway. Due to the soupy, billowing fog, the lanterns appear to cast a dim, yellow halo around the little pools, forming a path lining the streets. Up two blocks, in the second story of an old boot maker's store, aptly named 'THE HEAVENLY BOOT…we put our sole in every boot we make', is a small apartment, and currently residing there is the Ontolli family…

It's dark out. The rain won't stop. It's been raining all day. I'm trying to sleep, but dad's home and I can hear him hollering at mom. I know he was hurt in the war, but whenever he drinks, he yells at or beats up mom. I've never been able to help her. He's always been bigger than me. I tried once, and he floored me. He says he needs the booze to cope with the pain, mom says he does too. She ALWAYS forgives him. It just isn't right. I'm big enough now to go help mom, but she never lets me. I leave tomorrow to go to the United States to work for my Grandfather. He runs a very successful antique import/export business. He says that Americans are starting to enjoy our English Victorian furniture and rug styles. I've been well educated, and can converse in Americas' form of English as fluently as I can articulate our Motherland's.

Well, Grandpappy always said, a real man has to stand up for what he believes in, I recall as I pack my meager belongings. So, sorry Dad, before I leave you're going to get what's coming to you.

I make my way into the kitchen. Dad is standing over Mom. She's collapsed on the floor, cradling her face in her hands, crying. Dad, in just his pants and tank top undershirt, is holding a bottle in one hand, and making a fist with the other. He's yelling at her at the top of his lungs…something about the vino being the wrong brand or flavor or something.

"Papa. Please stop this now. You've made your point. Leave mother alone."

He spins around; spit splatters form his mouth as he tells me to shut the hell up. He approaches me, clenching his fist hard enough to turn his knuckles white. Oddly enough, I sense the move he's going to make, or at least guessed it. I immediately dodge to the left, his fist flies by me and cracks up against the wall, plaster crumbles to the floor, leaving a section of boards and mortar bare. He drops the bottle and grabs his injured hand. Gritting his teeth, he calls me another name I don't much care for. I reel back, and turn his head with a right hook to his jaw. He stumbles momentarily, and I step up to catch him as his legs give way. I pull his putrid, wine soaked face to mine and simply explain that I will indeed return, the moment I hear that mother is hurt again. I make it quite clear that, whatever pain he causes her will be returned on him tenfold. For every bruise, he'll receive a broken bone, etc. I drop him to the cold tile floor. I go to help mother up. Instinctively, I catch her weak hand as she attempts to slap my face. She yells at me for daring to strike my own father…and breaks down again crying. I hug her, tell her I love her, and head to the boat docks without a backward glance. I'm heading out one day earlier than I'd planned, but I figure I'll just sleep on the dock, and board the boat in the morning.

It is said that every man makes at least one life-altering decision. For some it's marriage, for others it's having children…and for others, like me, it's leaving a single night earlier than planned. The difference is, my decision led me to meet Antoine Cadrebra, definitely an Italian, Sicilian I believe. My father and he had to be the only Italians in England at this time.

I'd never met, or even heard of this man prior to that evening on my twenty-fifth year of life. I'd made it down to the docks. The rain had let up, leaving behind a wispy, gaseous layer of fog that appeared to be omnipresent. It was fascinating, like standing on a cloud, and seeing boats and crates protruding up through the misty night, like some time lost city. I'd found quite a nice spot actually, in between three walls of crates. I prepared to settle in, when I felt a chill run through my whole body. Shivering a little, I turned, only to come face to face with Antoine. He was a tall fellow, slender mostly, with an olive complexion. His hair and eyebrows were black as midnight, he was quite clean-shaven. His hair was a bit long, not for those days, but by today's standards. It was pulled neatly back into a ponytail. He appeared to be around twenty-five or thirty perhaps. He was wearing a stark black fog coat. He looked quite the gentleman I must admit.

"Kendall, are you ready for your destiny?" He asked.

"And that would be?" I replied, quite calmly I might add. I was surprisingly sober for such a meeting.

"To join the ranks of the immortals. Those who command the night?" he smiled, and brandished quite a mouth full of choppers. Quite unsettling, I assure you.

"I would have to pass on this offer? That wouldn't offend you would it, Mr...?" I was feeling a bit uncomfortable at this point. His eyes appeared to see right through me.

"Cadrebra. Antoine Cadrebra. At your service." He then bowed to me, and being of little faith in my ability to talk this guy out of whatever his plans were, I decided to swing my bag, with all my strength, at my new friend. It struck him, but unfortunately did not seem to faze him. He callously smacked the bag from my grasp, flinging it off into the fog. I decided to run, only to find him standing in my way at every attempt. I straightened up...and stood my ground.

"It would appear you have me at somewhat of a disadvantage sir. Now then Mr. Cadrebra..."

"Antoine, Kendall. Call me Antoine."

"Very well, Antoine then, how is it you've come to know my name?" My attempt to delay the inevitable was feeble at best, but I was attempting to buy some time. Perhaps a plan would pop into my head, given time.

And indeed, one may have, given the time. Unfortunately, time was, as they say, a luxury I wouldn't be afforded on this foggy eve.

"Kendall my boy, this is the eve of your final passage. You are to embark on the journey of the immortals! You have been chosen to become one with the night! Rejoice boy! This is to be your final destiny!" Antoine raised his arms, spreading his trench coat, which blocked out most of what little light there was.

My heart began to race, sweat formed on my brow, I began to panic as he brandished his fangs. Suddenly, and without any reason, I decided to dart to my left. As I did this, Antoine reached for me at my right. I was able to step around him. As I broke free, I started to yell for someone, anyone, to come to my aid. Unfortunately, the only one who showed up was…Antoine.

"Kendall, why fight it? It WILL happen. You are as a newborn human babe, refusing to come into the world, out of the safety of the mothers' womb. Yet, it is simply because you aren't yet aware of the wonders that await you! Come Kendall, be mine, and join me on my journey to dark perfection." Antoine reached out his open hand, palm up. As if I would just grab it and bare my throat to this monster…yet, I was beginning to become curious. Immortal he said, master of the night. What could this mean? Would it be so bad?

A picture flashed in my head, a scene actually. I saw Antoine grabbing me and biting deep into my neck. I saw the blood dribble down and stain the collar of my shirt. I fight, but eventually my body goes limp. Antoine looks up and smiles. His bloodstained teeth appear black in the absence of moonlight.

I turn and run, I don't want this scene to take place. It's as if I saw into the monsters brain, into what he pictured the night turning out…and I wanted to avoid it at all costs. It could have easily been my imagination running wild, and normally I'm quite calm, but this was just too eerie for me. And the scene seemed too real. As I run, I see again in my mind, that Antoine runs ahead of me, and waits for me around the corner of the third stack of crates. I don't know why I envision this, but choose to act on it, on the off chance there's something to my hunch. I turn at the first set of crates and sprint with all my might, hoping I won't run directly into the arms of this…demon. As I continue running, I taste nothing but the salt in the air from the water. I begin to grow angrier at the thought of being treated as a plaything, like a cat that's caught me like a mouse, and holds the tail, letting the mouse struggle at getting away.

I finally reach a building; I grab the old door by the iron rung, and pull with all my might. And, true to form, it wouldn't budge. I have another flash, I see Antoine standing behind me. I slowly turn to see that my flash was correct.

"No! Damn it man! I haven't the desire to become your eternal companion!" I blurt out so violently, spit leaps from my mouth.

"Pardon me Kendall? I didn't ask that, sir." Antoine looks at me in shock.

"But you…I just heard you…didn't you say…" I didn't know what to say.

"It is what I was thinking however, and I've decided that you will indeed join me. I must admit, you gave me quite the chase, but shame on me for expecting any less, from one who will rise again."

"I suppose begging is out of the question…Antoine…sir…I beseech you…let me go, find another, please?"

"Don't lower yourself thusly, Kendall. I merely bestow the gift of eternal enlightenment, I am but the messenger. You are Kindred already; I merely need to finalize the transfusion. You are ready to elevate to your true position as one of the masters." Antoine smiles and moves in toward me.

I start to struggle, but in an instant I feel the pain of his fangs pierce the flesh of my neck, starting as any stab wound would, but then, as I feel some of my very life essence ebb from me, my whole body warms, and every limb and extremity tingles. What a short, horrible life I'd thus far lived, and it flashed before my eyes. I began to tire, feel lethargic; my arms seemed to weigh a ton each. I no longer felt the pain in my neck; in fact I started to feel extremely excited. Actually, sexually turned on. Not toward Antoine, I've always preferred the fairer sex, but the feelings that rushed over me where overwhelming, quite enjoyable really. It's kind of like when you wiggle a loose tooth, a very pleasant-almost pain. This continues for quite a while, longer than ever before. As suddenly as it comes, it stops. My stomach starts to tighten; my insides act as if they'd been set aflame from within.

I hear…or at least think I hear Antoine say; "You're mortal shell dies now, and you will be reborn." Although, I'm not sure how he'd say that with my throat in his mouth. Aaaaargh, the pain stabs at me, at every fiber of my being! So much agony, like knives ripping through every part of my body. I can hear my heart beat, coming like thunderclaps. My head throbs in unison with the beating of my heart. I scream out, I can't hear my own scream. Damn this demon! I can feel my self-dying, how do I know? All I can say is, you definitely know when you're body is failing. I suppose you have to experience it to know. I fall into a deep slumber, darkness quickly overtakes me. I succumb to a sweet bliss of darkness. I fall into obscurity's arms as if it were my own mother. The cold, nothingness embraces me as if I were her favored son. I suddenly feel a shiver, and open my eyes. Hunger pains stab at my stomach. As my vision clears, I can see it must be morning, I can see very clearly. I turn my head and see Antoine perched over me like a bird of prey.

"Welcome Kendall, newest ruler of the night. You have been born again, to rise alongside those who have risen." He smiles, and I no longer fear him. This creature that frightened me to the core of my being no longer scares me; in fact, I almost felt a certain kind of kinship.

"How long have I been out, what time is it…?" I stop and realize that it's still night, I can simply see so much clearer now. I can feel that I've changed. I don't feel cold or warm, tired or rested, simply hungry.

"I hunger Antoine."

Antoine smiles and scrapes his fingernail along his wrist, blood bubbles out; I immediately latch onto his wrist and drink. The salty warmth tingles on my tongue, fills my mouth and smoothly glides down my throat. I feel my strength returning, I feel invigorated. The pleasant feelings are, again, akin to sexual pleasure. Apparently, it's as satisfying for the drinker as the victim. I don't want to stop, the warm liquid satisfies my every urge, but there's more, my aura feels regenerated, my spiritual self feels whole again. Antoine rips his arm away from me. He collapses to his knees, grasping his wrist.

"E…Enough…you can't over do it, it's dangerous for us both." Breathing heavily, he smiles at me.

Dangerous? I went through more emotions and feelings in the last…however long it's been, than in the last several years of my life. This bastard bit me! He killed me and brought me back. Dangerous indeed! I'll show him dangerous!

Admittedly, as tired as I feel, I feel energized as well, not unlike playing a full game of football, after scoring the winning goal.

I feel his hand on my shoulder; I turn and await his question.

"Kendall, where are you going? I expected you'd stay here with me." He looked puzzled, but carried himself quite well.

"I fear not Antoine. I've things to do in America. I thank you for your assistance, but nothing more. Good eve, sir." I turn to walk away and hear

Antoine talk about striking me from behind, I turn and still I hear his threats. But, his mouth is not moving as he speaks...wait...I get it now...he's THINKING it, and I'm picking it up. Fascinating! I suppose I've always had this gift at some lower level, similar to deja-vu.

"No Antoine, you're in no condition to attack me right now. I owe no obedience to you sir, I am kindred. You are NOT my Sire, only those who have risen before, do I owe any obedience to. Be smart Antoine; find yourself another victim to make your little Thrall. Again, good eve, sir!" I smile at my own brashness. Hours ago, this creature of the night could have broken my neck before I saw him coming, and now, I feel as though I could snap his.

I swing around to see Antoine gone, but I still hear him thinking. He's on the boat, awaiting me. How'd he get ahead of...oh, he's a flyer. He actually flew to the boat...I can almost feel the rush of wind that blew against his face as he flew...everything he felt I can sense. How does this work? How can I do this? Well, I'd best not waste my advantage. Very well then. I decide to let the proverbial cat out of the bag.

"Antoine my boy, your thoughts betray you sir. Be careful seeking revenge on one who is your better." It's kind of a rush to be toying with this man, as he did me earlier. I believe I can empathize with him; he sought out a mate, I understand now, a mate when one is Kindred, is not defined by human standards. During my humanity, a mate would be a female for me, as a male. For those of us who rule the night, a mate is one to share existence with, for you feed off one another, to energize one another. Any so-called sexual gratification is attained by feeding on a human, male or female.

I wonder now, how I can know all this? T'was but an hour or so ago, I knew none of it, including the very existence of such creatures of the night. I find myself almost feeling sorry for Antoine...almost. I mean, he did attack me and turn me against my will, but I have a much deeper understanding of why he did it now. You see, eternity is a long time and no one wishes to face it alone. Imagine outliving any whom you learn to love or even grant friendship too. You never age, all your friends and loved ones die around you, forever. I have read of Vampires, and they've always seemed so cold, uncaring, and unemotional. Now I can honestly say that I understand why. Any who have been betrayed by someone they let in, one time too many, grows callous toward all others, and will refuse to let anyone in. Does this mean...I'm never to let anyone grow close to me again? Must they be Kindred to live as long as me? Are there more Kindred out there? How will I know?

Well, my new found ability, perhaps this will allow me to know whom I can trust. I wish to know even more about my abilities. Perhaps Antoine can guide me? Am I being to hasty in my judgment of him? He did attack me, against my will! I clearly need to know more.

Well, I suppose I should walk up the ramp, where my 'surprise' awaits me. As opposed to an all out battle, I believe I'll try the gentlemanly way first.

"Antoine, my friend, I'm aware of your pending sneak attack. Please, sir lets not resort to fisticuffs. Come down and let's discuss this like gentlemen."

I hear a flutter behind me, spin to find Antoine standing behind me; his coat covers all but his head. His once neatly pulled back hair is a bit mussed up now. His facial expression screams of betrayal. His eyes appear hopeful, yet his visage demands revenge. I believe he is quite confused, angry, and even hurt.

"Antoine, I beg of you to understand...I must go to America, people are expecting me. I could learn a lot from you, why not join ME, and go there." I extend my hand in hope of a favorable response.

With a speed that surprises even me in my new state, Antoine swats my hand away, and slashes at my throat. Immediately I raise my hand and catch his by his wrist. Somehow, I knew that would be his next move, though I'd hoped differently.

Slowly I twisted his wrist forcing him to the ground, his once overwhelming strength, was barely enough for him to attempt to stop me from tearing his arm off. His forehead began to form larger, Cro-Magnon like eyebrows; his mouth and teeth start to protrude out, almost animal like. I can see the bone structure change under his skin, to resemble…well…a bat face I guess. His eyes go flat yellow, with no pupils. As this transformation ends, with a sudden burst of strength, he throws me, and I find myself sailing through the air, and smashing into a wall of the ships cabin. I immediately leap to my feet, and feel the anger building up in me. My vision turns red; I feel the muscles and bones of my face twist and contort. I let out a growl, and leap to meet Antoine in mid-air. We lock in each other's grip, and in each other's eyes. We smash down on the decking. We both scramble to our feet, never taking our eyes off one another.

"You will NOT make a fool of me boy! If you won't be mine, than you will be no ones!" Antoine hisses out.

"Stop! I implore you Antoine, don't force me to destroy he who brought me through!" I believe I saw a tear swell within his eye, but no sooner did I see this, that I saw Antoine look behind me, and then leap at me. Before he met me, I see a broken wooden cleat, for tying off the boat when you moor it. In my mind's eye, I see Antoine forcing me back onto this wooden cleat. As my vision dissipates, I react by side stepping his attack, catching him by his mid section and slamming him down on the cleat that is behind me. The broken part pierces into his back and protrudes up through his chest.

"I…I'm sorry Antoine, you now endure the fate that you had in mind for me."

"Ken…Kendall…your gift is that of foresight, use it to lead…the Harbinger will seek you out…you must prepare…Damnation! I wished for us to share in The Final Harvest…damn…"

Antoine closes his eyes, jerks one final time, and I turn and walk away.

* * *

It would appear that until I learn more about my newfound condition, it would be wise for me to go below deck. Upon arriving below deck, I find a relatively stocked storeroom. It's stacked from floor to ceiling with bags of grain and barrels of liquid. I'm able to these objects around to form a nice little retreat for myself. I figure it best to attempt to get some rest, and try to figure out all that has transpired. Sleep doesn't come easy, Antoine. My mother and father, my Grandpa, and others haunt my mind. I can't tell if I ever actually sleep, but I do know that I awaken with hunger pains.

Muffled voices penetrate my barrier. I decide to investigate. Prior to reaching the area that where the voices originate, I picture two portly sailors. Poorly dressed, unshaven, heathens if you ask me. Oh, well, I suppose I've eaten worse. I cannot believe I think this.

I walk confidently into another holding bay, where these two chaps are taking inventory of the ships supplies. To their surprise, I approach them. I'm calm and quite polite about my request. They, of course, do not respond as cordially as I'd hoped. I have already played the scene through in my mind, so I was aware of their every move, even before they were. It was child's play really. Within mere minutes, I had fed on these hapless lads. I felt quite wonderful really. However, before I could enjoy it, I saw another Englishman enter this hold. He was well dressed, well groomed, quite the opposite of the two seamen I just fed on. He would appear to be royalty, or an officer at the very least, I'd guess. Only he didn't act as amiable as one would have expected from royalty. Quite to the contrary actually. He actually prepared to attack me. So, obviously, I turned to defend myself.

This red clad gentleman, with his powdered wig, which is a quickly going out of style, moved far too quickly to be human. Although I foresaw him striking me, still did his phenomenal speed take me a bit unawares? The first blow went to him.

The force of his strike sent me twisting through the air as a rag doll would, smashing full force into a stack of barrels full of…fish. By the Dark Gods, the smell was putrid. Here I sit, with dead fish lying all around me, and my clothing soaked in fish water. I suppose it would have been quite a sight. As the Englishman chortled at the scene, I did indeed catch a glimpse of his fangs. A jolly Vampyr, this one is. His error? He stopped his attack to survey his handy-work.

Quickly, I darted across the room. Before he could react; I clamped him by his throat and locked onto his eyes with my own. He attempted to tear my hand free; he was contemplating attempting to claw at my face with the elongated nails of his right hand. I immediately latched onto his right hand and began crushing it in my own. I continued to pull his face closer to mine. When we were but inches apart I spoke; "William…Bill…I have decided to allow you to live. Your blow was well struck, I respect that. Do, however, remember this; you will never again be given an open shot."

"How do you know my name? Who are you, old boy?" He choked out, grimacing, somewhere between a smile and pain.

"Kendall Ontolli, and I know your name because your very thoughts betray you."

"William Wetherton the III. And how do you mean that exactly?"

"Exactly, sir. It is indeed, exactly as you are thinking it works."

"A mind reader? What a wonderful gift! I say, could you release me now?"

"I could sir, and will. Were I you however, I wouldn't try it again."

As I release him, he immediately lunges at me, with a simple side step; I grab him by the scruff of his coat and smash him down onto the ground. Pinning his head, face down onto the hard wooden planks of the floor, I lean closer and speak;

"Billy, I'll not warn you a third time. You will become my mentor, and you will do so on my terms. If you ever defy me again, the Undead Elder Gods themselves will not be able to protect you from the fate I have planned for you. And no, your 'dream walking' gift shall not be of any assistance to you."

I release him, and he shakily gets to his feet. He smiles as if unshaken, but his thoughts are of pure terror. He now knows who is master.

"Yes, of course Kendall. I believe we'll become fast friends, you and I. What would our plans be then, sir?"

"We go to America. The rest you'll learn as we go along. Sir William, together we shall become instrumental in ushering in "The Final Harvest!""

Chapter One
Sleepless

I startled to a quick, although foggy consciousness. My bedroom was varying between pitch-blackness, bright red, and deep blue. I've got to tell you, this was quite disorienting at first. As I got my wits about me, I could hear voices from outside, through my open window. After just minutes, I decided to throw off my warm, safe quilt, and put my bare feet on the cold wooden floor. As I did this, I recalled last Christmas, when my brother Russ sent me a pair of big fuzzy slippers, pink of course, and being a guy, I had to throw them away. Russ was my younger brother. He and I were the only survivors of a car crash that killed the rest of my family some years ago. This made us close of course, but we still live two distinctly different lives.

Anyway, in lieu of wearing them and risk being seen, I now had the pleasure of putting my bare flesh in contact with a highly polished parquet floor that, according to my feet, must have registered in the low teens, which is, of course, below freezing. Just to prove how accurate my feet are to registering the temperature, understand that since as long as I can remember, I've always slept with one foot out from under the covers as a temperature gauge.

As I made my way across my bedroom, watching with a little amusement, as everything I own flashed from red to black, to blue and back again, I finally reached my heavily painted window. It took me three hours with a hammer and paint scraper to finally loosen it enough to open it about ten inches, and after that, I wasn't about to close it again, no matter how cold it got. I then silently cursed at myself for liking it "a bit nipply" as Russ would brilliantly phrase it. Ten inches was just enough to fit my head out, and as I did, I hadn't realized just how cold it had gotten, or how accurate my temperature gauges actually were, (oh, for a nice warm pair of fuzzy slippers.)

As soon as I stuck my curious head out the window, the bitter cold stung my eyes and nose; this sent a shiver down my spine that shook my whole being. I swear, even my nostril hairs froze together. Luckily, only my head was facing the elements.

My room is one of two in an older, one and a half story white church. It wasn't much, but not bad on an insurance salesman's straight commission. My two bedroom hovel was quite a buy, even in a town on the upswing of tourism, where property values should have been sky rocketing, but instead were quite stagnant. This didn't dissuade people like me who grew up here, and were returning to start a new life or continue the one's they'd already started.

Upstairs it contained two bedrooms, a bathroom, and a large closet connecting the two rooms; this must have been where the pastor and his assistant slept. As you descend down the back stairs, there's a partition or false wall hiding the staircase. The only door is a curtain in the right, back corner. This old servant's stairway leads into what must have been a kitchen of sorts; an old stove and plenty of cabinetry still existed, and was in pretty good shape. Being single, I normally eat out or order in. I've added a newer refrigerator, the kind with the ice and water in the door, of which only the water works, and a large table, actually built out of old pews, my personal handy work. In exiting the kitchen, you enter a large open area, obviously where the services were held, but is now just a huge great room.

I recall as a youth, coming to services here, and listening to Pastor Frank, who I nicknamed Frankenstein, and always being enamored by the large leaded glass window at the entrance of the building. The cross was almost as colorful as my room was when I woke up. I decided to keep the leaded glass window, because I just felt that I should.

My father used to say "We're going to listen to FRANKLY FRANK, because he tells it as it is." Pastor Frank was an elderly man, hair black as night with gray sides, looking more distinguished than old. He was a man of thin build, but always appeared stable and strong. His voice, though a little raspy with age, was commanding in its own way. I'd heard, that about two years after I left for the big city, a large church 'The First Church Of Havenhill' was built and quickly grew to a congregation of five hundred members that put old Frank out of business. Oh, my family and a few others continued coming for a while, but old Frank decided to throw up his arms and retire.

I pretty much littered the big room with unmatched furniture; some older tables and a super cool entertainment system including a 64" big screen TV and major speakers! The old cherry double pocket doors and stained glass window remained undisturbed.

As I rubbed the sleep from my eyes, I made out three of Haven Hills finest, in full uniforms, and apparently a plainclothes in a trench coat, standing in the background, with a couple cruisers parked across at the Peacocks. All their lights were flashing, and a small crowd of people, mostly all neighbors I recognized, gathered around. Judy Peacock seemed quiet, wrapped in a gray blanket, being comforted by Officer Malley, and

John Peacock was the voice that startled me awake. He was up in arms about something, and we all heard about it!! The poor rookie cop, whom I didn't recognize, was getting the brunt of the old army sergeants' full wrath!! Quickly, I dressed myself and grabbed my coat on the way out the door, feeling, for the first time, the full icy embrace of the midnight air.

* * *

I immediately slowed down after exiting through the old wrought iron gate that surrounded my little front yard. As I stepped onto the glazed black pavement of E. Church Street, I was careful not to do a graceful face plant onto the street. In my excitement to see what was happening, I slipped on a pair of loafers with soles as slick as the ice-coated pavement itself. Trying to go relatively unnoticed, I quietly clip-clopped across the street to the Peacocks.

The Peacocks were your average American family of a mom, a dad, a teenage son, and a teenage daughter. They even had a golden retriever named Candy. Judy was a stay at home mom, as close to a TV Mrs. Cleaver as you can get, and John was a retired army drill sergeant. Sgt. John was about 6'2", stocky, and wore his red hair in an army issue crew cut to match his walrus like mustache. Very few people challenged this man to anything, except for his wife of course, who seemed to be his soft spot. Of course, I'd be lying if I said his teenagers didn't challenge him once in a while. Overall though, from what the neighbors have told me, Mike and Sarah are pretty nice kids. Sarah was the brain of the family, she was the kind who would take S.A.T's simply for the practice, and beat her old score. She was a little awkward and skinny, but had a smile that lit up her little freckled face, that you couldn't help but return the smile. Mike on the other hand, did not inherit his fathers red hair or skin pigmentation, but rather has stark black hair, with an almost olive complexion like his mother. He did manage to receive his fathers' physical side, which made him a great linebacker for Havenhill High. Mike was well known around town, and a good apple overall.

As I made my way to the group of neighbors, I made out the face of Jeffery Stockton through the fog of several peoples frosty exhales. I new Jeff as a kid, we were never close then, but since I came back, he's been very friendly and helpful.

"Hey Benjy, what kept ya?"

"Hey Jeff, what in the world has got ol' sarge Peacock in such an uproar?"

"Well, near as I can tell through all the yelling, there was some sort of accident with Mike."

"You mean like a car accident or a football accident or something?"

"Yeah, a car accident."

Sarge Peacock raised his volume another notch at the poor rookie cop, who, like anyone, cringed at the volume of this man's voice.

"...and what in the hell do you mean you can't find a body! Then he's probably hurt, laying somewhere, while you're standing here making excuses as to why I should continue paying my taxes, to pay your paycheck, because it's too damn dark or cold or whatever other sorry ass excuse you can come up with!!"

The rookie cop, Officer Beatty according to his jacket, was playing by the book; "Sir, we're doing everything..."

"You're not doing a damn thing but pissing me off! Now get in your nice warm squad car and find my son!"

"I assure you, we are making every..."

As if to strike Beatty, 'Sarge Peacock raised both of his massive arms, and guillotined them down on the hood of the police cruiser, causing a thunderous explosion, leaving two craters the size of watermelons in the hood. This was enough to stir ol' Officer Malley to enter the commotion.

Officer Malley was an older Irishman, with a temper to match his famed heritage. I've never witnessed his temper, but it's the stuff of legends I'm told. This would have appeared to be an ideal time for Malley to go off, but to my surprise, he allowed his years of training to take over. Officer Malley calmly sauntered over to the much larger 'Sarge Peacock, and, without even a hint of anger, smiled and stated;" Now John, I don't think wreckin' this fine cruiser, that yer tax dollars paid fer, will help us find yer boy."

Officer Malley calmly laid his weathered hand on the 'Sarge's shoulder and said; "Look boyo, let's you and me go back to the site of the accident and see what we can't figure out, eh?"

The 'Sarge, who's visage dropped from anger, to the innocent look of a man who, maybe for the first time tonight, has received a slim ray of hope, just whispered "I just need to know about my boy, that's all."

"We'll get 'er done tonight, ye have my word." The old Irishman smiled kindly, and they both climbed into the dented cruiser, and slowly turned west, down Church St.

Wow, this is like, my first few months back here, after graduating from State U., and I almost immediately got hired by Lifelong Insurance. I've spent most of my days and evenings convincing people to pay for something, that they will never get to see the benefits from. Probably, my favorite question to ask is "So, tell me Mr. Husband, will your widow, be as well taken care of as your wife is now?" What a colorful variety of responses I get from that one.

Other than working and fixing my new home, I get to shoot some hoops with my buddy Jeff once in a while, and watch HD sports on my big screen. It's funny, Havenhill seems so much smaller than I remember, and quite a bit less exciting. I suppose that's what is making me feel all giddy right now. Finally, something exciting, although I hope everything turns out ok.

As the commotion calms down, most went in for the night, a couple of the lady neighbors went in with Judy Peacock, and Jeff Stockton and I simultaneously caught each other's gazes. With a quick smile, we understood each other perfectly, and both ran to our houses.

Chapter Two
My First Taste

I immediately pulled out my favorite pair of blue jeans; they're the kind with flannel lining. I also pulled out a thick t-shirt and my old State-U sweatshirt. My, gray, red-toed wool socks and Timberline hiking boots almost completed the ensemble. My black and gray, thinsulate ski jacket, and old Raiders ball cap were the finishing touches on my 'Let's go adventuring' set up.

As I prepared to join my erstwhile comrade, Jeff, I hesitated...thinking about grabbing my Beretta semi-auto, just in case. I then remembered that the police would be there, so it probably wouldn't be necessary.

Being an insurance salesman, there are times that I carry large amounts of cash, like deposits for policies. One of my clients, an old coot named Rusty Ferber, was the kind of guy that was sure everyone was out to get him. He constantly ranted and raved about people not being what they seemed, but rather that people were out to get us all. He wouldn't buy a policy from me, but he did sell me the semi-auto for $1. He said that if I promised to watch my back, and never trust anyone, I could have it for a buck. I couldn't very well pass that up.

I exited my home, locked the large wooden doors securely, and turned to walk to my car. As I spun around, I almost knocked Jeff off the stairs.

"Wha…well, excuse me Jeff, let's go. By the way, take a breath mint will ya? I normally have to buy someone dinner before we get that close!"

As we ventured to the car, a newer, thin layer of snow was crunching beneath our feet.

We sat in my burgundy, 1992 Grand Am, I could feel my cold seat stiffly give way under my weight. I, of course, opted for the charcoal interior, with the leather sports package, and moonroof. As I flipped on the lights, I had to wait a few minutes for the windshield to defrost.

"What do you suppose happened, Jeff? Did I hear right, no body was found?"

"Yeah, supposedly, it wasn't in the car or near the wreck."

"That's weird isn't it? I mean, who was driving then?"

"I guess we'll find out, if you ever get us there!"

"Oh, that's where you want to go, why didn't you just say so?"

Jeff looked like a lumberjack in his overstuffed down vest and red flannel shirt. Jeff was quite the hero in high school. He was popular, played all the sports, and even got a scholarship to some junior college, until some knee injury benched him. He's planning on taking over for Coach Dickerson at Havenhill High, when the old man retires. It's funny, Mr. All-American, blonde hair, blue-eyed high school stud, is now sporting darkened hair with blonde highlights, and a goatee to boot.

I shifted into drive and off we went. The roads weren't really that bad, certainly not bad enough to lose control on without alcohol or sleepiness being involved.

"How are the roads?" asked Jeff.

"Not too bad at all." I replied. Up ahead, we saw red and blue flashes, and the heat was just now warming the car to a comfortable level.

"Up ahead, that must be them!" exclaimed braniac. He obviously made it to college on a football, not an educational, scholarship!

"Ya think?" I sarcastically replied.

As I brought the car to a halt, the rookie cop, Beatty approached us and motioned for me to lower my window.

"Yes sir?" I said.

"What are you boys doing out here at this hour?" questioned Beatty.

"Just wondering if we could be of assistance, Mike's our neighbor, and we'd like to help."

"Well, I can appreciate your offer," Beatty replied, "But I think we've all the assistance we need."

"Sir?" interrupted Jeff, "Judy Peacock asked if we'd lend a hand, what should we tell her?"

Beatty started to reply, then turned and headed over to Malley and 'Sarge. Malley nodded yes and Beatty waived us over.

"I didn't hear Judy say that." I smartly said.

"It was implied dude, didn't you notice it?" Jeff smugly grinned.

As we neared the cruiser, we saw Chief Malley, 'Sarge Peacock, Officer Beattie, and two other officers standing over the dented hood of the cruiser. By the time we arrived, two of the officers headed off into the woods with flashlights. The detective or whoever was in the Dick Tracy trench coat and hat must not have come. Malley, 'Sarge and Beatty were holding plastic cups with steam billowing off the top, and a flashlight, being held stationary over a large piece of paper, that appeared to be an area map.

As we stepped into their group, Malley looked up, smiled and said "Lads, it's good of ye to be pitchin' in like this, we're going to be needin' another pair or two of eyes. Ye'll be with Beatty here; I'll stick with John. Beatty, ye've got the ditches on either side, radio if ye find anythin'."

We set off into the usually damp, but now frozen ditches. As Beatty and I took one side, Jeff took the other. After roughly twenty yards, we came upon the wrecked vehicle.

"Can I check this out Sir?" I asked.

"Ummm…yeah, I suppose, we're done with it. Look I'm just going to keep going, catch up, ok?"

"You got it." My voice trailed off as I focused on the vehicle. It appears to have gone off the road, and smashed directly into a bungalow of trees. It took down several saplings, but an old oak, stopped it in its tracks. Looking inside, the dashboard was pressed against the driver seat headrest. If someone were in there, it would have taken the Jaws of Life to cut him or her out. The little 4x4 had a black interior, so it was hard to make out much. As I fished around with my beam of light from my flashlight, I did manage to catch a glitter of some sort. I continued attempting to spot it again, and as I did, I felt a chill slice through me. The glitter was located on the passenger side, back seat near the floor. A coin perhaps? The night was quiet, it's as if the cold dampened any sound. I lifted my head and looked around, I didn't see any body. I saw the cruisers, and heard Sarge bellowing out Mike's name, but it seems so far away, he must really be moving. The cold stings my nostrils, but smells fresh, clean. I make my away around to the other side the vehicle, trying to get a better angle, to see in the back seat.

"Ben…." I hear whispered.

I jump up and stab my flashlight beam all over the place. I can barely hear 'Sarge now. There is no one around. Maybe Jeff is calling for me, not a whisper but a yell from far away. Yeah, that's what it must have been. I walk around the vehicle again.

"Officer Beatty? Jeff?" I call out. I don't hear any answer. It's too damn quiet!

I close my eyes and settle myself. I hear myself breath. I slow down my breathing, calming myself down. I've always been a bit hyper, probably ADHD. You know, Attention Deficit Hyperactive Disorder, or whatever…anyway, I'm thinking usually highly intelligent people have this…

Whoa! A warm breeze on the back of my neck…aw God, what's that smell? I open my eyes and look around again, nothing! The smell has faded away too…yech! That was awful! Weird too, really…a warm breeze? Odd. I shiver again, probably from the opposing warm and cold air, hitting my neck. I suppose that's what scarves are for. I never found a cool scarf though…what the…? Ok…I totally heard something that time…like wind blowing a coat, or something flapping in the wind…but there really isn't any wind…who's messing with me?

"Jeff, come on dude, I think I found something, here in the backseat"

That jack ass! Fine, forget him. I'm going in to the back seat…

I heard someone approaching from behind. Excited, I went to turn and share my discovery, "Jeff, you idiot, look…" but as I did, my sentence was cut short as an icy cold hand clamps around my throat, I could neither speak nor turn my head. I did feel warm breath on the back of my neck that made my hairs rise. That smell is back. I felt the strength of whoever was gripping me as I fought to pull the hand clamped around my throat away. Dropping my flashlight, I used both my hands to try and tear his hand away, but could not budge it.

A raspy, low, yet oddly calm voice spoke the words, "The Final Harvest Approaches." I started to panic and thrash my whole body with all my strength, needing air desperately. I started to lose consciousness as I felt my head be pulled back and quickly shoved forward. I heard a loud thud, and slowly felt a stabbing pain crawl from my forehead down to my chin. A warm liquid started to cover what seemed to be my nose and then my mouth, making it even more difficult to breathe. As I opened my mouth, attempting to inhale, I gagged on what could only be the salty taste of my own blood. In a pseudo state of consciousness, coughing in an attempt to clear my mouth, I fought to open my eyes, and through blurred vision watched as a figure, with blood-red eyes, standing over me now, dark as the night, in a robe or trench coat I'd guess by his silhouette, gracefully stealing off into the night.

I slowly settled into a dreamless slumber, but the words echoed in my head like thunder.

"The Final Harvest Approaches…"

* * *

I felt my self-shivering, this only irritated the massive headache I felt. This was one that felt like a localized migraine, in the front region of my skull. I winced as I realized that, if I was feeling this, then what I recall happening, must have happened. I found my stomach dropping, fearing to open my eyes. I was terrified that the individual that did this to me would still be standing there.

Officer Malley must have seen me stir, for his thick Irish accent was the first voice I'd heard, and I couldn't have been more elated.

"Laddy, are ye with us? Ye took quite a spill, bumping your head a mite. But ye look like ye'll make it."

I struggled to open my eyes. I jumped as I felt a warm, damp cloth press against my face. Soon enough though, I enjoyed its warm embrace. As my eyes were wiped, I could open them, I was on my back, staring up at Malley, and 'Sarge Peacock.

"There now laddy, that's better. What happened and where's Beatty?"

Still groggy, but enjoying the warm water slowly cooling on my face, I blurted out, "There's a…a…metal thing in the Jimmy…and a guy…he grabbed me…I couldn't…too strong…"

Malley interrupted "Slow down now, ye say a feller grabbed ye?"

"Yeah, from behind, by my neck, he said…he said…a final harvest was coming…or something…then he smashed my face into the car door…and ran off…"

"Ok son, let's get ye to the cruiser and warm ye up, an ambulance is on the way."

"NO!" I surprised my self with my violent reaction, "I'm ok, you've got to find the guy, and he ran off…that way!"

"Laddy, I'll cancel the wagon, but let's go in the cruiser and warm up." Malley and 'Sarge picked me up and escorted me to the cruiser.

The cruiser was very warm inside, I grabbed a tissue, because almost immediately, the heat made my nose run and eyes water. "Sir, the guy, are you going to look for him?"

"Perhaps tomorrow laddy, ye see, the direction you pointed in, there were no tracks in the snow, except yours and Beatty's…"

"Jeff! Is Jeff ok?"

"Yes, he's fine, standing outside right now. I need to keep helping to look around, would ye like to come? Or should I ask Pete to stay with ye?"

"I…I'm fine. I'll just stay by the cruiser with one of your guys. Hey, did anyone find the metal thing in the back seat? It was like a pin or disc or something."

Officer Malley smiled, if he didn't believe me, he didn't show it, and said "Laddy, I'll go look fer it right away. Ye relax, and I'll be seein' ye soon enough."

I anxiously awaited the radio response. When it came through though, Malley said there was no such item in the Jimmy. Officer Pete Bandy leaned over and said, "It could have been a piece of glass or something. Don't worry about it."

I slowly started to wonder if what I recall really happened or not. The pain was real enough, even after Malley gave me some aspirin, but the whole story did seem far-fetched. Out of 7 guys, only I ran across this dude?

"Benjy, you ok man, what the hell happened?"

I couldn't believe that the same guy who used to be called the "wedge master" was genuinely concerned.

I related the story to Jeff, and his expression didn't change as I expected. He simply stated, "That's shitty, dude. Hey, why don't I run us home, I'm cold anyway."

"Wait, don't patronize me! Someone did this to me…I saw him! This didn't happen from slipping or anything, a dude, grabbed me and face planted me against the side of the Jimmy!"

"Yeah, yeah, I heard ya bro. Malley said he'll look into it. Let's get home and get some rest; we can figure it out tomorrow. Whoever it was, isn't sticking around with all these cops here, right?"

"Oh, so now you're the calm, intelligent one, huh, Jeff? This is bullshit! Fine let's go. I try to help out, get my face smashed and everyone wants to sleep on it, whatever man. I'd believe you, I'd try to help you find out who did this! I guess we're not in high school now though, huh, you're not big man on campus anymore, it's cool, and I'll just go myself. You go sleep on it…pansy…"

As I try to open the door of the cruiser, Jeff grabs my arm "Look, Ben, Officer Malley told me directly to either take you to the emergency room or home. He's in charge here and he has a gun, remember? I would go find this dude and whoop his ass for you, but I don't feel like getting arrested right now, dig?"

The look on Jeff's face was priceless; my emotional outburst got the exact response I wanted out of him. It angered him, and he's a pretty straight shooter when he's mad. I decided to alleviate the situation.

"Fine, Ok, you're still BMOC, at the Hillcrest Wack Shack, anyway!"

In one of his patented, brilliant come backs, he says "You belong in a Mental Hospital!"

We both started laughing at his ridiculous come back, probably more out of exhaustion, than anything else.

The officer saw us off, and Jeff carted us home. On the way, a light snow began to fall.

* * *

I awoke in a damp sweat in the car upon my arrival home. My sole concern became locking everything up, including my bedroom window. After a couple swigs of Nyquil, I managed to stop shivering enough to pass out.

As I turned over to squint at my clock radio, I saw it was 11:03 a.m. I grabbed the phone, and cancelled my appointments for the day. I only had two re-ups anyway.

I was surprised to find myself a little leery about looking outside my bedroom window, but as I did everything seemed normal, with the exception of the world having been blanketed in a layer of snow. The sun reflecting off the snow was just bright enough to re-start my headache. In the Peacocks' driveway sat the wrecked Jimmy, and an uncontrollable urge came over me to go see if the shiny object was still there or not.

I was still dressed from my previous excursion, so I finished getting ready and headed out across the street. The snow split under my boots, crusty on top, powdery underneath. As I reached the driveway, I immediately went to the passenger side and peered in through the broken window.

I heard snow breaking behind me and immediately spun around, both of my hands clenched into fists, raising them as if to block a punch.

"Hey, Ben, sorry about last night, I hope you're ok." It was 'Sarge Peacock, He appeared as though he had no sleep, the bags under his eyes glared from the sunlight.

"Yes sir, I'm fine. Did you have any luck?"

"Hell no. I...I don't know what's going on. Look, thanks for your effort, take care son."

The old soldier was a broken man. No parent should outlive his or her kid, that's the rule.

I immediately began riffling through the vehicle, and under the back seat, was a medallion. It's chain was tangled in the springs. If the medallion was laying sideways, you couldn't have seen it in the dark. I don't know why I was so persistent on retrieving this item.

The medallion was a circle, about the size of a silver dollar, made of aluminum and sported a skull with elongated teeth, and what looked like insect or maybe bat wings attached to it, in front of a smaller circle. This was probably part of some Halloween costume, or maybe a motorcycle gang or something.

"Hey, Mr. Peacock," I yelled, but received no answer. I went to the front door and knocked but received no acknowledgement.

I headed over to Jeff's place. It was empty; I remembered he got out of work at 4:00pm. I decided to take my prize, and go clean up and eat. In four hours Jeff would be back, and I'd go see him then.

I held the medallion up and said "I got it anyway. And screw you pal!"

Feeling a little goofy, I headed back in.

Over a grilled cheese, (which I'm famous for making) and a coke, I started letting my fingers do the walking. A-ha! It's still in business, "The Archives: Proprietors of the Strange and Old". I figured we'd head there after Jeff came home, excited to get his take on the medallion.

Chapter Three
Legend

The loud thumping of someone knocking upon my massive wooden doors startled me out of my daze. I went to the front door and upon opening them, was Jeff, grinning ear to ear.

"Jeff, what are you doing here? I mean, you work 'til 4:00 don't ya?"

"Dude, whatever, listen coach retired at the high school, I'm going to be the new coach! Cool huh?"

"Congrats, man! But, hey, is coach all right?"

"Yeah, now he is…he had a heart attack, but is recovering quickly."

I've known coach for my whole life; the man was built like a brick wall, ran ten miles a day, and looked thirty, not fifty-two. But I guess stranger things have happened. "Hey, c'mon in Jeff, I got something to show ya!" I handed him the medallion, and as he fixed his gaze on it, he lost all facial expression.

As I was about to ask if he were ok, he looked at me and said, "What is this thing?"

"I don't know, but I found it in Mike Peacocks' car. This was the thing that was shiny, the thing I tried to get before I was attacked. See, it's proof that what I remember was real!"

"Yeah, but dude, no footprints, right? Look, I believe ya Ben, but I say we drop it, and move on. Have you heard if they found Mike?"

"No, I was waiting for you to get home, then I thought we'd go over to Archives, to talk to Mr. Stiltworth."

"Look Ben, that old relic can't tell what this thing is, it's probably just a foreign coin or something." Yeah, I thought, from the castle of Frankenstein or something.

"Jeff, what's up? Last night you were all up for this and now, it's like you've got no interest…"

"Ben…Ben, last night we went to help the cops, I'm sorry you got messed up, but I'm sure it's not exactly like you think it was. Look, let's go to the gym and shoot hoops or something, I still don't start for another week, but I've got the keys!"

"NO! Uh…no thanks Jeff. I got some stuff to take care of, but thanks "pal" for the invite."

As I extended my hand to retrieve the medallion, Jeff's hand closed around it. When I looked away from his hand and into his eyes, he turned away and dropped the medallion in my hand. Why was he being so weird?

"All right dude, your loss. You know where I'll be, IF you decide to drop this nonsense."

As he walked away, I wondered what nonsense he meant.

* * *

I threw on my jacket and jumped into my 'AM, and took off into town. What nonsense did he think I was up to? I didn't say anything other than I wanted to know what this stupid medallion, that I got clobbered over, was. And "IF" it was anything unusual, Stiltworth is the guy who'd know.

Orvin Stiltworth was the town know-a-little-about-everything. If, by chance, it were something strange, he knew the most about it. It's been said that he even helps the police on occasion, solving strange crimes. Orvin's store was the store, that as a kid, you loved going in, because he sold anything from magic tricks to the coolest Halloween stuff. He always would take you to the counter and show you a magic trick or give a real spooky story about some whacked out artifact. I used to visit Orvin every afternoon on the way home from school. He always took the time to visit and amaze me with something. Dad didn't much care for him, probably because Pastor Frank spoke badly about him. Dad said Orvin was mixed up in some weird stuff a long time ago. Mom said, if I enjoyed visiting with him, she didn't see any harm in it. I've found Mom's are unconditionally supportive, and Dad's are supportive if they like the idea, in my family anyway. Orvin and I became close on the summer of my junior year, I helped him out around his house doing tasks he didn't seem to enjoy, he'd rather pay a kid to do it than do it himself. Oh, the stories he'd tell…witches, warlocks, gargoyles, monsters, demons, and so many more. I tell you, as a kid, there really wasn't anyone much cooler than old Orvin Stiltworth.

As I hit the main four of town, sitting kitty corner from me was a red bricked storefront, one in a row of maybe eight-ten storefronts, that although different in height and color, it appeared to be one large building, where the lower level was store fronts, and I guess the upstairs is pretty much storage or apartments in some cases. As I parallel parked and got out of my car, old James, a legless war veteran, was sitting on his corner, pretending to be blind too, he says this will up his profits off the tourists. Downtown was charming. Old, but neat in a nostalgic kind of way. People come from all over to shop for antiques here, but mostly civil war souvenirs. Havenhill is one of the unknown, yet major battlefields in that war. We got our butts kicked by the South, so I guess that's why we're not very infamous up North. More and more people are figuring it out, and that's why the rising tourism. A relatively unknown general, William Havenhill, was the guy who led us to defeat. Apparently, reinforcements arrived to keep the town in their power. We're not very strategically located or anything, so I don't know why the South wanted this little town.

As I entered the glass door, a chain of cowbells rattled to announce my arrival. This place had no organization, and was full of old, weird stuff. Cobwebs connected all the items and a thin, gray layer of dust blanketed everything except a small desk with a lamp, scattered with papers. There was an old tome, in a leather binder, which had more than just its pages in it, apparently Stiltworth kept notes in here too. I called out "Mr. Stiltworth? Is anybody here?"

From the back of the shop, through a couple of burgundy curtains, stepped an older man. His hair, white as snow, was pulled back in a ponytail. His white beard matched, except around his mouth where it's been yellowed, perhaps by cigarettes smoke. He appeared physically to be in very good shape; in fact he didn't look any older now than when I was a kid. Although, as a kid, I guessed his age at one hundred plus years old. But now I would say he's in his sixties. I guess, as I get older, old people appear younger, or something like that. He was clothed in jeans and a white T-shirt, with a burgundy velour smoking jacket or robe. Sticking out of his pocket was the stem from a pipe. That could explain the mild scent of applewood in the air.

"What can I do for you, son?" He inquired.

"Orvin, hello, how are you?" I enthusiastically asked.

"Fine sir, of what service may I be to you?"

"Why are you being so weird? It's me Ben Ruden!" Now I was puzzled.

"Imposs…really? Well, how are you my boy!" His puzzled look changed to a smile.

"I'm good. You ok? I know it's been awhile, but heck, not that long!" I exclaimed.

"Ben, things are going just fine, I think I've got a line on where the fountain of youth is, but get this, by the time I reached it, I'd die of old age. Ironic isn't it? You search for something your whole life, and when you finally find it, you're too old to go get it. But I'm sure an old man's dreams are not what brought you here today?"

"Right, I mean, that's interesting, but I really came to see if you'd ever seen anything like this before." I handed the medallion over to Stiltworth. Without even looking at it, he sets it upon his cluttered desk, dons a pair of old looking, circular glasses, pulls out his pipe and packs it. He lifts a gargoyle paperweight and presses something that ignites a small flame; he uses this to light his pipe. After several puffs, applewood scented smoke rises from his pipe, writhing in the air like a python. He exhales, and as he speaks, a small amount of smoke trails out of his mouth.

"Now, let's see what you have here."

As he examines the coin, he doesn't show any reaction. Suddenly, he sets his pipe down, in an ashtray that appears to be a skull with a whole in the cranium. He looks up at me and says "Where…" he clears his throat "where did you come by this…trinket, Ben?"

I parlayed the story to him, he started to look paranoid. He'd look at the door every few seconds, and hush me time to time. He'd then ask me to continue. Upon completing my story, he asked if anything odd had happened to me, so, begrudgingly, I explained about the attack. The pink of his face drained to white. He slowly, with shaking hands, set down his glasses and said "Ben, I'd give you $100 for this right now. I'd like to add it to my coin collection."

Was he kidding? A reaction like he just had, tells me there's more to this than he's letting on.

"Mr. Stiltworth, I don't want money for it, what is it? I can tell you know something. Please, Mr. Stiltworth, don't make me wait as long as you did for your question on the fountain, if you know something, please tell me."

"Ben, I…ok, here goes. You said Michael Peacock was in a car accident, and no body was ever found, right? Did the Constable also mention that he's the 4th teenage male in the last 18 months that has had the same situation? Ben, none of the boys or their bodies has been found."

"I didn't know that. Malley seemed honest enough, and Beatty's too green and by the book, I can't believe they wouldn't tell me."

"The police are, as in the dark as anyone Ben, I don't believe that they are anything but confused. The attacker, male or female?"

"I…I think it was a male, he was so strong."

"Yes…well gender isn't that important any way, insignificant actually. Ben, what this medallion symbolizes…"

The cow bells tell us someone just entered the store, Stiltworth slides me a card and the medallion, he stands up, and heads to the front of the store. I follow to discover him greeting Jeff.

"Jeff, what's up?"

Jeff looks to Stiltworth, then switches his gaze to me, he smiles and says "Benjy, you're not letting old Stiltworth fill your head with spooky stories are ya?"

I immediately responded "Yeah, did you know the old man has found the fountain of youth? Oh, and he offered me $100 for that old coin I found."

"Good, now you know that's that. Come on, let's go hoop." Jeff strolls out of the store without a backward glance.

I follow, looking back once. Stiltworth appears relieved, and fumbles in his pocket for the pipe he left back on his desk.

As I catch Jeff, I grab his shoulder and turn him around. "That was pretty dickey of you to tease the old man like that. I came to him, so back off, huh?"

"Oh? Sorry dude, I just think he's weird. He buries his nose in fiction for 100 years and starts to believe it. So, did you take the $100?"

"No, not yet, I thought I'd offer the Peacocks to have it or turn it in or whatever. I mean, technically, it should go to the police as evidence, don't you think?"

"Yeah, I'd say so. Hey, let's drop it there on the way to the gym!"

"Look, Jeff, I've already told you, I still have some things to do. We'll hoop another day, ok?"

"Sure, whatever, catch you later."

As Jeff leaves, I pull out the card Stiltworth gave me. It's a local Chinese restaurant, Yat Wang's, great egg rolls! On the back he wrote, "meet me here in the banquet room at 10:00, ALONE."

I look back at the store; it appears peaceful enough, so I thought I'd follow up on what Stiltworth said about all the disappearances.

* * *

I pull up to a great, gray stone building. Out in front, the steps travel the entire width of the front of the building. They lead up to 4 huge pillars that suspend a great stone porch roof. The rest of the gray building looks more like it was carved out of stone as opposed to built out of small bricks. This is the Havenhill Honorary Public Library. It kind out sticks out, there are no other buildings as unique as this one in town.

I enter the stale air and paper scented filled library. Before I can stop myself, a yawn escapes me. It's too damn quiet; all I can hear is the stamping the librarian is doing and a couple guys flipping through newspapers. Could you be any cheaper than reading the libraries newspaper instead of splurging thirty-five cents and getting your own? I don't get that.

I approach the librarian, she's not your typical stuffy old broad going "SHHHH!" all the time, to my surprise she's a younger thirty-ish year old gal, slim build, about 5'9",(roughly my height), with golden blonde hair pulled back in green velvet scrunchy. Her oversized glasses clarify that she has green eyes, very unusual.

"Excuse me, Miss…"

"Ellen. Well, not Ms. Ellen, just Ellen. What can I do for you?"

"Well Ellen, my names Ben….Ben Rudin. I was wondering if you could help dig up some old newspaper articles, over the last eighteen months or so."

"Well Ben, all you do is go over to the Microfiche and scan them yourself"

"I see," what the hell is microfish? "Ellen, if you could maybe point me in the right direction…I never…"

"M-hmm, come on then, I'll help you." Within minutes I'm scanning all the old newspapers, this fish-doohickey is pretty cool.

"If you don't mind my asking Ben, what are you looking for?"

"Well, I just got back to town, and my neighbors' teenage son disappeared in a car accident, and then I heard that several other teens have also disappeared."

Her face turned a bit red, she swallowed hard, and stammered "My…little brother…disappeared six months ago in a drinking and driving accident, they never found the body. Keith, his name was Keith."

"Oh, I'm sorry, I didn't know…I was just looking into it."

CULT OF THE VAMPYR

"He's not dead Ben, I can't believe that. But I don't know how to find him, help him, he was such a great kid, and I can't do anything to help him."

"Ellen, I have a…theory on these disappearances, I'll know more tomorrow. I could be completely wrong, but if not I'll fill you in. You work here tomorrow?"

"No. But here's my number. Please call me."

"You bet. Take care."

Every article I outlined almost the exact same set of circumstances. What could be happening?

I decided to get home, and get ready for my evening meeting with Mr. Stiltworth.

* * *

At 9:45 I grabbed my Barretta and 1 clip of ammo. I tucked the gun in between my jeans and my shirt on my back and pulled my coat down over it. The clip went in my inside pocket. I left for Yat Wang's, and intentionally drove off the opposite way you'd normally take into town. I left before my windows were completely defogged, and without any results, tried wiping the frost off from the inside. A small area where my defrost blows out, at the bottom of the window, cleared up. I found myself preferring to drive, hunched over and looking through my steering wheel at a 5"x5" patch of window, to risking Jeff coming over while my car warmed up.

As I arrived at the restaurant, my window was clear and my car was warm, just in time to shut it off and start all over again. I entered the red and black, dimly lit lobby. A nice young lady, the owner's daughter I believe, offered to seat me. I explained I was meeting someone, and she immediately took me to the back banquet room. The scent changed from MSG and hot mustard, to a very pleasant applewood. The lights went off and the front of the restaurant closed for the night. A young man, probably a busboy, offered to move my car around back, so I let him. In the banquet room, Stiltworth was sitting, a glass of rice wine to one side, and his leather bound tome on the other. Applewood scented smoke curled up into the paper wrapped ball lights.

"Hungry Ben?" Stiltworth inquired.

"Yes sir. A couple of eggrolls and some General Tsao's chicken would be great."

The room was pretty large, maybe 30'x40'or so, they had large parties back here, wedding receptions, things of that nature. There were 4 large tapestries, red and black with gold insignias on them. The walls were stained a dark brown, almost black really, with ceremonial Katana's and other swords, fans with pictures on them, and all the tables were black with red and black chairs. The cushions had plastic on them, to stop food from staining them I guess. Lights hung all over the place, casting a dark red hue over the room entire.

"Ben, about this afternoon…" Orvin started.

"Yeah, look, sorry about Jeff. He seems to only care about himself." I interrupted.

"I don't necessarily agree Ben; he seemed to be concerned with what you were up to. Perhaps you should follow his advice and move on with life." Orvin sat back folding his arms awaiting my reaction

"I appreciate that Orvin, but I'm just too curious to go home and just watch Music TV." I sat back and folded my arms.

"Impetuous to the end, eh? I recall that about you." Orvin allowed a small grin to escape his visage.

"Orvin, has it been so long, I mean come on, I don't look that different, do I?"

"Son, I remember you all too well, it's just been a while, and I'm afraid I feared the worst about you and your family. I heard things, but obviously they're not true. I'm delighted to see you, really!" Orvin reached out and touched my hand, when he removed his hand, my watch, the one I was wearing, was buckled and laying on my hand, having been stripped off my wrist.

"That was always my favorite trick, and I was glad to see you were still up to your old tricks! But look, you know I respect you, everyone else thinks you've lost it, and I almost did to this afternoon, but we need to talk about the medallion."

"Ben, did you bring the medallion?"

"Yeah, here."

"Ben, there's nothing but stories behind this medallion, I'll tell you the story, but realize we've no proof. It's just a legend, alright?"

"Yeah, sure, so what's the legend?"

"Ok, look, this medallion is the symbol of an ancient evil, supernatural in nature. I'm not sure who is claiming this symbol as their own right now, if anyone, but it used to belong to a Cult of the Undead Gods. Ben, I've not seen this in 40 years, but if its back, we've got a major problem. If the Cult of the Undead Gods is going again, I need to meet with the Nine."

"Wait, we don't even know if they are active again, right?"

"Correct, we don't. But allow me to fill you in on some 40 years ago. fifteen teenage males and twenty-five teenage females were abducted over a period of two and a half years. They were never found again, but the Cult took credit for their abduction, and the town was held captive, never leaving their homes at night. All communication was severed, but eventually the National Guard came in and shut down the cult. It was a major bloodbath, no cult members survived to our knowledge. Mayor Sewet kept it very quiet, no publicity, and only a handful of people stayed here after that. Only nine of us that experienced it still live here."

"That's insane! Havenhill had a major bloodbath, and no one knows about it?"

"Yes, but Ben, the town would never have survived if we hadn't done it that way. And to some of us, this is where our lives were. We, of course, had thought the threat dead, but if it's back..."

"Wait! If this all happened before, the kids disappearing and all, why since it's happening again, hasn't anyone informed Chief Malley?"

"Malley was here the first time Ben, if he's not called us together, he apparently doesn't believe it's happening again. However, that medallion may be all we need to assume the worst."

"Then we gotta go see him! Now!"

"I understand your concern, remember, that's only one possibility. This Mike kid may have run across this by error, and that's all."

"Look pal, that doesn't explain the missing bodies, does it? Something is going on, if you don't call Malley, I will!" Again I sense someone approaching from behind, assuming it's the waiter I slowly turn, reaching for my Barretta, but not pulling it yet.

"Calling me won't be necessary Laddy, I'm here now."

Malley, in full uniform, stands in front of seven other recognizable men and women. All of them have a leather bound tome tucked under one arm.

Chapter Four
Meeting of the Nine

I tightly grasped the clip in my inside jacket pocket. Attempting to be brave, I asked, "What the hell is going on here?"

Completely ignoring me, Malley said "Orvin, why is this young lad here?"

Orvin Stiltworth tossed the medallion over to Malley, as Malley caught it and looked at it, the Irish temper I'd heard so much about finally flared up.

"I'll be damned! Men, show the lad out, it's time for a Meeting of the Nine, here and now! God be willing, we'll stop these demons before they get started!" The men moved immediately at Malley's orders. One of the men, Sam Crotchet, the barber, grabbed my arm, and attempted to lead me out. I tore my arm from his grip, and yelled "Will someone tell me what in the hell is going on here!"

Malley spun his head around quick enough to cause most people whiplash, and slowly, but sternly, said, "Laddy, ye need to go now, there're forces at work here ye don't understand, nor do ye want to. Leave now, or ye'll be spending the night in a stone cold cell!"

Bravely, or stupidly, I blurted out "What? The Undead Gods? I found the medallion, and I'll be damned if I'm not included in this."

Malley, whose face was as red a tomato, stepped toward me, then stopped himself. He looked over to Dugan Manchester, a 6'3" walking tank, and Yat Wang, a man renown for being of the heritage of Samurai. These two moved toward me, I found myself stumbling backward, and pulling my Barretta out, (the clip still in my coat pocket), and managed to say, "Back off guys…I mean it, back off." I glanced around the room, and caught myself in a stare down with Malley.

Malley didn't flinch, as I stood there staring into his ice blue eyes, I realized that this man scared the hell out of me.

"Malley, it's my fault," Orvin spoke up, a little unsure of himself, "the boy was attacked by one of them, you know that. We can't let him walk off without educating him a little first." This allowed me to pull out of the stare down and find Orvin. He motioned for me to lower my gun. I did trust this guy, but these others, I don't know. I slowly relaxed my arms, but kept the gun pointed at the big guys.

"Put it away lad, it's not loaded anyway." Malley turned his back and slowly stepped away, motioning to Dugan and Wang to back off.

Malley stood with his back to me and asked, "How bad do ye want to know?"

"Sir, I…I want to be involved. Until I know what's going on, I can't see going on with my normal life."

Yat Wang, the restaurant owner, interjected, "He has the aura. They'll seek him out."

"Damnation! I know, but I thought that perhaps he'd go about his business. They're back, aren't they Orvin?" Malley turned his head to Wang with an expression of: 'tell me I'm wrong, please.'

"No, Malley, this time it's different I think," Orvin Stiltworth packed his pipe, "this time is different."

"Not that much different lads, tonight was number five, the Johnson boy." Malley slumped into a chair. "And what's worse is, this time" Malley had to stop to swallow, "this time there was another vehicle involved in the accident. A child, a four-year-old girl, killed in the accident, Damnation! Now the bastards are killing children! It's bad enough, the teenagers, but now children, too?"

Wang locked the large banquet room door. He and some others started to move the tables into an octagon formation. Wang then swung a large tapestry, red with a gold dragon on it, aside and pulled out burgundy robes. He proceeded to hand them out, he even handed me one. As I slipped it over my head, the musty scent of mothballs told me it had been a while since it was last worn. Orvin lit nine candles, and then motioned for me to take a seat opposite Dugan. Everyone took a seat in front of their candle and untied their leather bound tomes, except me that is.

Malley stood up and without a downward glance started speaking some strange words. The others all started in, I couldn't understand most of what was said, but one section spoken in plain English, went:

"Ancient Ones, Thou Art not Welcome Here, Enow!
We Defy Thy Vile Implications Toward Our Plane,
Get Thee Away, No Ancient Magic Shalt Thy Evil Weave,
Keep Thee Astral, Nay To The Corporeal Plane, Away Evil Incarnate,
Thou Art No Longer The Source Of All That Is! Thou Art A Lie, A
Venomous Serpent Of No Power Here. We Don't Recognize Thy Will,
Thou Art Naught But A Lonely Elder, Thy Time Is Past, Keep Thee
To The Plane Astral1."

This chant was repeated three times, I'm assuming the other two chants, were also repeated three times. All the chants were spoken in unison, and as the final word was spoken, the nine candles were extinguished all at once. By the time my eyes adjusted, all nine candles, one at a time, re-ignited. As the ninth candle re-lit, all the members slumped back into their chairs, exhausted.

"Did…" Malley took in a deep breath "Did the prayer take Orvin?"

"I believe it did Malley, but it took too easily, that's what I meant by this time being different. Does everyone recall the Soaring Skull's true meaning?"

Wang was the first to speak, "The Soaring Skull signifies the Harbinger of Doom from the Undead Gods, right?"

"We thought so, and in a way it still does. That description was misinterpreted by us originally. It is a symbol of the Harbinger of the end of humankind, or The Final Harvest."

Final harvest? Holy shit, that's what…"Hey everyone, sorry to interrupt, but that's what the dude

who attacked me said! He said The Final Harvest approaches! Remember Malley, I told you he said that last night!"

"Ey, so ye did lad. I recall now. So what does that mean Orvin?"

"Well, what that means is that the Undead Gods aren't coming themselves, our spell has seen to that, but that it worked the first time, tells me the Undead ones have no interest in any extended visit. Remember, in your tomes, it speaks of the Elder Undead Gods all being loyal to a serpent or dragon of some sort. This beast is the mainstay of all their power. The Cult of Undead Gods fell so easily, because the Undead Gods never visited them, they all remained faithful but unchanged, mortal still. The communion with the Undead Gods never happened. Look here, in your tomes" Orvin continued, in early Slavic:

"He who art Harbinger, having been fully communionized, who art one with the Elders, as servant and king, shalt rule. As we are one, and he who art communionized, and brought to the abode of the Elder Undead, in spirit, body, and soul, shalt bring about the Final Harvest, the cleansing and communion of humankind."

"Who is the Harbinger? How can we identify him?" Inquired Malley.

"There's nothing more than the amulet and personal aura to help us ID this individual, and we have the medallion now."

Wang stood up white as a ghost, "It's the boy, Ben, and he had the medallion of the Soaring Skull!"

"Relax Wang, it's not Ben, he'd have attacked by now, our chant would have forced him to in defense of the Undead Elder Gods." Orvin looked over and smiled at me, putting me a little more at ease.

Dugan Manchester, the owner of a sporting goods store, finally spoke up "Orvin, I'm a little rusty at my interpreting, but I did notice something about needing sacrifice to entice the Undead."

"Correct, the Cult of the Undead Gods, made the error of inducting everyone into membership, and offered no sacrifice to the Undead, thus no Communion, no Undead Gods presence, and no true Harbinger."

I couldn't stand it, they were all too calm about this, I stood up and exclaimed, "So, what do we do about this, and what did you mean this time is different?!"

"Ben, what I mean by it being different, is that the Elder Undead has made no attempt to make themselves known. They made no attempt to interfere with our ceremony, they are clearly very confident about something. My guess is that they've placed a Harbinger here already, and it's building its forces as we speak."

"How can you all be so calm? I don't know if this is just a bunch of old men playing devil worship or what, but if you believe it, how can you just sit here and talk about humankind being harvested like so many crops?" I was shaking furiously, I couldn't sit, and my mind began racing.

Dugans' deep voice brought my attention back to the matter at hand. "Ben, none can enter the inner sanctum once the ritual has begun."

"Knights of the nine, we must prepare for the worst. Malley you'd best set curfew again. James, you're the local TV station owner, help with curfew, and get the message out that now is a good time for everyone to consider vacations. Mr. Mayor, contact the businesses, let's get them to give paid leaves of absence." Orvin stopped only to puff on his pipe. I had no idea this balding, portly old guy was Mayor Villiard.

"Orvin, we can't afford to start a panic..." the Mayor suggested.

"Bloody Hell man! We're talking about the Harbinger! It is death walking in human form! Panic is exactly what we need! The citizenry must know this time! There'll be no saving Havenhill for John and Mary Lunch bucket and their one-point-five kids this time! We've all got to get out of Havenhill now!" Dugan buries his reddened face into his callused hands.

"Dugan, that's very logical, but logic has no place here. I realize you're standing in for your father, God rest his soul, but mankind's sole defense starts with The Nine. We must fortify our defenses, or the Final Harvest will be ushered in at the end of the first trimester, one year exactly, after the new millennium."

I've never heard Orvin Stiltworth's voice sound so painstakingly measured.

"Orvin, how do we fortify our defenses? We can't even identify the Harbinger. Even if we did, we've no idea how to stop it." Dugan sounded very concerned. These guys seriously believe all this crap!

My head is swimming; this can't be real, can it? I did get attacked and no one believed me. Aw jeez, what's going on here? Deciding to act without thinking, I said "Somebody needs to go find out if this Cult has been reformed or not, wouldn't that tell us a lot?"

All nine were silent, after brief glances to each other; they focused their attention back on me.

"How involved did ye want to be getting' again, lad?" Malley sarcastically remarked.

"Whoa, fellas, wrong idea. I absolutely refuse to get within ten miles of some evil, dragon worshipping, Undead-worshipping, Harbinger-following, psychopathic teen killers! You Nine fella's best work on a plan B. Bad idea by me, ignore me, let's take suggestions, ok?"

"He does have the aura." Repeats Wang.

"The lad has had a run in with one o' them and survived." Malley followed up.

"Ben is young enough looking, and with some training, could pass for a potential convert." Pete chimed in.

"Yeah, but if he really did run into one of them, why didn't his guy kill him or abduct him?" James questioned.

"He's too damn unknowledgeable guys, he'd never survive!" Dugan added, with what, in my opinion, was the only voice of reason tonight. "But then again, maybe Ben is the only one that wouldn't be discovered. He does radiate the aura, and isn't one of The Nine."

"Ben," Orvin iterated, "If you don't wish to do this, we'd understand. You are, however, our only hope as we see it of infiltrating their cult, assuming it exists. If you're having a hard time believing this, imagine if we attempted to talk someone else into doing this. You ran into one of them, potentially, and even you can't believe this."

"Hello? Is anybody here that can hear my voice? NO! Forget it! You're all nuts! I…."

Orvin interrupted "Ben…your parents, they…"

Before he can finish his sentence, all nine candles extinguish at once. I can barely make out the sound of the rustling of cloth. The room is lit up momentarily, six times in succession, each time followed by the crack of a fired bullet emitting from where Malley was sitting. Through what looked to be strobe lighting, from the gun barrel, an ominous, dark figure moved cat like across the octagon of tables, and a sickening cracking sound ripped through the darkness, followed by a thump.

A pair of seemingly floating red dots momentarily mesmerized me. They then sped toward me and disappeared as I raised my hands to protect my face. A horrible smell, like sulfur or rotten eggs, floated across my nose, I felt nauseous and again felt warm air pulsating against the back of my neck. I was frozen, I couldn't move, I then heard a whisper. "The Final Harvest approaches. Join us."

As quickly as they went out, all nine candles relit, and I felt a warm liquid run down my inner thigh.

Chapter Five
Decision

Wang ran to the light switches, and quickly flooded the room with blessed light. As compared to the candles, even lights wrapped in red and black paper was momentarily bright and disorientating. As my eyes adjusted, I wondered if anyone else knew what had happened to me. As I searched around the room

I spotted Orvin Stiltworth laying face down in a pool of blood, his neck twisted at an impossible angle. Again nausea threatened to overtake me as I realized what all the other sounds I'd heard were.

"We're screwed." Villarreal whispered.

"Lad, I fear we haven't seen the worst of it. Damnation! How did that thing get in here?" Malley smashed his still smoking revolver down on the table.

"Without Orvin, we can't do the ceremony! He was our caster!" Villarreal yelled out in a panic.

"And that they knew, and that they knew." Malley appeared thoughtful. "Wang, ye were second circle, weren't ye?"

"Yeah, but with Orvin, I only ran the ceremony once, years ago. We'd need time to study and we'd need Nine to cast!" Wang responded.

"We can get another or two with the aura, they'd be learnin' as we were, but time is of the essence. Our stronghold is no longer safe…" Malley trailed off.

"My God! Orvin is dead, and you're all worried about your freaking ceremony! How can you all be so cold!" I ran over to Orvin's body. On a note, the letters running off the page at the end read…Ben's Tome.

"What…who knows what Orvin meant about my parents? Do any of you psycho's **know** what Orvin meant?" I looked around; they were either in deep thought or weren't paying attention to me. "Hey! What did Orvin mean…" Well, it was time to get their attention, "How much training?"

"Sorry Ben, what was that Lad?"

"How much training? What do I need to know? I got an…invitation, they'll welcome me in, I think. Train me, and I'll go in, for Orvin. We'll do some harvesting of our own with these bastards!!" I met Malley gaze for gaze. He turned away first this time. With the exception of wet undershorts, I felt surer of myself than ever.

"Lad, ye'll do fine. We'll train ye. We must find a new inner sanctum, though…"

"I live in the old church…" I winced as I heard myself say it.

"Perfect, we can fortify a church with very little effort! Bravo, Ben! Let's not waste anymore time dawdling. Wang, Pete, bring the supplies! We're off lads!"

Malley radioed for an ambulance, and we all entered our separate vehicles. Wang was waving two torches around each individual vehicle, some protection spell I heard, and as he finished, each car headed off toward my home.

* * *

The night was unusually bright as the snow magnified the moonlight, casting a bluish hue over everything. It was very calm, no wind to speak of, and very cold. The crisp night air added to the shakes I was already feeling. These were the kind of tremors that attacked in uncontrollable waves. I'd been shaken down to my bones, they almost ached. The cold wasn't the real reason I was shivering, the heat blowing out of my vents was ineffective, and I'd put a hand up to the vent until it almost was too hot on my skin, and realize that under my skin I was still cold. The thought of that vile, stinky…creature, breathing on me, and my being too scared to do anything about it, scared and angered me at the same time. "Join us" It said, I wish I'd have thought about my Barretta, and pulled to "join" its barrel with that creature's mouth and blown away its putrid smelling breath!

I can't remember feeling this angry before, I suppose I feel kind of violated. 'It' made me piss my pants! Nobody's ever done that to me before, and just thinking that it had the upper hand, had me at its' mercy, why couldn't I fight it? I, for the first time in my short life, feel angry enough to actually want permanent revenge. Pictures of Michael Peacock, Ellen's brother Keith, and poor old Orvin, flooded me. None of them could do anything, I'm sure they were all as helpless as I was. Even a four-year-old little girl was victimized by these guys. And, what did Orvin mean by bringing my folks up? No one else should have to go through that, and as these Undead Gods are my witnesses, no one else will! I've never even thought about taking a human life, and still won't, but this…this thing is going to learn how to die again!

As I pulled up to the front of my home, several of the nine were already on my front porch waiting for me. A young lady was also on the porch, engaged in conversation with Dugan. As I left my 'AM, I saw that it was Ellen.

"Hey, Ellen, what are you doing here?"

She ran over to me and threw her arms around me as if we were long lost lovers. (I wish)

"Ben, my God, Ben…I saw him, Keith, I saw him! Tonight, on my way out of the store! I yelled to him, he looked my way, smiled and ran off. I swear it was him." Ellen was shaking in my arms; I touched her hair and then slowly turned her shoulders, forcing her to walk with me to the front door. I pushed through the members of The Nine, and unlocked my massive wooden doors. As we entered, I felt a wonderful rush of warm air.

All were accounted for but Wang and Malley. I sat Ellen down, and went to the kitchen to start some hot water for coffee. Upon my return, I saw Wang enter followed by Malley, Beattie, ol' sarge John Peacock, and his wife and daughter, and all were carrying several firearms. These were the most able bodied individuals in my opinion. Toss Dugan Manchester in with them and you've got Havenhills' four biggest, strongest, or best-trained warriors you could find. I almost started to feel optimistic for the first time in two days.

I let Ellen explain her story to Malley. Malley suggested she stay within the safe house for now. I decided to sneak upstairs to change. As I did, I glanced out my window and saw Jeff strolling across the street toward us. I immediately thought we should let him in too. I finished and ran down stairs. As I threw the curtain open, I saw Wang speaking with Jeff.

"Hey, let me see Ben, ya blasted Sichuan slingin'…"

"Wang, why won't you let Jeff in, He's a friend, and…" for a change, Malley spoke up, surprise.

"Wang, tell Jeff he's not welcome, and secure the door." Malley turned and continued sorting out ammo.

The door was forced shut, Wang couldn't do it himself, and so 'Sarge threw his body into it.

"Excuse me, this is my house, Jeff's a guest, you can't just…"

"Ye've *invited* Jeff in yer house before, Ben?" Malley spit out, almost angrily.

"Uh, yeah, once to see the amulet. Why wouldn't I?"

"Lad, we can't be having any more than this fer now, sorry to be rude, ye can apologize to him later. Ye're to avoid contact with anyone else right now, 'till we've sorted this mess out, OK?" His face didn't look as if it would accept no as an answer. Not knowing what the hell was going on; I decided to play by their rules for now.

"Well…OK, I guess."

I got Ellen settled in a guest room, went to bunk down for the night and several others did too, but the "warriors four" took turns at watches. I slept sounder than I remember sleeping in the past several years.

* * *

The sound of constant movement from down stairs stirred me awake. I groggily threw on some fresh clothes, a ball cap, and tucked my robe under one arm and headed down stairs. I could smell bacon filling the air from down stairs, my stomach growled hungrily. I entered the kitchen to see 'Sarge' surrounded by steaming pots and pans.

"Mornin' 'Sarge, what's cookin?" I smiled sarcastically.

"Grab a plate and some grub, training starts at 0700." He didn't even look up, he was in his element now.

"In the other room, everyone was milling around, Ellen sat on the couch with her feet tucked under her legs, looking very tousled and sleepy, and was holding a large cup of steaming coffee. I smiled.

"Ben," she quietly stated "What is everyone doing, Malley wouldn't let me leave, this is strange."

"Ellen, if you'll just stay a while, everything will become clear. Remember, I promised you a theory on your brother. Hang tight, and you'll see. Trust me, ok?"

She nodded yes, her eyes questioning, and continued to scan the room. Wang and some others were chanting that weird language again, making odd gestures, and placing weird objects around the doors and windows. I guess I see Ellen's point, watching it, it does appear strange…very strange.

They were all in their robes, so I threw mine on. Dugan approached me. "Ben, we gotta get going on training. Finish your food and let's get rolling." Dugan slapped my shoulder, hard, and turned away. I didn't even flinch. After he turned away, I rubbed it.

* * *

Entering through the front door was Mayor Villarreal, carrying a box. He motioned to me to join him.

As I walked over to him, Dugan met me there.

"Ben, go clean up and put these clothes on, and come back." Villarreal shoved the box in my hands.

I went into my bathroom and took a quick shower. The warm water started to finally warm me up. I didn't realize how cold I still was until the shower. I got out and opened the box. It had "POLICE EVIDENCE" stamped across it in several places. Inside was a pair of black Levi jeans, a black silk button up shirt, with a black ring collar, and a flap that covers the buttons. Also, there was a black leather three-quarter tie-up army boots and a shin length black wool trench coat. I put on everything but the coat and looked in the mirror. I got a shiver from my own reflection; I immediately turned and vomited up my breakfast. I guess I was a little nervous. Tossing cold water on my face, I went back out and met with Dugan. He rubbed gel my hair and combed it back, and placed the medallion around my neck. I felt freaky. As I entered the great room, Ellen screamed and dropped her mug, covering her mouth with both hands.

"Are all you people sick!?" She stood up and raised her voice with tears in her eyes, "What are you trying to do?"

"Whoa, Ellen what are you talking about?"

"Ben, that's how Keith looked, last night, when I saw him."

"Oh crap. No Ellen, it's not what you think." I stood next to her. "Ellen, it's Keith, he's mixed up in a cult. A lot of people are. I'm going in to see just how many."

I felt the firm hand of Dugan land on my shoulder. "Ben, it's time come with me." Officer Beatty quieted Ellen down and explained how undercover works for the police and tried to comfort her.

Dugan, Malley, and Wang took me upstairs to the empty bedroom.

"Alright, Ben, Y'er gonna learn to use that Barretta quicker and more accurately." For the next three hours I practiced dropping a clip, slapping one in, and practicing on a target. I did well enough to move on.

Malley showed me two ju jitsu moves using an enemy's weight against him, and how to snap a knee via hyperextension, to stop someone from pursuing you. These are apparently two basic training moves you have to learn in order to join the police force. They were relatively simple to learn, but would take practice to do well. Four hours later, I decided more practice will come later.

We were brought food, which we took less than fifteen minutes to devour. Sweat beaded on my forehead, these freaks dress warm. I had to excuse my self, and go vomit again. Some cult guy I am!

Then it was Wang's turn. "Ben, I'm going to teach you a chant. You must memorize it, for it could save you later on. Once you use it, all will be aware that you aren't who you say you are. So, keep it for extreme emergency. The chant is: APITU APITU TIAMET—FORAY FORAY DRACO-LEPIDIPUS ANTSWONG."

"Ok, got it. What will it do?"

"It will give you the opportunity to escape." Wang left the room.

* * *

Exhausted, I went down stairs. I sat and drank a warm cup of tea. Professor Burton, a nearby college professor, stood up and ran over to Wang. Wang in turn approached me.

"Ben, Bill just deciphered something new." Pull out your tome.

I did so and went to the page marked by what appeared to be a flattened lizard tail, and in looking, found that the weird hieroglyphics were already deciphered and written in plain English on Orvin's notes.

Upon perusing them, something caught my attention and I realized that I couldn't swallow. Orvin was right, this time would be different. I felt the blood rush out of my face. I felt dizzy, I staggered, literally falling into a chair. I dropped Orvin's tome to my side.

"Everyone...according to Orvin's notes, he's here, the Harbinger is here. Nothing...nothing in the tome tells how to stop The Final Harvest, once the Harbinger is here. Nothing." I closed my eyes, wishing this to be a bad dream, and as I kept them closed, I saw the red eyes piercing into my soul.

Nothing. Nothing...

Chapter Six
Graveyard Shift

As I reopened my eyes, I saw everyone standing around me. Ellen walked over and knelt next to me. She took my hand in to hers and pulled it up to her silky soft cheek. Her cheek was warm, but had a cold area where tears had cooled the flushed temperature of her skin. Quietly, gently she spoke, "Ben...I'm worried. I can't pretend to have any idea of what's happening here, but to see you like this, acting like there's no hope. I...I...what's happening?"

I scanned the room, all eyes were on me, but these guys are supposed to be the experts, what do they want from me? Again I felt nauseous, but a little hungry, kind of like a hangover. I worked up enough strength to continue. "Ellen, everyone, I'm not very knowledgeable about any of this, I don't even know if I buy any of it. All I know is, Orvin's notes indicate that the Harbinger of The Final Harvest, is already here, on this plane of existence. Orvin also states that the tome's power is meant as a preventative measure, not something that can be used, once the Harbinger is here."

"So it's over, we're just awaiting doomsday, eh?" Mayor Villarreal whined.

"So long as we're alive, we've a fightin' chance!" Malley assured.

"Look, I don't know how much this counts, but Orvin does indicate that once The Nine has set up all the defenses, there is one possible ceremony, that is unknown to any, but a communionized member. So apparently, they can destroy themselves." I now looked up and around to The Nine for an answer.

"That would only make sense, how else to keep discipline in their own ranks." Wang stated twisting his mustache.

"So, what? We go capture one? What if he don't know it?" Dugan pondered.

Surprisingly, Ellen spoke up "Hey, if you guys are talking about that cult from 40 years ago, that was just a bunch of kids acting like they were something they weren't. Officer Malley, you should just be able to call the State Police and march in there and stop this now."

"It's a mite past that option now lass, trust me."

"I don't understand, a cult's no big deal, just…" I was forced to cut her off.

"Look, I've got some more bad news. Apparently the Harbinger doesn't work alone, he surrounds himself with many." The Professor was kind enough to back me.

"Yes, a recent conversation with Orvin…it makes sense now. Orvin was saying, that the minions for protection form first, then the Harbinger is revealed, the minions becoming a shield for the Harbinger. In fact, the Harbinger, though here already, can't yet be active. There has to be a certain amount of followers set first in order to safeguard him, if that makes any sense."

"So our time is limited, we must act now!" Wang excitedly added.

"Look, it sounds to me like, all we gotta do is stop the membership drive. No members, no Harbinger." Dugan looked as though he'd stumbled onto an easy answer.

The professor contradicted with, "Well, not exactly, you see '*He who shall bring about the cleansing and communization…*" more or less states, we either will join or be wiped out."

"Ey lad, but only if he's able ta be active, right?" Malley questioned.

The professor, a little unsure of himself came back with "I don't really know, I guess that's all we've got to go on, so we might as well continue with the plan, if Ben's still up for it."

"Wait, your big plan is for all you big, gun wielding guys to bully people out of joining up and Ben gets to go into the lions den all alone? That sounds cheap to me! Why don't all you gun slingers go blow the place apart?" Ellen interjected.

Wow, I'm getting to like her! But…as much as I liked Ellen's plan better than ours, I grudgingly answered her for everyone.

"Ellen, if one of The Nine went in, they'd be found out immediately. Conveniently enough I received an…invitation, if you will, from an old friend. A friend I *really* would like to meet up with again, and deliver a little message from Orvin." My stomach fell about six feet at the thought of another meeting with stink breath.

Ellen looked into my eyes. Hers filled with doubt, mine with conviction, and she lowered her head and nodded.

"Look, Ellen, and Mr. and Mrs. Peacock, and Sarah, my first mission is to find your brothers and son, and bring them back, you have my word." I was so scared; I felt a shiver go through my entire body. I'm not sure where I was getting this courage from, but something made me feel like this was what I needed to do. I felt like a kid in school who knew that on his way out to the bus, he'd have to face that one kid that just had to set up a fight. You have butterflies, but excitement at the same time, because if you win, you will be cool for like a month.

Mrs. Peacock started to cry, ol' Sarge Peacock, gave me a look of gratitude, and saluted me. Sarah's face matched her fiery red hair, and she simply said, "Please bring my big brother home."

If nothing else made me want to do this, that simple statement, by a little girl who wanted her big brother back, was enough to solidify my decision. Dusk started to fall, and I knew it was go time!

* * *

I stood up and put on my long, wool trench coat, and black gloves. I looked to Ellen, and then the others.

"Remember Ben, you have the aura, they will seek you out. Just head out and beware." Wang warned. As I headed toward the door, quite unsure of what was going to happen, Ellen intercepted me.

"Ben, I want to go with you. Let me come with you."

"No, I smiled softly… I mean I'd like nothing more, but I don't know what will happen, and can't involve you, yet. Wang? Can I come back at all?"

"Not until you are finished, otherwise they will know you don't really belong. I'm sorry." Wang lowered his head.

"None of you expect Ben to succeed, do you? You're just sending him off, knowing full well that they'll kill him! Just to buy you time! Ben, don't do it! They don't care about you; they only care about stopping the threat, no matter how many sacrifices have to be made!" Ellen looked to me; a tear was streaming down one cheek.

"Ellen," Wang interjected, "Its true Ben is entering into danger, and none would blame him for backing out, but realize he volunteered, we didn't ask him to do this. We've prepared him to the best of our abilities, now the choice is up to him and him alone."

"Look everyone, I don't have any idea what I'm doing, or how to do it, but someone has to find out if the cult is reforming or not, at the very least. I plan on finding that out, and then coming back, with Mike and Keith if at all possible. The actual stopping of the cult is up to The Nine." As I swallowed, I felt like my Adams apple was the size of a Golden delicious.

"Then I'm going, too. Malley get me some clothes like Ben's, we'll leave together. It's my brother." Ellen demanded.

"I'm afraid the cult is picky, lass, they seek out their members, members don't go to seek them out and survive. Ye see, Ben has the aura; they've already made him the offer. Ye'd only be puttin' Ben in danger, lass." Malley warned.

"Fine! Ben, I still think this is stupid, I don't need you to end up like Keith, but since no one else seems to care, bring Keith back, ok?" Ellen's voice shook, she turned and weakly walked away.

I turned and headed to the door, as I pulled the door open, I saw Jeff with his back turned looking back toward his house. "Malley, Wang," I whispered, "I need some interference here." Malley called on his radio for a squad car, minutes later a cruiser arrived and stopped in front of Jeff. They motioned him over to the cruiser, as if to question him. As he walked over to the cruiser, I took off in the opposite direction.

* * *

The night was quite peaceful; I can't remember the last time I was out, just walking in the cold evening air. The briskness of each breath constricted my breathing a little, but felt cold and clean. The snow gave way beneath my boots. You know, the crusty kind of snow that pretends it can support your weight, and at the last second gives and you break through up to your shin. Of course, the game is that you continue to try and step lightly enough for the crust to support you, but of course, it can't. As I continued down the sidewalk, I noticed all the homes that have their lights on and smoke billowing out of the chimneys. I think about all the families, cozy and going about their lives, as if nothing will ever change. I almost find myself envying their apparent naiveté. I find myself noticing weird things, things I've never really thought about, like, how some houses had their addresses posted out by the road, and others didn't. How is 911 supposed to find your house if there's no visible address?

I see a small quick shadow darting around me on the ground, as my eyes adjust a little more; I see it's a black cat, with a white chest. It approaches me and meows loudly. I look for tags, there's no collar, so it must be a stray. I learned that if you ignore them, they'll go on their way. So I did just that. Unfortunately, it decided to follow me. Oh well, at this point I've reached town. It's lit up with assorted Christmas lights, some of which are burned out, and oversized decorations that look older than me. The lampposts are entwined with gold and silver foil strips. Many of the storefronts have cheesy X-mas scenes painted on their windows and fake snow sprayed all over. I continued down the sidewalk of the main four intersections, and passed Orvin's store. Anger, once again, swelled up inside of me. I looked in the window, half expecting to see Orvin wave me into his applewood scented abode, but instead saw a dark, locked up shop. I turned away and continued down the sidewalk. Upon reaching the Quick-e-Mart, I noticed several teenagers hanging out. I scanned the area, looking for any that might be dressed like me. There didn't seem to be any. Today's fashion is obviously, oversized jeans or corduroys, with tattered bell-bottoms, hanging halfway down their butts showing off whatever boxers they were sporting. Thick-soled canvas tennis shoes, dark colored coats or dull colored flannel shirts with thermal underwear shirts underneath. They wore dark, knit ski hats and sunglasses, at night.

I'd like to tell you that the girls dressed differently, but they didn't. Did you know that there are stores that sell just this stuff? I really don't get this 'style'. Apparently, with people dressed up this freaky, I didn't stand out too badly.

I entered the store to grab a pack of gum and a coffee. I almost went for the Friutstripe gum, it's been years since I had that. The problem is, the flavor doesn't last very long. As I went to pay, the guy at the cash register, widened his eyes, and said, "You…you want ta pay for that?"

"Well, yeah, what else…" I stopped myself; I guess it's time to play whatever role I'm supposed to play.

"So, you gonna try and make me pay?" I asked, leaning closer. He backed up and shook his head violently back and forth 'NO'.

I grabbed my stuff and left. I approached a group of teens. They started goofing around and getting cocky. When I arrived, they looked at me and starting acting as if cops just pulled them over.

"Hey, punks, I'm lookin' for some dudes, you seen 'em?" I said as gruffly as I could.

"No, no, sir…not tonight, not yet." A guy in a letterman's jacket said.

"Well, I guess I am early. Hey, any of you pukes know when these other dudes usually show up?"

From the back of the group a voice shakily said, "Uh…about 12:00 usually, after curfew, but I've only seen 'em once. They look kinda like you, that is who you're lookin' for, right? Guys dressed like you, wearin' them necklaces?"

"Necklace? This is the soaring skull flesh bag! I oughta just…" I stopped myself, wondering if I over did it or not. The closest kid darted off, and then the rest scattered. I smiled, I hated doing it, but it was sort of a rush. 12:00am was a couple of hours away. I figured I couldn't look too tough, gingerly sipping coffee, so I figured I'd best drink it and get rid of it. Yech! No wonder that dude didn't want to charge me for this muck! It tasted burnt. I popped a piece of gum in to try and cover the taste left by the coffee, but the coffee was so strong I couldn't even taste the gum.

Ok, so, let's go over my brilliant plan. I infiltrate into this cult, and un-brainwash Mike and Keith, I then find out all the Cults secrets and we all go home. The Nine, then do the ritual to stop the Harbinger, and I make my Monday morning appointments. While I'm at it, then Ellen thinks I'm a hero, and wants to be my eternal love slave. How hard could this all be? What am I thinking? This is ridiculous! Wha…?

I feel a presence; it's one I've felt before. I scan the area, I don't see anything. Perhaps it's just the cold this time. I continue to walk, more cautiously though, looking around.

"Ben", I hear my name said in a loud whisper. I stop and look around.

"Show yourself or beat it!" I bravely yell out. Over near a large oak tree, I make out a silhouette of a figure standing there, red, glowing eyes staring at me. It looks like a Jawa, but taller and with red eyes. I stammer backwards, I feel the fear welling within me. I start to reach for my gun, but stop myself.

"Ben." The whisper repeats.

"What? Who are you? Why don't you come over here?" I nervously ask.

"Join us."

"Join who? I don't even know who the hell you are, or what to join." Damn! I was losing him.

"We are real. We exist. We are reborn to rule. Join us."

Wow, a full sentence this time. But why does he want me so bad? Something about my aura?

"I need to know more, who are 'we'?" I nervously inquired.

"The grave yard. Haskins Tomb."

He was gone. How does he do that? I was looking at him the whole time! Off to the graveyard I guess. Figures, a graveyard, how cliché can you get. Meet the evil, demon guy, leader of the undead cult in the graveyard, what is this, some bad novel? Well, off I go, I'm in this deep, might as well go deeper.

I continue down the sidewalk, the graveyard is actually in this direction, so I guess I unconsciously chose the proper direction. Again, I start looking around, looking at the houses differently this time, and no matter how hard I try, I can't get that guy out of my mind. Hey, at least I didn't get my nose broke, or piss myself this time, that's a good start. I notice a pair of headlights hit the trees ahead of me and a car come to a halt just behind me. I don't turn, but hear

"Hey Benjy, is that you?" Crap, it's Jeff! I quickly try to come up with a story, but continue walking, as if not hearing him. I hear him running up from behind me, I immediately set myself and at the last moment, grab Jeff, and help his momentum carry him past me, sending him sprawling into a snow bank. I take off at a dead sprint, cutting through yards, trying to lose him. I'm pretty certain he never saw my face. Hey, that move worked, maybe not in the way Malley meant, but it worked. I'll probably be cool for like a month at Havenhill High. I turn to look, and see no Jeff pursuing me. I re-direct and head for the graveyard.

As I spot the graveyard, I see that the front gates are locked, but anyone could just walk around and get in on the sides. *That* makes a lot of sense. I find myself stopping at the edge of the graveyard. I really don't want to step onto it, as if, once I do, I'm going ahead with this. This is it, no turning back, do it or quit. I hear tires squeal, I turn and see Jeff's car coming around the corner. I dive into the graveyard, and roll behind a tombstone. Jeff's car passes by.

* * *

As I pull myself up off the ground, I look around the graveyard. Haven hill, being as small as it is, doesn't really have that large of a cemetery, but it probably covered eight to ten acres. Of course there were only two tombs or mausoleums, Haskins, the richest family in Havenhill, and Jefferson's, the richest family in Naperville, the next town up. Why they bury their family here, I don't know.

There were several younger trees littering the landscape, all without leafs at this point of course. In the dark, in a cemetery, they fit the description, of scary, winding trees, that resemble whatever your imagination comes up with. One thing I've always wondered is why there is a ring around the base of some trees, about a foot in diameter, where there is no snow. It's always a perfect circle, and no matter how deep the snow is, there's always that circle.

This is your classic cemetery, about one-third of the tombstones are broken or unreadable. There does seem to be an eerie glow lighting the cemetery. Again, probably the moon reflecting off the snow, but it's somehow spookier here. The iron fence is rusted and broken, and even missing in some areas. The graveyard leads back into the woods. The deeper you go, the more foliage there is, and the less kept up the grounds are. There must be a couple of hundred tombstones, peppering the acreage, but I always wondered, if there were only two hundred tombstones, where is everyone else who ever died, in the history of Havenhill or any other town for that matter? Take your larger towns for instance, if they'd been around for a couple hundred years, how many people died in that period of time? With the exception of cremation or moving the bodies elsewhere, there would have to be thousands of people who died from old age or disease or accidents, wouldn't there? I don't care where you go, there are never enough tombstones to account for everyone that passed and didn't get cremated. Especially towns like ours that had a couple of major battles in the Civil War.

Anyway, I guess standing in the middle of a cemetery, waiting to go meet 'skunk breath the Jawa', tends to make one question weird things. Or perhaps, I'm just weird, case in point; look at what I volunteered for.

I started to head back toward Haskins Mausoleum; of course, Haskins is in the furthest most back corner of the cemetery. I suddenly stop. Why is it I know this? I do feel, as if I know this place, in fact, I'm not even all that scared. Ok, maybe a little scared.

As I wander deeper into the cemetery, my eyes and ears, start to play tricks on me. I start hearing one thing, but as I stop and focus, I either no longer hear it, or it is actually something entirely different. I often think I see a figure, but upon further investigation, it's not a person at all.

I finally reach Haskins Tomb; it's a smaller, gray building, quite overgrown. It doesn't appear as if anyone has been back here in years. The face of the building was at one point, nicely designed with twin statues, one on either side of the door, both since having been broken up a bit, and lots of designs carved into the actual face of the building. The door appears to be wooden, with huge, rusted metal, hinges and rusted bands of iron supporting the wood. There is no way it had been opened in years.

As I focused on the door, feeling confident that it hadn't been touched in years, a loud scraping noise emitted from within the door, as it slowly started to open toward me.

Chapter Seven
Infiltration

The scraping sound of old, rusted hinges, not having been opened in years, was similar to thirty people scraping their fingernails down a chalkboard at school. The cracking and splintering of age-old wood added to the orchestration of sounds screaming from the simple opening of this door. The door was opened about a third of the way, when all the noise ended, a puff of dust floated out as if being forced by a leaf-blower. I froze in my spot, waiting to see if my "buddy" was going to stick his pale, featureless face out at me. I stood for approximately five minutes, which seemed like hours. 'Not a creature was stirring, not even a mouse', came to mind in this numbing silence. I eventually came to realize that the next move had to be mine. I looked around, as if hoping the voice of reason would take human form and drag me out of this mess. Look as I might, such a summons went unanswered.

I approached the steps to this mausoleum, that the building itself only stood seven feet high and appeared to be approximately ten by twenty feet. There were three steps leading up to the partially opened door. The steps went the whole width of the face of the building, and in the center was the door, again, statues on either side held pots one could put plants or flowers in. Both statues were horribly disfigured from age and weathering. As I stepped on the first step, I felt lightheaded. I started to pick up the scent of death. A very old, dusty scent, like that of raw chicken left out in the sun too long. Add a cup of sour curdled milk and break open some rotten eggs, and there's the recipe for the odor that's reaching out to me, failing in its attempt to entice me to enter.

I decided to 'buck up', so to speak, and reach for the door. My gloved hand grasped the door handle, and with surprising ease, the door groaned in protest, and I was able to pull the door a little bit more open. Looking into the mausoleum I saw stairs leading down. They went a surprising twenty to twenty-five feet down and led to a large, dimly lit room. Descending into the mausoleum, it seemed that no matter how I tried to avoid it, I would still get slapped in the face by sticky spider webs. Just as I wiped one web off, I'd walk into another one. What a pain. When I finally reached the bottom, I started to adjust to the odor, and thick dusty air.

The room was lined on two of the walls with nameplates; each placed every three by three foot square. This would appear to be a similar set-up like a morgue, where the nameplates are where the drawers would be. I'm assuming there's a body behind each nameplate, or at least a coffin. I'm not sure how they get them in the wall or anything.

I continue looking at the walls and come to a section of six three by three foot open chambers. Yep, a coffin would slide in perfectly. Maybe, they just cement it in and slap on a nameplate, who knows? I decide to head to the wall opposite the stairs where a door is shut. Again, with a minor groan, the door opens, inward this time, with very little effort. I suppose this door doesn't quite get the weathering the upstairs one does. Through this door, a long narrow hallway stretches off into the darkness.

Odd, who or whatever opened the upstairs door, is no where to be seen. I half expected my "buddy". With few other options, I decided to enter the hallway; my vision seemed to adjust, slowly, but surely as I continued down the hall. There really wasn't much on the walls to notice; in fact the only noticeable things at all were those famous cobwebs. Since there were so many webs, it would stand to reason that no one had been down this hallway, right? So, I decided to turn around, and head the other way, back to the main room. I entered the main room to find a young male standing in the staircase, leaning against the staircase wall. He was about sixteen-years of age I'd guess, black slicked back hair. He was wearing clothing similar to mine, and sure enough, he was sporting the same medallion.

He smiled, and sarcastically said, "He said to meet AT the Tomb, not IN it."

"Who are you?" I inquired.

"Your guide." He turned away.

"Wait! I'm not going anywhere until you answer some questions pal!"

He continued up the stairs. For fear of being locked in, I hurriedly followed. Once again, I was outside, this time however, the cold air was sweet as molasses, and I drank deep of its freshness. I looked and saw my 'guide' walking deeper into the woods. I ran to catch him.

Upon reaching him, he said "So, you've met him, huh? You made a good impression on him."

"Who? Who's him? And what good impression?" I think I knew the answer to the first part, but I wanted a name.

"If you didn't impress him, he wouldn't risk bringing you in like this. That's pretty cool, man."

"What's your name?" I asked nicely, hoping for a straight answer.

"Well, I was Keith."

Holy shit! It's Keith! Ellen's brother!

"Keith Krenar?" I nonchalantly asked.

"Yeah, but that's in the past, y'know?"

"Right, I was Ben Ruden."

"You still are, dude, but that'll change after you're Embraced."

"Hey, Keith, you ever think about your family, or sister, you ever miss them?"

"No, they're not my true family, after being a Thrall to the master, he'll Sire me. Dude, it's incredible, you're making a wise decision. The power of becoming one of the Kindred makes being a Thrall way worth it!"

"What's a Thrall?"

"You'll find out soon enough, we all start as Thralls. Hey, we're almost there." He picked up his pace, as if he were actually excited to arrive. He sure doesn't seem to be here against his own will.

We were traveling deep into the forest, I had no idea it even went this deep, I haven't even seen a deer blind for the past twenty-minutes. I felt myself starting to tire and my head still ached. "Almost" there is apparently a relative term. The trees were bare, but there were enough of them to block out the sky, I expected pitch darkness, but oddly enough, I could see as if it were dusk. I attempted to hear an animal or bird, but heard only Keith's footsteps, on crunching snow, leaves, and snapping twigs. I didn't see myself talking Keith out of this, and getting him to come home with me, he seemed pretty sold on this Thrall business. I finally started to hear noise. Noise…like people talking or singing even.

"Is that the place? Where all the noise is coming from?" I brilliantly deduced.

"Yeah, come on." Keith pushed through the thickets with ease, until an orange glow ahead made him appear as a silhouette to me. We broke through to a rather large clearing, with a large bon-fire. Several people were yelling and doing crazy dances around the fire. Some stood while others were on all fours, like Indians doing a rain dance or something. I could smell the burning embers and wood from the smoke. Little glowing embers danced into the dark sky like a group of fireflies. I could feel the heat from where we were standing.

Keith turned to me with a smile like a kid on Christmas morning. "Let's go join the festivities! The Undead Ones favor us this night!" Keith ran to the group, joining in, and I quickly lost him in the swarm of dancing bodies.

"It is good you came. They are pleased." I heard an almost familiar voice from behind me. I spun around, attempting to keep my cool.

As I spun, expecting to see Ol' Death-Breath, I see instead, a fully cloaked figure. It could be D.B., but he wasn't usually shy about showing me his face, and this man was taller, stockier.

"Yeah, it's great to be here. Look, I was invited by some guy, I don't know much, but I do know that this is the best place for me, if I want to make it past the upcoming Harvest." I weakly smiled.

"Yes, you are who we were seeking, now the circle is complete. My manners, I seem to have forgotten manners, come we shall sit, and feed…er…dine, hmmm?" He swirled around, his robes flowing, and he starts off past the fire. His cloak hides everything quite well, except of course his medallion. I follow, meanwhile I'm telling myself, so far so good, it's even a polite cult. Approximately one hundred yards or so in, I see a bungalow, quite large really, about the size of a football arena, with one obvious entrance. It had been constructed of many trees, and is in the shape of a dome. As we reach the door, my host states, "Our Haven is your Haven." He reaches for the door, and without touching it, draws his hand back, and the door swings outward, as if connected by fishing line. He steps in, I peer in through the opened door, and it appears to be pitch black. My vision does adjust shortly, and I see my host standing in the door way.

Startled, I jump back, placing my hand over my heart, I sigh and say, "Sorry, I thought you'd gone in, I almost ran into ya."

"Ben, enter, I invite you." He solemnly states.

"Uh, yeah, thanks. I guess I will." I look back over my shoulder, having just realized that the chanting and singing had stopped. Approximately twenty to twenty five guys were standing shoulder to shoulder in a perfect line. These were all the guys dancing around, even Keith was there. They were silent and perfectly still. Although the fire was blazing behind them, it must have been hitting their eyes just right, because every single one of their eyes were glowing red, as if caught in a flash, in a picture, or like a deer in headlights. I turned back toward my host; he extended a candle out to me, probably to help me see. I took it from him, and a rousing round of cheers erupted from the kids behind me. My host lowered his hood, the flame from my candle revealed his face to me. My God, I knew I'd recognized his voice…

Chapter Eight
The Inner Circle

"Believe! It is written as the very words of the almighty! So it is written, so must it be done! Believe in that which lends itself to common sense, not haughty stories, not unproven hearsay, but that which cannot be disproved! Hold no belief that is in defiance of simple reason! Know the difference between truth and fantasy!"

I was flooded by a single sermon Pastor Frank once gave when I was very young, yet, I recall every word. His sermon continued, "We are made in the Lords own image, He Sired us, and He gave us life. He also gave us, of all Gods creatures, the gift of reason! We use reason in a court of law; one is innocent until proven guilty! And yet when we are asked to believe, we say there is no Lord until it is proven to us! Why would we believe that humankind, Sired by our Lord, is innocent until proven guilty, but our Lord can't exist until He proves he exists? Were we to lend the benefit of the doubt to our Lord, that He exists, until it is proven he does not, then and only then will we be treating our Lord and Father equal to that of our brethren. To treat our Sire equal to our brothers is once again a crime. We are proof of His presence, and I defy anyone to prove otherwise!"

The passion and conviction in Frankenstein's sermons is why my father loved listening to him, these sermons having earned him the nickname 'Frankly Frank'.

Standing before me, his facial features highlighted by both the raging bonfire behind me and the candle in front of me, stood Pastor Frank. He looked identical to the way I remember him. He doesn't look any older, but I remember vividly, his charismatic smile.

"Ben, I've looked forward to seeing you again. Please, follow me; let's get out of the elements." Frank turned. When entering, I noticed, the walls were indeed intertwined branches, similar to a giant bird's nest turned upside down. It was dark, but the candle gave off enough light to make it bearable. It smelled of fresh pine and sap. We traveled quite a while, through twisting passageways, until we came to large circular room. Looking straight up, there was a hole in the center at the top of the dome. This room was pretty much bare, with the exception of a large, wooden, circular pedestal. It was probably ten feet in diameter and maybe three feet thick. It lay face up in the center of the room. All around it were six candles, and upon further review, this disc had the Soaring Skull carved into it. In four edges of the room, there were octagon-shaped mirrors on stands. The floor was dirt, and there were exactly two doorways, one that we entered through, and another directly across from the first one. The walls were the same, large branches, intertwined like a bird's nest.

"Excuse me, Pastor Frank, um, what is this room used for?"

"All your questions will soon be answered. Continue with me." Frank stated as he headed for the far door.

Upon entering this next door, it appeared to only be a storage room, some robes, boxes and other items I couldn't very well see. Frank walked up to one of the wooden shelving units, and stood before it. As if alive, the branches forming the walls, creaked and snake like, pushed the shelves aside and parted like curtains being drawn open on a stage. Beyond was a staircase leading down. Only my candle was emitting any light. Frank was walking with no light, and seemed to have fewer problems than I did. The steps were actually carved out of the very earth itself. They led down for; I counted forty or forty-one steps, and opened into the town sewer system. The smell gave this away. There were twin sidewalks on either side of a stream of…well you can guess. Every hundred feet or so, steel rungs led up to a manhole cover, then about every two-hundred feet, until I no longer saw any. I had no idea Havenhill was big enough to even have sewers, or service tunnels, or steam tunnels, this extensive. There were even a couple of tunnels splitting off now and then. We, however, continued straight, or at least what I guessed was straight. I got pretty turned around in that birds' nest, but I would guess we were heading away from town. I deduced this by the fact that there'd be no need for manhole covers deeper in the woods. We eventually reached a third turn off tunnel, heading to the right.

"Where are we headed Pastor Frank?" I inquired, trying to force a smile onto my face.

"Ben, just call me…Frank. We're almost there."

Again with the 'almost there' routine. Everyone in this cult thinks that within an hour walk is 'almost' there! I followed in silence for at least five or six miles.

We reached a dead end, where a cast iron door stood. It appeared to be riveted into the very wall. There was a keyhole however. I would guess that city service men would have the key to this door. Frank turned to the right of the door, and reached into the solid cement wall and pulled open a door that didn't exist. No big deal right? Trees moving on their own, doors appearing out of no where, I guess next we'll just board an invisible air plane and fly off to some Amazon island of warrior women, who need men to procreate…anyway, Frank steps into the door way, and because I've been doing it all night, I follow.

The thought does cross my mind that now would be the opportune time for me to turn and bolt! I mean, I know the cult is reformed, I know where all the missing kids are, I could lead whomever to the hideout in the woods, that's all I said I'd do anyway. Of course, I'm beginning to think that the dome in the woods is a fake hideout, and I'm about to enter the real one. I guess I've no common sense, I mean, its not like Frank has threatened me or anything, and he is or at least was, a Pastor. Ahh, let's face it, I'm just plain curious!

As I step through the solid wall that now has a wooden door protruding out of it, I enter another staircase of only six steps. This leads into a boiler room. This boiler room is probably two thousand square feet. There are four large boilers, and more pipes and meters than I'd care to count. Of course there's a lot of other machinery in here I can't identify, but the main thing is, none of the machinery is currently operating. The webs stretching from pipe to pipe have been undisturbed for some time. The metal door with the keyhole in it, next to the invisible door, also leads into this room, but clearly hasn't been used in years. Apparently that's what these guys want anyone checking the area out to think as well. Frank leads me to one of three doors. He opens it and enters. We continue down an unlit hallway, in the small amount of light that my candle emitted, the hallway looked like one in a school or a hospital…no way!

"Frank, is this Hillcrest?" I questioned.

"Excellent, Ben. Yes, this is our true Haven. It has been abandoned for years."

Yeah, Hillcrest Mental Institution, nice freaking place! This used to be a premier, nationally known mental hospital. It was almost as well known as the Mayo Clinic, but that was over fifty years ago. I heard it was shut down because some plague or something was spread via the food, and this was causing some of the infected patients to go even crazier and attack other inmates and staff, actually tearing their throats out. This was such a violent outbreak; I'd heard that over three hundred people died during it, until the State sent in help to relocate the patients and staff. They could never find the agent or virus that caused this, so they closed it down. This was like a fifty-two million dollar facility, just closed down, never to be re-opened. It was even rumored, that the infected patients were burned, as to not spread the plague. Some said several escaped, never to be found. But, being sick, they couldn't have survived very long. In fact, the only attempted cure was to do a complete blood transfusion, replacing infected blood with new, but I guess patients quickly polluted their new blood and reverted back to their almost anemic state.

Well, regardless, you can't help but get the creeps in a place like this. I remember in high school trying to come out here once, in a drunken stupor, but we couldn't find it. You know, a thirty thousand square foot, three-story building is pretty hard to locate. Actually, it is. The government ordered all roads and access blocked off, which coupled with fifty years of vegetation, hides this mammoth pretty well.

Frank manages to find another set of stairs heading down, this set led to a door that has been used quite a bit, based on the half moon shape the bottom of the door has made due to it being opened several times, sweeping the dirt away. This opens up into a large room, of poured cement-like the sewer walls. It is very dry, and actually warm, the opposite of what I expected. The floor however is dirt, very compact dirt, but dirt none-the-less. There are three doorways located off of this room. This room is also circular, and has a disc-like pedestal in the middle of it, but this medallion replica appears to cast out of silver or chrome. There are four octagon mirrors around the room and nine candles, of which eight are lit, surround the giant medallion. This is the only discernable difference between the dome and this room except, no hole in the roof, or at least I don't see one. Two robed figures sit in two of the nine over stuffed chairs. The chairs are constructed of wood and burgundy velour. Sitting in a third chair with one leg dangling over one of the arms of the chair, swinging his foot, as if sitting still is pure torture for him is my old pal Death Breath. His lips curl up, in either a silent growl, or a smile. I've never seen him this close up before, I've been closer, but never actually seen him this close. His pale face appeared to be that of an albino, his eyebrows and lips, unlike an albino, were stark black. He had long, wild black hair and blood red eyes. He almost looked like a rock star with make-up on. He wore a black leather body suit. He was slender, but muscular. When he curled his lips to me he brandished two fangs, exceptionally longer than the rest of his teeth. He nodded hello to me. Anger swelled up with in me. I wanted to pull out my gun and finish him now!

"I see you two have met...of course you have. Than I suppose other introductions are in order." Frank started with the two cloaked men. "Ben, this is Barry Haskin, and Bill Jefferson, and you've already met Jessup. Please sit." Frank clapped his hands and a young lady in her teens brought out a decanter and five pewter goblets. One was handed to me, I decided to sit and hear them out. I almost spilled my drink as I hit the seat; it gave way like a beanbag. I managed to upright my self with a little dignity. I sniffed what was in my cup and it had the smell of berries and vinegar, wine obviously.

"Are you hungry Ben?" Frank asked.

"Yeah, but that's alright. You ready to fill me in or what?" I was a bit sharp, but didn't know how else to say it. I drank deep of the wine, it tasted fruity at first, but it didn't take long for the wine aftertaste to kick in. All wine, no matter how expensive, tastes like vinegar to me eventually. I'm a beer man.

"Ben, what questions do you have? I have a couple of you, who would you like to go first?" Frank asked.

"Ok, so like, what in the hell is Jessup supposed to be?" I stared at Jessup with stone cold eyes.

"He is just one of us...of the aura, one communionized under the natural laws." Frank said.

"Ben, what do you think I am?" Jessup asked in his hoarse voice.

"I can't tell. Frank I'm not comfortable with this creep in here. Can you and I talk somewhere else?"

"Aw, Ben, after all we've been through?" Jessup springs to a standing position and starts toward me. He makes his snarl or smile or what ever it is, and brandishes his canine like incisors. I struggle to get up, flinging my goblet to the ground and reach for my Berretta...

Jessup reaches out and strokes my cheek, as I swing my Berretta around and plant it on his forehead.

"Don't ever touch me you piece of filth!" I yelled in my most pissed off voice, feeling his gloved hand touch my skin reminded of both times he had me at his mercy and of what he'd done to all the others.

I don't know if it was the conviction of my voice or the fact that I had a semi-auto pressed into his forehead, but Jessup widened his eyes, and quickly backed away, clearly frightened.

Jessup slumped back into his chair. Frank chortled at the whole scene, I thought I blew my cover, but Frank found it funny.

"Well Jessup, perhaps you should do as Ben requests, excuse us, if you will." Frank asks.

Jessup springs back to his feet, and skitters quickly through one of the doors.

"Now Ben, could the others stay, they may be of use in answering any questions you might have."

"Sure, I just don't like that Jessup guy."

"I'll go first. Ben, why bring a gun?"

"I guess I had no idea what was going on here, it all felt right coming here, but I guess I was being cautious." I'd hoped that my years of sales training were helping me sound legit.

"Fair enough, now then, how is it you came by the amulet?"

"I found it in Mike Peacock's car, something drew me to it." I figured he'd know any part of the story Jessup was involved with.

"And the clothing? Is this how you dress now?" Frank asked.

"No, but I did visit with Orvin Stiltworth and he filled me in on the old cult, so I kinda figured that would be how you guys dressed." I picked up my emptied goblet, immediately the young lady refilled it.

"Yes, and your meeting with The Nine, how did that go?"

"Well, Jessup kind of screwed it up, you know, killing Orvin and all."

"M-hmm, I see, was the spell cast?" Frank sat back and folded his arms; I learned in sales training that this means the guy closed his mind, which meant he knew the answer.

"Yeah, it sounded like gibberish mostly, and all that happened was the candles went out and re-lit."

Frank looked to the other two and smiled, as if perhaps I passed his test to see if I'd lie or not. "Ben, what else did old Orvin tell you about us?" This time Frank leaned forward, which he was seeking information.

"Basically, that this amulet is the Soaring Skull, the amulet the old cult wore. And that if the cult is back everyone is in trouble because of a Final Harvest." I drank again.

"I see," Bill Jefferson interrupted, "And so do you know what the Final Harvest is?"

"No sir, I just felt I'd be better off with you guys than The Nine, not to mention, Jessup is quite persuasive." I nervously raised my goblet to my lips, but did not drink.

"Ha!" Frank blurted out. "Son, are you at all aware of why we invited you here tonight?"

"I guess it's to join your cult, become a…a Thrall?" I answered.

"A Thrall? Well, very good then. Ben, do you know what a Thrall is?" Barry Haskin asked.

"Uh…no." I couldn't think of anything.

"Ben, a Thrall is a mortal held under a mind bond, or blood bond, to one of us, as a servant. Is this what you wish to be?" Frank asked with a sarcastic smirk on his face.

"Isn't that how everyone starts?" I questioned.

"Not you Ben, you are of the aura, you are Vampyr." Frank assured me.

"Vam-peer? What is Vam-peer?" I was starting to feel real uncomfortable.

Barry stood up and dropped his robes revealing an old, yet very well kept gray confederate uniform. Following was Bill, dropping his robes, his attire was something you'd see in the 'Amadeus' movie, complete with ruffles and a white wig with a pony tail. Frank kept his robes on.

"Those are neat outfits, but how does that answer my…" I closed my eyes and swallowed. Even I could put two and two together. I was hoping they would speak and dispel my dread.

"Ben," Frank interjected "Vampyr are those of humankind with the aura and ability to become immortal. Bill and Barry are wearing their original clothing from when they were first Embraced."

"So, you're saying they're wearing real old clothes. I'm still a little confused here, what's Embraced mean?" I'm guessing Frank could read the concern in my face by now.

"What he's saying," Bill interjects "Is that I was once in service of the Queen, before America was founded, and that I am as old as the clothing I wear."

"That's impossible! You'd have to be…oh yeah, you said immortal." Shit!

"Vampyr, Ben, is what one is, before becoming Vampire! Some call it Vampir, Vamphyr, Vamphyre, Vamphire, or one of several other terms, meaning Vampiric."

"Ok. So like, these guys are vampires? Like Nosferatu or Dracula, like blood sucking, wooden stake through the heart, sleeping in a coffin, vampires?" Frank curls up his lips and hisses brandishing fangs, Bill and Barry follow suit. I freeze, dropping my goblet once again, attempting to make my body move. Frank closes his mouth and his face returns to normalcy once again.

"Ben, relax, we just wanted to show you we were on the level. If we wanted you dead, Jessup would have finished you the first time. Ben, death is the destroyer of life, there is no afterlife, and so death is a waste. Also, to simply kill humans, is wasting food. Jessup doesn't agree 100% with us, but the rest do."

"Yes," agrees Barry, "Jessup calls us Cunctatols. But never Cauchemals! Ha, ha, ha!"

All three burst out in laughter, what is this, like, vampire humor or what? This is sick and can't be real, can it? I guess, if an old man, a cop, a sports storeowner, and a few others can cast spells, these guys could be vampires. Oh, by the way, I'm ready to wake up any time now.

"The rest? How many…vampires are there?"

"Well, we've nine in our inner circle, ten if you include the Harbinger. As far as vampyr, there are several hundred all over the world. Thralls are as many as we decide to make. Let's not forget those infernal Footpads, uh, wanderers, if you will, they have no class. These are the…creatures Hollywood is so big on making movies about. They really give us a bad name. Poor Lineage, poor form really." Bill expressed.

"Bad name? Excuse me, but with all due respect, you DO suck people's blood right?" I boldly stated. That would be like saying Hitler gives Nazi's a bad name.

Frank fields this one, "Ben, Footpads aside, we are Kindred, and you could be too. It's my guess, that when educated you would like to choose the side that most benefits you, eh?"

"Bully! Be in line for the buffet, or BE the buffet, eh chap?" Bill smiles. He could go on stage as a stand up vampire comedian, and just eat anyone who doesn't laugh.

"So, Frank, you've killed people, sucking their blood? Where you a vampire when I was a kid? Back when you were my families Pastor?" I felt choked up, until now it didn't really sink in. I'm sitting here with guys that could kill me before I could raise my hand. I thought Frank to be a man of God. My family trusted and supported this man. I didn't want the answer I knew I was going to get. How can this be happening? I'm helpless to stop it. What do I do?

"Ben, I…" Frank stopped mid sentence, regrouped and sternly stated, "I've been Kindred for one hundred-nineteen years. Yes, as your Pastor, I was Kindred. Ben, I never spoke of humankind's false Gods, only of our Lord and Sire. I fear that the Bible is nothing more than a best selling novel of fantastic stories." He looked at me with conviction, but sorrowful eyes.

"That's a croc! I heard your sermons! My Dad believed in you! I believed in you! You couldn't have been…Hey! How could a vampire live in a church?" I figured I had him, but as always, Frankly Frank had an answer.

"Ben, Vampirism predates Christianity or Judaism by thousands of years. That alone explains why a cross can't harm us. I've grown rather fond of them over time actually. Again, many who've learned a little about true vampirism, were appalled by what they knew, so added that we can't walk in sunlight, it takes a stake in the heart to kill us, a cross burns us, decapitation followed by burning, destroys us. Oh, and of course we can turn into bats, rats, and gas. Look, humans who fear us, turn to their organized religions as ways to kill us off in movies. We are superior to mere mortals in virtually every way, but we are not the creatures you've read about, and post dated religions are just Greek mythology to us." Frank sat back and drank from his goblet.

"Why take a chance on telling me all this? What if I decided to bolt and tell everyone?"

"Then we'd deal with you, like the vampires you've read about." Barry snarls out to me.

I like Bill better, jokes are better than death threats, call me kooky on that one, huh?

"Fine, but The Nine…" I was interrupted by Barry again.

"…are weak. They can't touch us, never could, never will be able to. I figured Jessup showed that to you."

"True, so let's say I'm in, I want to become…Kindred. When do I meet the Harbinger? Or is he one of you?" The room erupted in laughter.

"Ben, my boy, when you meet him, you'll understand the humor in asking if one of us were him." Frank walked over and put his hand on my shoulder like he used to when ever we'd leave church. It almost put me at ease, almost. How was I going to get out of this? Oh, and supposedly retrieve some tome or scroll with the spell of stopping them on it? I doubt it's lying on their coffee table. The young lady came around and refilled our goblets, giving me a clean one, and handed us all cigars. Cubans of course, in a redwood humidor. Of course I half expected the box to be in the shape of a coffin, but it wasn't.

I heard the door creak open, I spun around, as best I could in this gentleman's club of the undead, only to see Jessup standing on the stairs, with his sarcastic, snarl/smile. He casually tossed a body, fully clad for winter, onto the oversized floor amulet in the middle of the room.

"A piece offering Ben." Jessup hissed out.

I got up and walked over to the body on the floor, I couldn't tell if they were alive or not, as I rolled the body over, I saw it was...No!

Chapter Nine
Unholy Communion

Now what? I can't just sit by and let Jessup or these others just kill people. Then again, I can't really stop it, or at the very least, don't know how to stop it. If I turn on them without any idea of how to stop them, I'll probably end up dead, and the slaughter will continue. I guess my best bet is to continue to learn about these creatures and hope I discover something that either The Nine or I can use to stop this...this nightmare from spreading.

As I rolled over the body, I realized it was Russ, my brother. He was a bloody mess, all torn up, swollen, black and blue. Damnation! That tears it! Russ opens his eyes, he weakly grabs my arm, and "B...Ben...help...me." He closes his eyes again, and his hand drops limply from my arm. He is still breathing however, but his breathing is shallow. In one swift motion I jump to my stance, slap in a clip and unload four shots into Jessup's' chest. The shots all hit their mark and send Jessup flying up against the door. I immediately swing around, fully expecting one of the others to be coming after me. All three however, are still sitting in their over stuffed chairs puffing on their Cubans and sipping their wine.

I find myself yelling, "You can't fuck with my family! No one touches my family! I don't care who or what you are! So, who's next?" Frank points his cigar at where Jessup was. As I spin around, I see Jessup standing five feet behind me.

"Ben, that hurts like a bitch! But, relax, I didn't do this. Some of our Thralls found him and some other guy snooping around the graveyard. They caught this one, they say the other one made it to his car and took off. I brought him here so you could help him. Ask him; just don't shoot again, ok? It stings."

I kneel down again, "Russ, is this the guy that did this to you?"

"A…a lot of guys…Jeff…" Russ passes out again.

"I got to get him to a hospital! Frank? You gotta let me get him there."

"It will do no good. You may take him if you wish, but he'll die before you get there. Ben, only you can save him. Become one of us, become immortal, become a ruler. You are vampyr, you were born to be one of the elite. If you choose to do so, it will be within your power to save Russ." Frank stuffs the stogie back in his mouth and settling back into his chair.

This is bull! This is a set-up to get me to join. If it's true, I don't want to be one of them! If it isn't and this is some elaborate set-up, than I'm no worse for the wear.

"Jessup? How did *you* manage to come by this scene?" I sarcastically asked.

"Ben, have the old Cunctatols taught you nothing in my absence? The Thralls bring all their victims to us, like a cat showing off a mouse it just caught. This one just wasn't dead yet, drained, but not dead." Jessup grinned again.

"Jessup, this one is my brother! Hey, shouldn't he have the aura too? Same family? Why would they attack someone with the aura?" Answer this, big mouths.

"Yes, he has the aura. Thralls can't decipher auras. Just as The Nine couldn't decipher yours. See, to the Thralls, he could have been one of The Nine, and naturally they are ordered to kill any of The Nine they run into." Frank answered.

"Hey, foods food to predators, if it moves and bleeds, its fair game." Bill states, using his cigar's trailing smoke like a piece of chalk on a chalkboard, like he's writing it out for me.

Oh man! I guess I don't have much choice. I put sadness aside and concentrate on how I can help my brother. Guess I gotta go through with it for Russ. I guess I'll give these bastards what they want, but when it's done, I'm going to make them pay! Nobody manipulates me and messes with my family and gets away with it!

"Fine. You win. Frank," I say in a resigned voice, "why can't you save Russ? If you do, I'll join you and swear allegiance."

"Alas, I can keep him alive, but if I Embrace him, he'll become my Thrall, bonded both by mind and blood to me in eternal servitude, or you could Communionize, and have the power to save him either as a Thrall, Kindred, or let him remain a mere mortal."

"Where's the other six of your inner circle? How long does Russ have?" I had a million questions flood over me.

"Again, I can keep Russ alive for you, for as long as you need. I wouldn't wait too terribly long, however, the longer you wait, the weaker his constitution will grow. If he grows too weak, his system may not survive his re-birth, and certainly will not survive remaining mortal. The mortal spirit is so weak."

Frank assures me. "As for the whereabouts of the others, that is their own business. I would expect them back soon, however."

"Re-birth? You mean becoming a vampire, right?"

"Of course. You see Ben, your mortal body must die, your mortal spirit ceases to exist, and then you are re-born Kindred, one communionized with those who have risen. Those from the Astral plane."

"You don't mean some kind of air plane when you say that, you're talking about some plane of existence, like in that Dungeons &Demons game, right?" If only I'd played that more in college, I might understand this stuff better. I bet they tell you how to kill vampires in that game.

"Exactly Ben," Frank sucks on his cigar until the tip radiates orange, and then, releasing the smoke slowly, he continues, "Everyone has a Primaterial plane existence and an Astral plane existence. Your aura is from the Astral plane. Look, you've heard of outer body experiences? People floating above their own bodies, and watching as their Primaterial body gets surgery done to it? Or people state they've gone down a long tunnel with a bright light at the end of it, and just as they almost reach the light, they are pulled back?

They say this is a death and back experience?" I ponder aloud. "Well, yeah, I've heard stories of people saying this." I leaned forward, seeking more information.

"Ben, all Biblical or famous people from centuries ago, before film, had pictures painted of them, correct? What did every picture have in common?"

"Well, I don't know, I guess I've never paid much attention." I was showing my confusion.

"Ben, every picture has a halo or glow behind them. Think back, Mona-Lisa, Plato, all of them. This glow or halo was their personal aura. Their aura showed up to the artist, simply because true artists can see things differently than anyone else. Your aura, or life energy, is larger than your mortal shell. Your mortal shell or Primaterial existence is what your aura would look like if it manifested itself onto the Primaterial or mortal plane. Ben, your aura is what others call your soul. Here, answer me this riddle, if any of these Biblical or famous people didn't exist, how is it that every picture, in every country across the world, of each individual, is identical, down to the number of thorns in Jesus' thorn crown?" Frank drinks deep.

"So you're admitting that these people existed, even the Biblical figures, so why are you panning the Bible?" I, of course, expected an answer.

"Look boy," Barry interjected, "We never said they didn't exist. Hell, they had to for the text of the Bible to remain accurate over the centuries. Sure, there are gaps in time in the Bible, that's where faith comes in, but all we're saying is, for paintings of individuals and text of books to remain intact and exact, someone had to be alive all through the centuries, and those someone's were the Kindred."

"Wait, are you saying Moses was a vampire?" This is getting outrageous, I'm not too religious, but I'm starting to look for thunderbolts now!

"No. We have no proof of that, and vampirism is a belief of facts, not fantasies. We can't say who were the Kindred, and who weren't, all we can say is they all had a strong aura about them, and could have been or become Kindred, if they desired." Barry took his turn at relaxing now.

"So, all famous people have the strong aura, and could be vampires? So maybe people did see Elvis at a restaurant!"

If so, he wasn't there for a burger!" Bill threw in, in his own jovial way, "Maybe, the ketchup, eh?"

"Ben, not all infamous people are vampyr, but a majority was or they wouldn't have made it like they did. And, Ben, some unknowns, like you and I, have the aura. All the rest are grown here as food, food to be harvested, so that we Kindred can go on ruling the night." Frank added.

"Where do you think the term "Harvest Moon" originated, son?"" Added Bill the jester.

"Well, this is fascinating, but a lot of stuff to digest." I winced as soon as I said it. Bill of course followed up with roaring laughter.

"Of course it is. Enough for tonight then, Kalen, show Ben to his room, we'll talk again tomorrow evening Ben." Frank gestured to the servant girl, Kalen. I like that name.

Kalen led me through the middle door, this led down a corridor, it was dark, and I'd left my candle back in the other room. Oddly enough, I could sort of see anyway. I was led through another door, clearly a patient room, but one below ground. It contained a bed, a desk and chair, an armoire, and an oil-burning lamp.

"Kalen, are you happy here? Are you ok?" I inquired.

With no response, she smiled and closed the door. I locked it as she left. I figured even Jessup would wake me if he tried breaking it down. As I lay down, I couldn't keep my eyes open. I drifted off, probably drooling on my pillow as usual. I slept like the dead…

* * *

I sat up quickly as if being awakened by a loud noise. I then realized that I hadn't heard a loud noise, I think I was just awake enough to realize where I was, and that maybe sleeping wasn't such a good idea. I jumped up and listened at my door, I heard nothing. I went and turned up my lamp. I realized there was a mirror hanging on the wall, one I didn't remember, but then I noticed my medallion was hanging on it, and certainly don't remember taking it off and putting it on the mirror. I checked the door and it was still locked. Oh well, I was pretty out of it, tired and my mind was swimming with information. What a weird outlook on life, or afterlife, or un-death? Whatever. I lace up the boots, throw on the trench coat, swing the medallion over my neck, and look at my unshaven face. I had bags under my eyes, and for the first time in days, I felt hunger pains. I sure hope vampires can cook. Whoa! That was weird, I could have sworn I saw…in the mirror…nah, couldn't have been.

I open the door, slowly, and peek my head out. The hallway is dark; no one appears to be in it. I head back toward the main room. As I reach the door, I hesitate, but after taking a deep breath, I pull it open and enter. Leaning against one of the chairs is a guy I don't recognize. He looks like a CEO or maybe a presidential secret service guy. He's decked out in, what has to be a $1200 Italian suit. His shoes are snake or gator skin, he's wearing dark glasses, and is smoking a cigarette. He smiles upon my entrance. He sort of looks like Don Johnson, he even appears to be tan…but that's impossible, isn't it? Wait, maybe he's not a vampire!

"Yes, I am Kindred, Ben."

"How. how did you…" I brilliantly stammered.

"I heard you, each ones gift is different. So, they are right, you are of the aura. Why are you so unsure of yourself?" He inquired. I was afraid to think of an answer, if he can read my mind, he should already know why I'm unsure, I'm scared shitless!

"You…are frightened? They DID do a good job on you. Fascinating. Ben, are you going to communionize tonight?" He asks with a hopeful tone.

"Why is everyone so concerned with when I communionize? If you're all in such a damn hurry, why not just overpower me, and turn me?" I was serious, how weird!

"I'm sorry Ben, it's been awhile since I've met one of Lineage such as yours. It's quite exhilarating really." He smiles, brandishing teeth as white as on a toothpaste commercial, with the exception of those incisors.

"So, you know me, and you are…?"

"Oh, so sorry, Kendal Ontolli, at your service." Again with the kind of smile that has wooed many a victim close to him.

"Kendal, have you seen Frank any where? I was supposed to meet him…"

"You're early; Frank said evening, dusk if you will, if you think back, you'll remember that. Anyway, any chance of Communion tonight? Not pushing, just curious." No smile this time, he's serious.

"So why hasn't anyone tried to…to…Emb…" Again he interrupts me.

"Embrace you? That would be a last resort. We were so hoping for a voluntary Communion. It truly does get you there faster and there's less risk of becoming a Thrall." He stops me again. "I know and I'm sorry, habit you know, I'll attempt to stop reading you."

"Dude, is this, like, *the Ben* or what?" A teenager dressed in a Hawaiian shirt, long shorts, and sandals approaches from one of the other doors. His hair is bleached, and his washboard stomach gives away the fact that he's a genuine 'surfer dude'.

"Yeah, hey, how are ya?"

"Shaka Brah, how's it hangin'? Dude, is like tonight the kine' communion night, yeah?"

"I don't know, I NEED to see Frank. Look, it's been a pleasure; I'll be in my room if Frank shows up." I turn to head back down the hall, only to be met by The Road Warrior. This guy looked just like Mel in the movie, right down to the eye patch and white streaked hair. Oh, and we've another case of death breath here. I crinkle my nose and try to walk by him. As I put my shoulder into him, attempting to pass, he growls and stands his ground. I back off, he's a big mother.

"Look, I need to get by; you got a problem with that?" I receive another growl as my answer. At least Mel could talk, and was a little cleaner looking.

"Hey, Kendal, could you ask…him to let me by?"

"You might as well try it yourself, you want to. He won't touch you. Stand your ground, as you were born to."

"Fine, move it Death-Breath, or lose it." I walked directly at him, he wasn't moving, great!

I put my face about five inches from his stinky, hairy face and whispered; "You'll be the first ass I kick, but for now, you aren't worth a breath mint to me." I quickly spin on my heels, attempting to get out of his reach as soon as possible, and without looking as if I was running away, headed to a chair.

"Hey, Kendal, how does a guy get some food around here?" I look back at the big guy, he hasn't moved.

Kendal sits, as does the surfer dude, Mel keeps standing. By my count, I've only not met three of the inner circle, one of which is the Harbinger himself. Kalen brings out some wine again. It tastes great. I'm hungry and thirsty, and figure some wine will help settle my nerves. Crap, I don't know who's more unnerving, Mel or Kendal, I'm actually beginning to like Jessup now.

Enter the Countess of Monte-Crisco, a tall, slender; Elvira looking lady enters through the final door I've not yet been through. She's dressed in a slinky, black dress, her medallion gleams, her eyes are mesmerizing. I tear my eyes from her, two young men, wearing only loin cloths carry the train of her dress, and kneel on either side of her chair, both young men are handsome and muscular, but their eyes are glazed over and they have puncture marks and healed legions all over their bodies.

"So," She speaks in a silky voice you can only usually hear for $1.95 a

minute over the phone, "You must be the prodigal child. How yummy."
She licks her lips and closes her eyes.

"I'm Shanestra, and I've been waiting to meet you."

"Ben," its Frank! I can't believe I'm excited to see this guy. "Have you
met everyone?"

"All but Zephyr...and the Harbinger dude." The surfer dude added in
for me. Bill and Barry followed Frank. Jessup was close behind, "How's
Russ?" he said and smirked at me. I take it back; Jessup is the biggest
asshole of all the vampires so far.

"Fine, how's your chest feeling numbnuts?" What am I stupid? He just
rubs me the wrong way!

"Healed Ben, oh, did you get the mirror I left for you?" Again with that
infernal smirk.

"Enough!" Kendal spoke up, "Where is Zephyr? Anyone see him
recently?" He looked around, "Well, Seth? Were you going to enlighten
us with your last visit with him?"

"Dude, like it was for ten minutes, he went harvesting dude,
Footpadding. It's not like I didn't tell him, but you know, he's not one of
the Progeny, he's not gonna, like, listen to me, ok?" Seth sat back down
like a kid that just got blamed for something he didn't do.

"Yes, I suppose you did try, very well."

I interrupted, "Progeny? What's that?"

"Sorry, Ben, yes you're close. Actually, Progeny is the description for
all vampires sired under one sire. All in this room have the same sire
except Zephyr, Bill, and Denny over there." Kendal points to Mel.
Denny? That big, smelly, hairy son-of-a-bitch is named Denny? Ooo,
that's a tough name.

The door swings open, a large black man, dressed like a native,
complete with war paint, animal skins, and animal teeth for jewelry steps

through and tosses a body onto the floor. This man makes ol' sarge Peacock look like Barney on Andy Griffith. The light of the candles glitter off his sweat coated skin, "Dis be what happens, when we's all sits around and waits!" As my eyes adjust, I see fresh wounds on his hide, blood stains his lower jaw, he's shaking as if pure adrenaline or caffeine, I'm going with the first thought, was flowing through his veins.

"Is he one of yours Zeph?" Shenestra asks all innocent and lady like.

"Sit down Zephyr. You're late." Without hesitation the big guy sits, still shaking angrily, but not challenging Kendal. So let's see, from left to right we have Zephyr the big guy, Seth the surfer dude, Denny the road warrior, Frank, Bill the Englishman, Barry the confederate, Jessup the ass, and Kendal the telepath, oops, and Shenestra the Siren. They're all here and accounted for, except for the Harbinger, unless Kendal is him.

"No sir, I'm not the Harbinger. Ben as soon as you wish to become Communionized, You will be made aware of all that is transpiring, and you will then meet the Harbinger, the time draws near for Those Who Have Already Risen to reveal the Harbinger and usher in our final hour. 'The meek shall inherit the earth', do you know who said that Ben?" Kendal asked.

"Uh, no, not really."

"Me either, but Bill killed him for it." Kendal smiled and Bill burst out laughing, joined by Jessup's hissing and Shanestra's snickering.

"Ok, funny, Frank, Russ is he..." I looked to Frank.

"He's fine Ben. This meeting is for you. What questions do you have today, Ben?"

"Ok. Look, who is this dead guy on the floor?" I asked, since no one else seemed concerned.

"Dis is only a T'rall. But, dis is the t'ird dis week!" Zephyr spit out, like he'd just sucked out snake venom out of a wound.

"Yes, The Nine seem to be working overtime. Ben, you see now, we kill theirs, and they kill ours. Its war, son. Unfortunately, The Nine haven't the resources to stop any of the Kindred, only our Thralls. That is enough however to force us to take a personal hand in their downfall. Ben, the time has come for you to make a choice. Communion or Embrace, choose wisely. Again, Communion is your better bet, but the option is yours." Kendal extends an empty hand out to me, not for me to grab, but to show that about sums it up for my options.

"Well, as enticing as getting bit in the neck sounds to me, I guess I'll be choosing Communion. What do I do?" I close my eyes, knowing I'm relatively screwed at this point. The other thought I have is to yell out my chant and run, leaving Russ here. I can't bring myself to do this. I open my eyes, and see that all the Kindred are smiling and drinking wine.

"Ben, running is not an option, Frank will guide you if you'd like." Kendal gives me a concerned look, and then his face quickly breaks into that famous smile, and he lights up a cigarette.

"Frank is it always a celebration before Communion?" I inquire.

"Of course, we're adding another Kindred ruler to the Lineage. Come, drink, we start soon."

Kendal jumps up and everyone immediately stops the chattering and partying, they become silent. He looks around, and calmly tells Frank to stay and guide me. Kendal takes a last look at me, and then with a gesture of his hand, motions to the others. They all stand and quickly scatter toward the steam tunnel entrance. Kendal slowly saunters behind the others. He stops and turns, as if remembering something, and simply states, "Frank, be a gem, and bring Ben by my place tomorrow. I will expect he's been communionized. Damn! I really must go now, good luck Ben, may they be kind."

Kendal stops for a moment looking up; he then places his dark glasses on, and bolts down the hall. I hear his shoes clip clopping, but I don't see much more than a blur. Something upset these guys; I just gotta know what it is. I turn to ask Frank, he appears to be lost in thought, "Frank? You ok? What is it?"

"…of course, I understand." Franks eyes come back into focus on me. "Ben, Russ is just down the East wing. Read from the Tomb Of Uhr, it will explain all. I fear I must leave and join my colleagues, the Tomb is under the pedestal, I'll raise it for you. It shall remain raised for three hours. Make sure the Tomb is returned before the Communion is complete; you'll be too weak to raise it again. Ben, if you're not Kindred by tomorrow, Kendal will Embrace you, it's much…more pleasant communionizing. I'll see you soon."

Frank lifts his arms as if truly lifting something, but touching nothing, the pedestal or large medallion, rises to four-feet off the ground and levitates there. Frank rushes down the hall the others took, back toward the boiler room leading to the sewer.

Lying on the ground is a leather bound tome with large letters burned into the leather "UHR", centered perfectly under the letters is the impression of the Soaring Skull…

Chapter Ten
Aftermath

I've finally got the chance to grab the tome and hightail it out of here. With all of the Inner Circle gone, there's no one to stand in my way. Wait, Russ…I have to grab Russ and get him to a hospital. If he's made it this long, he ought to be able to make it to the hospital. Mike and Keith are to far gone for me to reach, I guess if I save Russ, and get the tomb to The Nine, and they stop the Vampires, and Mike and Keith don't leave the cult to come home, I can at least tell everyone that they're alive. I mean, hey, that's good news, right? That, coupled with me making it out alive with the tome, and helping Russ, what else can they expect from me…

"Please bring my big brother home." Oh, how the words rang in my ears. I picture little Sarah Peacock's freckled face, with a single tear clinging to her cheek. Can I look her in the eye and say that I tried to bring Mike home? He's the latest recruit, he may not be as brainwashed yet. Crap! Eventually I've got to look out for number one. This may be my only chance…

"Ben…that you?" I hear a weak voice ask, hardly louder than a whisper. As I turn, I see its Russ, using the door to keep him on his feet.

I immediately rush over to aid him. My God! He looks terrible. He's as white as a…never mind. I throw his arm around my shoulder and head out. I pause briefly to grab the tome. We head up the stairs and into the building; I decide not to risk the steam tunnel. Ok, so if I get caught, my story is…that I didn't get to finish the ceremony before the pedestal dropped, and rather than leave the tome unattended, I thought I'd seek out one of the Kindred, and guard the tome until I found someone. Yeah, that'll work. Ok, here we go.

I find myself aiding Russ with less effort than I expected. This is good, however, we're not outside yet, and we've many a mile to go through the woods to get to the hospital. I finally reach the main ground level. It's amazing, this building was constructed well, in fact it looks like, if someone just cleaned it up a little, and turned on the power, it could be up and running in no time. It almost looks as if everyone left in a hurry, some beds are still made, food trays are sitting on tables in patients rooms, notes strewn about the nurses station, wheel chairs tipped over in the hall way…I'd expect someone would have come in and pack up any useful items. Oh, well, I see the entrance. The doors are chained shut of course.

"Russ, you ok man? Look, hang in there; I've got to get these chains off. You ok, man? Russ?"

"Ben…just hurry…Pastor Frank…he's…he's a…" Russ' eyes roll back into his head, and then they close. Crap! I've got to hurry!

With no time to lose, I pull out my trusty firearm, and crack off a shot that shatters the chains. Grabbing Russ, we head out into the forest. Again, I get to feel the cold embrace my face, I don't even lick my lips for fear of them freezing. I've tucked the tome into my coat and am pretty much carrying Russ in a fireman's carry, legs and arms wrapped around my arms, his belly pressed against the back of my head. It feels ok so far, but I'm sure I won't be able to do this forever. I steer toward the paths with little or no snow, I figure these will be hard from the cold and I'd hate to step into a three-foot hole, covered with snow, and hurt something. The night is quiet; I don't even hear birds or animals. There's very little breeze, which helps keep the wind-chill factor, not a...well, factor. As I continue down the path, I'm brought to a sudden stop. Leaping out from behind a thatch of trees is what appears to be a Thrall of someone's. He lands on all fours in front of us, he looks up at us, and his eyes are glowing red. He smiles and then let's out a hiss that doesn't sound like a teenage boy trying to hiss, but more like the guttural hiss of a caged tiger. He leaps to the side and disappears into the trees. I set Russ down, and pull out my firearm.

"Come here little Thrall, come out and get me!" I swing from East to West to North to South, with my arms fully extended.

I hear the hiss again, and leaping out from behind me is the kid. As I swing around, I fire off a round, it doesn't hit its mark, and I feel my self being taken down under the weight of my opponent. I hit the ground hard, my gun being jarred from my grip, and bouncing off into the night. The Thrall opens his mouth, and brandishes fangs, the thread of saliva connecting his top row of teeth to the bottom row, glistens in what little moonlight penetrates into the woods, between the trees. Does this punk really think he's going to bite me? This gives a whole new meaning to the slang term 'bite me!'. Note to self, don't use that term anymore.

I twist, attempting to get some leverage, with all the strength I can muster, I manage to make him lose balance, and find my self able to roll out from under him. He immediately springs to all fours again. I slowly get to my feet. I grab my amulet and shove it in his face.

"Back Thrall, never attack a Vampyr! Your master will be displeased!" I was already working on Plan B.

The Thrall backed off, and lowered his head. "I'm sorry. Release me, please."

"You may go, but speak nothing of this meeting!" I pointed back toward the Hillcrest Institute.

The Thrall fled back in that direction. I went over to Russ, he still lay there unconscious. Interesting, the amulet may be my ticket past all the Thralls. I found myself fatigued after that last skirmish. Damn! I had to get Russ to safety. I picked him up again. I found my breathing labored, it was getting quite difficult to continue with the weight of Russ on my back. I find myself dropping to my knees; I have to set Russ down. Oh man, I'm sorry Russ; I can't make it with you. I look up, the moon through the trees appears to have tears in it, this is simply the branches blocking out parts of the moon. Have you ever had that feeling of being completely overwhelmed? So overwhelmed you just want to give up? You want to swear and cuss at everything, the feeling of abandonment. As completely uncool as it may seem, I really just want to cry. What in the Hell am I trying to do anyway? My brother is laying here dying, and I'm helpless to save him. He'll either freeze to death, or die from his wounds, but I refuse to leave him. Yeah, infiltrate the cult and report back to HQ. What a great idea, I mean look, best case scenario: I live, Russ dies, Mike and Keith stay in the cult, only to be killed later by The Nine, and mankind survives. Worst case? Pretty much the opposite, only with mass genocide on the side. It's hopeless. I should just stay here and freeze with Russ, then I'm out of the picture. They say freezing is one of the best ways to go…ah, hell, who am I trying to kid?

I guess I've got my second wind, at least I hope I do. I toss Russ back on my shoulders and head out. They say, whenever you get hurt, if you say 'ouch' out loud, that actually helps quell the pain. I've personally found, that if you swear out loud, when you're too tired to continue physically, actually get mad, it helps take your mind off your fatigue, and the adrenaline keeps you going. This may not work for everyone, but I'm not concerned with everyone right now, just with my brother getting help. If Russ makes it, no more Twinkies in his diet! Funny, I haven't seen Russ for like a year or so, and this is how we get to see each other, him coming to help me. Please Russ, hang in there bro!

I've been walking for about three hours as best as I can estimate, according to 'cult time', I must almost be there. I hear a car driving by; I can make out the sound of its wheels cutting through the slush. I don't see any headlights, but a road must be nearby. This new information makes me pick up my pace, I feel invigorated, excited, hot damn! We're going to make it!

"Russ, we're going to make it bro, hang tight, we're going to make it!" I push out through the last line of trees, and find the blessed road. I-98 never looked so great! All I need is a car now. After waiting for what would seem to be an eternity, I see headlights coming over the hill. I tuck the medallion under my coat, and step out on to the road, waving both arms wildly. The vehicle is a car, no wait…a police cruiser! Great! They pull over and turn on both their red and blue lights, as well as their spotlight.

"Young man, are you ok?" A voice yells out to me, but being blinded by the spotlight doesn't allow me to see who's speaking to me.

"Yes sir, my brother, over here, he needs a hospital!" I hear two sets of footsteps rushing toward me. I jump at the sight of their silhouettes, but relax as they come into view. They rush past me and pick up Russ, carrying him to the car, I follow, and they help me into the blessed warmth of the cruiser.

"Please, call up Malley, tell him you've got Ben Ruden, I have to talk to him, he'll understand…" I close my eyes and allow the heat to caress my entire being. For the first time in days, I feel safe…

* * *

I come to, groggy, but eventually I'm able to focus. I actually feel good; standing over me is a kind looking older lady, dressed in white, with a brown sweater buttoned over her uniform.

"Nurse, Russ is he…"

"Shhh, you've had quite a night. You rest, we'll talk more later. You've got an I.V. inserted to rehydrate you, so you'll soon be fine."

Geez, could her voice be any sweeter? Grandma is that you? We're talking about a voice that is as sweet as a marshmallow soaked in honey.

I feel too revived to sleep now. She left, I get up, pulling out my I.V. I go to the closet and find all my clothes, my medallion, and my tome there. Whew! That would've sucked, to lose that. Hey, my gun! Oh, yeah, in the woods. Oh well, I'm sure Sarge has an extra one. I start to get dressed, the clothes are stiff and cold, and quite dirty really. Well, they'll have to do for now. I decide to take it upon myself to remove my I.V. When I've finally got my whole ensemble together, I stick my head out the door. A cop is sitting across the hall from me, he's looking to his right and hasn't seen me yet, so I quietly shut the door. How am I supposed to get out of here? I scan the room, a phone! I pick it up and dial my number.

"Hello?" a voice answers.

"Hey, who is this?" I inquire.

"This is the Ruden home; I'm just looking after it while Ben's out of town. Who can I say is calling?"

"Dugan…is Dugan or Malley there?"

"Hang on."

"Hello? This is Dugan."

"Dugan! Hey, it's me Ben! I'm at the hospital; I've got what we need! Tell Malley to have his boys bring me over!" I excitedly exclaimed.

"Ben? Great! Hang on…ok, Malley radioed Officer Johnson, he should be right outside your room, he's going to check you out and come get you. Don't move until he comes to get you. See you soon, great job pal!" We hung up.

As I continued to scan the room, I saw a flip chart on me. Being nosey, I decided to have a look. Holy cow, it says I was to receive 2 units of PRBC's (Packed Red Blood Cells) Gross! They must have me mixed up with Russ. Man, I need to check on Russ. Ok, so I'll just call the front desk and ask about Russ, like a relative…which I am really, anyway…so I dial. I let it ring like fifteen times, I can even hear the phone ringing down the hall. Well, enough is enough; I'm heading out and looking for Officer Johnson.

I open my door again, and of course no Officer Johnson in the seat anymore, I suppose I could just check on Russ, and get back here in time to meet Johnson. I mean, if they really do have me mixed up with Russ, and he obviously needs those Pbr's or whatever, than it's got to be brought to someone's attention. So, since I make sense to me, off I go down to the nurses' station. The halls are a highly polished crème color with an almost marble look to the floors, the walls have a door every ten feet or so, and are peppered with posters and pamphlet holders, and like most hospitals I've been in, the pamphlet holders are mostly empty. Who reads those things? That's what I pay a doctor or nurse to tell me. Anyway, oh here's a good one, 'DRUGS CAN KILL', so like what is it exactly the doctors prescribe to us? Wait, 'DRINKING AND DRIVING DON'T MIX', I suppose the drunken driving accident victims are saying "Really? Shit, if only the hospital was stocked on those pamphlets when I was here

on my last cholesterol check, I might not be wondering why there's so little feeling in my legs right now!!! Thanks MercyThorne Memorial Hospital!"

Someone doesn't pay attention to the RE-ORDER NOW cards in the slots. Oh look, a medical humor poster, it states 'HOW MANY DOCTORS DOES IT TAKE TO CHANGE A LIGHT BULB? NONE, THEY HAVE THE NURSES DO IT!' Penciled in under it is 'That's the only way it'll get done properly and before tee-time.' Ouch! A little battle of the wits going on, huh?

I now hear several phone lines ringing, as my footsteps echo in the hall, I can smell the sterile cleansers used. I think every hospital uses the same cleansers, and only one company makes them, and the 'hospital smell' is like an additive. Odd, there's a supply cart blocking the middle of the hall, well it moves easily enough. Whoa! There's not a soul at the nurse's station. The phone lines are all lit up, someone's got to come answer them. Where's Johnson? As I look down the hall, almost all the little lights above the patients' rooms are lit up. I'm guessing that's the nurse call light. I decide to head over to the nearest room to see if there's a nurse in there. No wonder no ones around, it looks like all the patients needed service at once. Oddly, as I open the door, I find no one in the room, patient, nurse or doctor. A weird feeling starts to overcome me; I rush to the next room, empty. I continue, at a pretty quick pace now, flinging doors open and finding only empty rooms. The furniture is in there, some bed tables have food trays on them still, none of the beds are made, and the TV is on in most of the rooms. I decide to go to one without the little light on, sure enough, empty. The difference, is that the beds are made and it wouldn't appear that the rooms had been previously occupied, recently anyway. Ok...ok...settle down, I was just in a meeting with nine vampires, and I'm letting this psyche me out? So like, how come this is weirder? All right, let's think for a minute. I, of course, assume that there's a logical explanation. Not that logic has worked yet, but come on, it's got too eventually. Think, think, think…nope. Nothing comes to mind this is just plain eerie. Wait a minute, no…they wouldn't…I decide to head back to a room with the little nurse call on, and take a closer look. I approach the bed, there are some bloodstains on the sheets, but this is a hospital, people probably do bleed sometimes. I head to the next room, yep, blood stains. Damn! Those bastards, but why not find me? They've apparently cleared my floor, and who knows how much more? Fine, I'll just call my house and…dead. Ok, so this weasel didn't want to pay for phone service, wait…crap! I head over to the nurses' station; I no longer hear any ringing or see any lines lit up. As I pick up a receiver and hit lines, I hear nothing. They do however have a little green fuzzy thing with big sticky feet stuck to the phone holding a sign that says 'Don't catch the Y2K bug, get your flu shots.' Great. Ok, where are they, I can only think of one thing to do…get the hell out of here. I borrow a nurse's backpack lying on the counter and empty it out. It's black so it kind of goes with the whole cult look, oops, except that it says 'Trust me, I'm not a doctor.' Ok, whatever. So I put my Tome in it and cruise down the hall. Crap! I quickly head back and rifle through the patients file holder on the counter, here it is; Ruden, Russ: Room 601. I…I've been in that room, empty. All right, these bloodsuckers are going down! I rundown the hall looking for the elevator, and as luck would have it, I find them. I punch the down button and the first three of four elevators that arrive are going up. I think they do this on purpose too. So, I figure the elevator god didn't receive the right signals, so I decide to press the down button repeatedly, and sure enough, the elevator arrives. Happy that I figured it out, I hop on and go to push the 'G' button, only to find that every button is lit up. Oh good, that gives me the opportunity to stop on every floor on the way down, I hope the cute little kid that did this doesn't get any Yu-Gi-Oh for X-mas. I consider the stairs, but am curious as to see if any other floors have people on them, so down I ride, the elevator stops on the next floor down, floor #5, and the doors slowly slide open…

* * *

I step out of the elevator, only to stand facing two other elevators doors. I turn to the right, and walk out of the little elevator hall into an empty set of halls. Once again, I can smell the sterile chemicals, there seem to be no noises, except that of some machinery, little quiet hums. I look up to a sign stating the types of patients on the floor, this is the floor that houses the comatose victims. I guess MercyThorne is well known for its comatose unit. I immediately head for the nurses station, and again find no one. How in a matter of minutes, less than an hour, did everyone disappear? I head through the stainless steel doors marked with the yellow and black strips and a large 'personal only' sign. I head down the hallway and through another set of double doors. On my right side is a set of doors that states comatose in raised letters with Braille dots underneath it, what? Is this like for the blind doctors and nurses and personal that help to take care of the coma patients? I can see it now, 'Hey, Doctor Smith, is this guy still in a coma?' 'Gee, I don't know Doctor Jones, are you even sure it's a guy?' 'Good, question. Let's ask the blind nurse how the patient looks.'

Any way, I enter the set of doors, and find actual patients in here! Of course they're in a coma, so it's not like they'll be much help, but…why were they left here? This room is rather large; it contains six beds with six patients, four men and two women, all of which are hooked up to several different machines. All the machinery appears to be operating. Why?

Why just leave them alone? Well, regardless, it's just nice seeing people again, if you can call them that still, they say most coma victims, when they come out of it explain that they had an out of body experience...which would mean, according to Frank, their aura or astral form is not currently within the body, so it offers up no value to vampires...I shudder just thinking about that. Bottom line is that no one else is around, so I'd better make myself scarce as well.

I head back down the hall, peeking in windows as I go along, seeing no one, and reach the elevators. I call one and as it arrives and opens, I note that, this time, no other floors are lit up. I reach around and punch floor six and head for the stairs. I push open the heavy yellow door with a wire mesh twelve by thirty-six inch window in it, and head down the stairs, my mind is racing, I hardly feel the effort of racing down the stairs. Russ pops in my head and I stop abruptly. The sound of my footsteps however, continue for about six more steps...aw crap, those aren't mine, someone else is coming down the steps. I begin to call out, but come on, how many movies have I seen where the victim yells 'Jimmy, is that you? What are you doing standing in my closet with a running chainsaw and a freshly decapitated pig head pulled over yours? What? No answer? Here, I'll just come within your reach. Oh, still no answer? Well, are you Curt then? Rick? Mom?' So, at any rate, if they don't yell out to me, I will not be the guy to yell out first. I decide to continue down the steps posthaste. As I reach second floor, I decide to enter onto it. I rush over to the fire extinguisher and yank it off the wall. I stand to one side of the door, waiting for it to be opened, the fire extinguisher held over my head, ready to be used as a club for the first person through the door. I wait for what had to be several hours, or at least minutes, and then it hit me. I set down the fire extinguisher, and yank the fire alarm. This ought to...to...crap! No sound? How is that possible? Well, I'm finding a different way out! I

122

head full blast down the hall, again empty and silent, not even the hums of machinery. I skid to a halt in front of the doors of a lecture hall, I push through them, and head down into the almost pitch black room about fifteen rows, and then slide to my knees down between two rows of theater, fold up style chairs. I stop and take a few deep breaths. Ok, my only chance is to bust out of here and yell out the chant Wang taught me. Oh, that's right, Wang didn't know they were vampires…well, it's the only ace I have left to play, so… As I get ready to get up…blinding lights go on. I scrunch back down. Damn! I'm breathing way too loud, I can't hear if anyone is in here or not. As I bravely decide to jump up and yell my chant, the lights go back out. This is very disorienting! Wait, ever so softly, I hear, what I believe to be the pitter-patter of feet. Sweat drips off my forehead and hits the cold, painted concrete floor. The sound of footsteps, as light as it was, stops. Another droplet of sweat drops to the floor. I feel that if I get closer to the floor, there's less likelihood of being discovered. I press my cheek to the cold floor. I realize just how much I'm perspiring, because my cheek feels wet, as I press it to the floor. The cold strength of the floor feels good. It reminds of college, and how many nights I came to bring forth my offerings to the porcelain goddess. Next to sex, and that first piss after a six pack of beer that you've held in to the last possible second, because you know that once you go, you'll be going after each beer. Nothing felt as good as the cold porcelain of the toilet seat pressed against your forehead, supporting you until you were done giving your offerings.

I could hear my self swallow. I slowly raised my head to peer out over the back row of chairs, in the darkness I couldn't see a thing. Wait, a silhouette, or shadow dances across the rows of seats, it's moving, I think, heading right at me! Slowly, toying with me, but definitely heading toward me. In this darkness I can't be sure, but…

I yell out "APITU, APITU, TIAMET-FORAY, FORAY, DRACO-LEPIDUS ANTSWONG!!!" As I finish the chant, with an unbelievable force, I feel my stomach being slammed into, knocking the wind out of me. My head must have struck something because I feel like it's being split open by an axe! The pain doesn't end until I lose consciousness...

* * *

I awaken on the selfsame cold cement floor I passed out on after that viscous attack. Weakened, I reach out for the seats, attempting to use one of them to help pull myself to my feet. In my blind groping about, I grab onto what feels like soft cotton, surrounding a...a...LEG! "Shit!" I blurt out withdrawing my hand quickly. Who the hell is this? I dive and roll out of the row of seats, landing in the aisle, quickly, yet clumsily I stumble up to the light switch and flip it on, the room floods with brightness. As my eyes adjust, I see over two hundred backs and backs of heads sitting in the chairs. All the seats are taken. Doctors, nurses, interns, and patients fill the room. An odor or stench if you will, finally wakes up my olfactory senses. I start to dry heave. I now know this smell, the smell of the dead. One doesn't quickly forget a stench like that. I slowly walk down and turn to view the back row of people. I step back weakly, as the visages of the dead carve their way into the deepest recesses of my mind, my God, I can almost hear them. Helplessly the gray husks, the silent vessels that once stored a soul, their faces, twisted and contorted out of fear, hopelessness, and pain, reach out to me. They begin yelling to me, RETRIBUTION! RETRIBUTION! Good God, all of them are facing me, each and every throat has been torn out. This does not however, quench their cries! Louder than words could ever be, the frightened faces of these victims flood my senses, no man could stare death in the face like this and not go totally insane. All these helpless people, many having spent their lives in the pursuit of treating the ill and the dying, to have their own existence cut short in a flash. A quick death, but imagine, you'd be awake while you felt your life slipping away. You'd be reaching out for help, praying to be saved, but none would answer your prayer. The predator has come, and you're the game to be had. Like the rabbit finally caught by the wolf, you accept your fate, you stop fighting, but continue praying, and finally the final sleep overcomes you.

I continue down the aisle, more of the same, row after row. The front row has a different look to it. These victims are sporting a Colombian necktie. A Colombian necktie is when you get your throat slit and they pull your tongue out through the opening in your throat. This is a total mockery of human life! There is no respect for the dead here! This is wrong, I don't care what Frank says, this is wrong! They've gone too far. I don't know why they are playing with my mind like this, but leaving me alive was their final mistake!

I spin and run up the aisle, I don't care who I run into now! I burst open the doors and head back down the hallway. I head through the reception area and nurses' station, past the elevators, and blow open the door to the stairs. I take the stairs three at a time, until landing on the first floor. This doesn't add up! Why would they do this? I push open the emergency exit and rejoice in the scent of the cold winter air. As the frosty air stings my lungs, I drop to my knees. Its dusk out, lights are starting to go on, I look up to the sky, I scream out "WHY!!!"

All those people, their lives instantly extinguished, their corpses set up as trophies, much as a hunter does with a deer, mounting it to prove how he defeated a wild animal. Of course, he was sitting in a blind and had a gun, but hey, it's sporty. And Russ, I don't even know what happened to Russ…Damn them! I lower my head and stare at the ground; a tear rolls off my cheek and hits the ground, melting its way deeper into the crusty snow…

Chapter Eleven
Existence

It all happened so fast, over just two days I believe, I'd met with vampires, escaped their lair with my half-dead brother, and ended up in a hospital, where the entire staff and several patients were murdered, so I had to escape there as well. As luck would have it, I'm less than three miles from my house. With strength drawn from, I don't know where, I start off into a dead sprint toward my house. I pay no attention to any of the headlights of the passing cars. I kept focused and kept running full bore. In a short time, I rounded the corner my house was on. I allowed my self to slow down the pace, as I did this; I felt my self-running short on breath. When I reached my iron gate, I flung it open, and almost simultaneously, my front door opened and Dugan rushed out and grabbed me. He virtually carried me into my home. I heard the door being barred behind me. The whole gang was there except Ellen and the female Peacocks. My living room had been cleared of everything except a large round table and chairs.

"Ben, how are you my boy!" Dugan asked worriedly.

"Look everyone, I need rest. I haven't been safe in days. Not sleep rest, just rest." Sarge pulled in my lazyboy from the kitchen and helped Dugan set me in it. They pulled up the footrest and removed my boots. Malley threw a blanket over me, and Wang handed me a cup of hot tea.

"You guys haven't heard from anyone?" I asked.

"No, laddy, where's Johnson?" Malley inquired.

"Oh, probably dead, like everyone else at MercyThorne hospital." I nonchalantly added.

"What…do ye mean, dead?" Malley asked in his cop voice.

"Well, let's see, everyone over to the hospital has been murdered. Doctors, nurses, patients, and even some visitors. A lot of them are sitting in the lecture hall, there throats are ripped out, and their bodies are drained of blood." I sip my tea, the heat warms my insides and I lift my eyes and scan them all before speaking. "You see, we're not dealing with just a cult, but the Cult Of The Vampyr. Vampires guys, not cultists, blood sucking, undead, neck biting, VAMPIRES." I take another drink.

"Excuse me? Did you say…Vampires? I find that hard to believe…" Mayor Villareal declared.

"Hard to believe? Hard to believe! I can't believe you just said that! Aren't you guys the ones casting spells against Undead Gods? Look, believe it pal! I witnessed it. And furthermore," I reached into my backpack and slammed the Tome down on the floor. "Read that Villey, and then talk to me! Malley, I just told you that hundreds of people are dead at the hospital, you gonna make a call or anything?"

To my surprise, Malley followed my orders and immediately got on the radio and dispatched a couple units.

"Gentlemen, this is the Tome you requested, Mr. Peacock, I'm sorry, I never had the chance to try and get to Mike. It wouldn't have mattered anyway; he's a Thrall now, under the mind control of one of the vampires. I truly am sorry." I looked into his deep brown eyes. All he could say was;

"Then he is alive?"

"To the best of my knowledge, yes."

"Ok, son, I appreciate your efforts." He turned and headed into the kitchen.

"Wait," Wang interrupted, "It makes sense, vampires. Ben how many?"

"Well, nine big dudes, and the Harbinger, who I never met." The look on Wang's face was that of total acceptance.

Dugan picked up the Tome and started leafing through it, he closed it and said, "Uh, Ben…this book is empty…"

"What?" Again with strength out of nowhere, I jump up and rip the Tome from his hands, he drops his saddened gaze toward the floor as I remove the Tome. I fling it open and, sure enough, it's a bunch of blank pages. The bastards switched it on me! They let me go so they could…shit! "Dugan, Malley, Sarge! Get out the heavy artillery! Cover every entrance! Wang, you and the professor look for any anti-vampire anything in your Tomes!"

"Laddy, are ye worried about anything…" I cut him off immediately.

"Look, they switched the book on me and let me go. I imagine they've followed me at this point, they know where we are now and that I've betrayed them. I tried the chant you taught me Wang, it didn't have any effect on them. We've got to find something!"

"Incoming!" Sarge called down from upstairs. "Ellen."

"Let me answer the door, it's probably me they want most, but be ready!" I unblock the door; I swing it open to reveal a very cold, shivering Ellen.

"Ben…you're…you're here." The look in her eyes seemed almost frightened. She must have been worried sick. I reach out to her, but she shrinks away from me.

"Hey, Ellen, it's alright, I'm ok. I saw your brother. He's alive and well, but he's not coming home anytime soon. I'm sorry." Again I step toward her and she turns a shoulder to me. Dugan sticks out a massive arm and pulls her in. I step out onto the porch. The cold fogs around the street light, in what appears to be a perfect circle. I scan the immediate area. Instead of fear though, I feel anger swell up in my chest. I squint and attempt to find anything odd in the surroundings. Slowly I send my gaze toward Jeff's house. No lights are on. My own breath fogs my vision some. I defiantly stand on my porch, daring any of these bastards to show their pale visages. After a final look around, I re-enter my home and Dugan shuts the door and barricades it again.

I look over to Ellen; she has her face buried in Mayor Villareal's shoulder. I once again pick up the tome. As I flip through it a second time, I notice that the first page is stuck to the front cover. I slowly peel it back, leaving most of the words in good shape, but a couple end up missing some letters. Small black flakes of ink litter the page. The ink is flaking off; it's a burgundy in color, almost black. I use my fingernail to scrape at the words, they flake right off. This is no ink, its dried blood, and it reads:

"BENJY, THAT'S QUITE A SHOW YOU PUT ON. BRAVO! AN ACT LIKE YOURS DESERVES AN AUDIENCE. ALLOW ME TO PROVIDE SUCH AN AUDIENCE. IT LOOKS LIKE A FULL HOUSE! OH, SORRY ABOUT THE TOME, CAN'T HAVE THAT FALLING INTO THE WRONG HANDS AND ALL THAT, YOU UNDERSTAND. SEE YOU IN YOUR DREAMS, CHUM!"
    LOVE AND KISSES,
    JESSUP

That sick…written in innocent's blood! Oh, I'll be seeing you all right 'chum', but in your nightmares!

"Wang, it was the one who killed Orvin. His names Jessup, he's like a hit man for these guys. They send him out to do their dirty work, probably because he enjoys it so damn much! Near as I can tell, a guy by the name of Kendall Ontolli is the leader…" I get interrupted by Villareal.

"Wait, Kendall Ontolli? 'The' Kendall Ontolli? Multimillionnaire, English spice importer/exporter

Kendall Ontolli? I've met him, he can't be a vampire."

"Why not?" I inquired. "Why couldn't he be a vampire? Look, these guys don't run around in tuxes and black capes with red lining. They live day to day amongst us, and we don't even know it. There is so much to this whole vampire thing; it's actually more like a religion than a race of undead creatures…" Again, I'm interrupted, this time by Malley.

"The lad speaks the truth, there are several dead bodies, all drained of blood, many of which are settin' in an auditorium. Tell us more lad."

"Look, we could chat about this for hours, or we could figure out how we're going to stop this. These guys are serious. Something shook them up though; they all had to run off for something, left me alone. That's when I took off. Hey, Villareal, where does this Kendall live?"

"Well, all over the world, but he keeps a modest mansion out by the old mill, other side of the lake. You know, that big place with the stone wall surrounding the whole estate, on the edge of the lake? It's about forty/ maybe forty-five minutes from here."

"I was supposed to go see him tonight with Pastor Frank. I'm sure he's aware of my defection by now. I would lay odds though, that there's a Tome of Uhr at his place. Maybe a few of us should grab some heat and pay him a visit. It would be easier than getting into the underground lair."

"Wait Ben," Wang interjects "you say the chant did not work? It should have, even on vampires. It should have at least fazed them. It was created for all undead."

"Well, it didn't, or maybe I said it wrong, or not in time, but I said it and got leveled in the process. Apparently by Jessup." I turned my attention on Ellen.

"Ellen," I softly said. I slowly walked toward her. She looked up at me with a tear still hanging on one cheek. Her face was flushed, possibly from the cold outside, and then entering the heat inside. More likely though, it would be from crying. As I reach out my hand to her, she whispers,

"Don't…don't touch me. Just don't…"

"Ellen, I tried with your brother, really." I sympathetically pleaded.

"It's not that. Ben, you…you shouldn't be here. You CAN'T be here." Ellen appears to be gaining strength in her conviction.

It's odd, I feel like I'm being cold shouldered by my love of many years. I've known Ellen less than a week. Something is upsetting her a lot. I felt more unsettled by her rejection than I should have. Damn, I don't have time to work on this right now, and that's really unfair! Still, I couldn't let it go.

"Ellen, I want to have a talk with you, really. I want us to spend time together, just the two of us, and discuss whatever it is that is upsetting you so much, but…" interruption, shocking.

"But…we have to go get this book and save the entire human race. Can your little tiff wait until then?" Dugan brilliantly threw in, making an ass out of himself.

"Look lads, Dugan and John Peacock will be going with Ben to recover the tome. Ben's dealt with these boyo's, so he needs to be leadin' it. I'm guessin' you two will only be back up. They still must want Ben or he'd be dead by now. Ben, I'd go in with a change of heart if I were ye, and see if they'll accept ye still. If things aren't goin' right, that's when these two will be comin' in to get ye out. These aren't standard issue, but John

here is lendin' us these comms. Just push it, and the boys will be right in."
Malley turned to continue setting up guns for the mission.

I turn and start over to Ellen again, she stands up and tosses a wrinkled
up ball of copy paper at me. It hits my chest, and bounces off into my right
hand. I unravel it and attempt to straighten out the wrinkles. It's a
photocopy of a news article from over ten years ago. The headline reads
"RUDEN, LOCAL FAMILY OF FOUR, IN FIVE CAR PILE UP."

It goes on to state that "...Russ Ruden is sole survivor, and is in critical
condition at MercyThorne hospital. Relatives can be reached..."

* * *

I slowly raise my eyes to meet Ellen's. Her eyes start to swell up and she
brokenly whispers "Just who the hell are you?"

"Ellen, I'm Ben Ruden, I have no idea who made up this..."

"Ben, or whoever you are, I was researching for a patron at the library
and ran across this on microfiche. People don't 'make up' ten year old
articles!" Her eyes search me for answers. I find myself trying to recall this
car wreck. I truly don't have any recollection of this accident.

"Then how do you explain me being here, now. Ellen, really, my family
was never in a car accident. We're all fine, except maybe Russ. Please give
me the benefit of the doubt on this one. We'll...look into it more after I
retrieve the tome. Ok?" I gave her my best puppy dog eyes. She turned
away and rubbed her arms as she crossed them, probably attempting to
comfort herself. She spins back around and gives me a hard stare.

"Look, I don't care if you're Elvis. As long as we stop these vampires!
I think we're losing focus here!!" Dugan finalized the conversation. "If we
could worry a little less about an old newspaper clipping, and maybe just
a little more on saving humanity from total genocide, then we could all

argue about whether or not Ben here, is really here…or not!" Dugan looked over to me and rolled his eyes, nodding his head toward Ellen.

I walked over to Ellen and gently grabbed her by her shoulders, tucking one hand under chin and turning her to face me. "Hey, it's me…really. I promise you we'll get to the bottom of this as soon as we can. I am Ben, and I think you know deep down I'm telling the truth. And…I need to spend some time with you later. Can you just trust me until then, please?" Ellen hesitated a moment before she collapsed into my arms. She's been so strong since I've met her, and seeing her in this frail state makes it even more appealing to me to comfort her. I feel something…and I sure hope we get to know each other better.

Ellen looks up to me, slyly, and a semi-smile tugs at the corner of her mouth. She softened and says, "Ok Ben, I'll trust you. Just come back to me so we can put this nightmare behind us." Ellen slowly walks off into the kitchen, as I extend my arm, hoping to stop her. Dugan pushes his barrel-sized chest between Ellen and me.

"Hello…Vampires, remember?" Dugan smirks at me.

"Locked and loaded. Let's tear up some grass and kick some ass!" Ol' sarge announces.

Dugan straps on his guns and tosses me a nickel-plated Berretta. I tuck it between my belt and the back of my shirt. I throw on my favorite black leather jacket. It has a pretty thick lining in it. I pull on my black leather gloves, my favorite hiking boots and a head wrap. It looks like a headband, but is made to cover your ears. I feel surprisingly ready to go attempt this coup.

"All right guys, lets go meet 'The Lost Boys". I head toward the door, with sarge and Dugan following behind me. I unbar the door and pull it open. With a groan the old door swings toward us. A flash of lightning, followed by a clap of thunder, startles me as I make out the sillouhette of someone standing on my front porch. There's a light sprinkle coming down, and it seems to be turning to steam as it pelts the figure standing there. The figure steps forward, and as it does, I feel myself being yanked off my feet backwards, and sarge swings his AK-47 like a baseball bat and clubs the figure on the head, forcing him to drop to his knees, groping at his injured forehead. Another flash of lightning and clap of thunder illuminate the figure on his knees before us…

* * *

"Shit!" Sarge yells out. He bends down and helps the figure up.

"Ben…what's happening? I was dropped here to give you this note…" Jeff collapses into Sarge's arms. A note floats to the ground. Sarge drags Jeff in and we all go back in. I tear open the envelope. Once again, the crusty black writing drops dried blood shavings to the ground. It reads;

"BEN,

IT HAS BECOME OBVIOUS TO US, THAT YOU ARE NOT YET CONVINCED OF YOUR TRUE DESTINY. WE GIVE THIS BOY'S LIFE TO YOU AS A GOOD FAITH GIFT. WE REQUEST YOUR PRESENCE AT ONTOLLI MANSION. BE FORWARNED, ANY WHO ACCOMPANY YOU WILL BE DOING SO AT THEIR OWN RISK. WE ONLY REQUEST THE SIMPLE BOON OF ONE MORE CONFERENCE WITH YOU, IF YOU STILL CHOOSE TO DO SO; YOU MAY LEAVE AS YOU CAME.

Ever your obedient servant,
KENDALL ONTOLLI"

"I think maybe I ought to go by myself…" Wang snatches the letter from my hands; he quickly skims it and says, "It would appear that they have good intentions."

"Oh, well, so long as the blood-sucking, flesh-feasting undead, bringing about the end of mankind, vampires, 'appear' to have 'good' intentions, we might just as well give them the benefit of the doubt, eh?" Dugan not-so-subtlety adds.

"Well, I know, but…I really don't want you guys putting yourself at risk…they haven't made a move yet…" I can't even convince myself.

"Perhaps, it's because they haven't the necessary power, laddy. Perhaps The Nine are more of a threat than these vamps led ye to believe, laddy." Malley interjects with that cocky grin he's so famous for.

"Yeah, maybe…" Again I can't seem to convince myself. There has to be something else.

"Look gang, the note said at our own risk, so I'm risking it, capiche?" Again, Mr. Subtle jumps in.

"All right, how's Jeff?" I check.

"He's out of it boyo, but don't be worryin' about him. We'll see to the lad, you see to your business." I take one more quick check of Jeff, while Malley and Villareal drag carry him out of the living room, arguing over the best way to take care of him.

We head to the front door again. This time we open it and there are no surprises. We step out into the misty, cool air. I take a moment to look around off my front porch. We step down and head for Dugan's truck. We hop in, and Dugan fires up his oversized engine. As he shifts into gear and starts moving, the snow and slush groans as it splits beneath the tires. We head out toward the lake. Slowly the cab warms up. I look to sarge and Dugan; both men are completely stone-faced. Their visage is unchanged, frozen in a permanent frown. Their concentration regarding the task in front of them reminds me of boxers entering the heavyweight championship fight.

"What the hell?" Dugan asks, breaking the silence.

Behind us, a car is flashing its lights at us. Dugan, surprisingly pulls over, and gets out. I decide to get out as well for backup. As I step down, I look up only to see Dugan staring at me in complete awe.

"What's wrong? Who is it?" I sidestep Dugan, and realize the car is Jeff's. A guy steps out and says;

"Ben, I've been trying to reach you for days, I figured this was you coming out of your house when you jumped into this truck…What…?" Jeff obviously can't understand why my jaw is hanging down to my belly button.

Chapter Twelve
The Warriors Three?

"What's the problem? Ben, what in the hell is going on with you?" Jeff asks in a semi-pissed off tone.

"Jeff...where have you been tonight?" I hesitantly inquire.

"I was headed home from the Quik-E-Mart, and saw you guys getting in this truck. It hasn't left your house in a couple of days...but, anyway...what is going on? All the shops close up at, like, 4:00, and you've had a ton of people at your house for the past few days..." Jeff halts his statements as he notices Sarge break off into a dead sprint back toward my place.

"You and the boy carry on, I'm headin' back!" Sarge yells over his shoulder as he heads back toward home.

"Look Jeff, if you do me this favor...aw, forget it."

"Dugan...?" I look to him.

"Let's go." Dugan jumps back into the truck.

"Jeff, I'm sorry, but explanations will have to wait. Jeff...were you with Russ at all?" I winced as I asked.

"No dude. Isn't Russ like your brother who lives out of state?" Jeff could definitely read the expression on my face. "Ben, what's going on, man?"

"I'll explain later, honest. Sorry, got to go." I ran and jumped on the passenger side.

Dugan floored the great beast, and swung her around back toward my place. We traveled nearly a mile before overtaking Sarge. He really moved for such a big guy. As if by telepathy, Dugan simply slowed down and Sarge swung himself up into the back of the moving truck. As we felt the shudder from the truck catching Sarges' bulk, Dugan picked up the speed again. What was happening? I couldn't answer that for Jeff. I can't tell which Jeff is the real one, but how can there be two? It has to be a trick by the vamps. We've only been gone like ten or fifteen minutes. I pray nothing's happened.

As we take the corner on almost two wheels, I see an orange glow down the street. As we finally reach my old church house, we see it engulfed in flames. Yellowish-orange flames lick the outside of my place through the first-floor windows. As I jump down from Dugan's truck, I land in unison with a crackling sound, a thundering boom followed by the tinkling of shattered glass. My prized possession, the stained glass window over the entrance, explodes outward. How could a fire of this magnitude occur in fifteen minutes? I ponder this question as I race toward the house, hearing the welcome sound of fire trucks from off in the distance. Sarge heads right toward the blazing inferno, and runs around one side, into the back yard. I race around the other side, but am blocked by walls of fire. As I race back around, the fire trucks arrive, firemen jumping out and unrolling the hose. Another fireman uses a huge tool to work on the fire hydrant, as two others run the hose over to attach it. Numbed, I grab it too and help them drag it to the front lawn. Within seconds, two separate hoses are sending out high-powered streams of water. Sarge races back around from the back yard, waving a Katana sword.

"This is all I could find by the door" he screams, "the blaze was too hot, and I couldn't get in from the back either." He drops his eyes and shrugs, shaking his head. I stare at him, struck silent by lack of comprehension, dropping to my knees.

"This was Wang's weapon. There's still blood on the blade. There was a fight all right. Damn! We're too late! How can we be too late? Why?" Dugan sticks the Japanese sword into the frozen ground.

Within forty-five minutes of their arrival, the Havenhill Fire Department douses the flames. Dugan and Sarge immediately head toward the gutted shell that was once my home. The stench of burnt everything and smoke was putrid. I haven't stopped the dry heaves, which rack my body. Sarge grabs me and slaps me hard.

"Let's go' he whispers urgently, almost kindly. As we enter the place in the one opening by the side door, we see that most everything was unidentifiable charred lumps. I allow myself to wonder about Ellen. Did she get caught up in this mess? Oh please, let Ellen be gone, be at home, safe. Well, as luck would have it at that moment, I managed to stumble across a body. I haven't seen so many dead bodies in horror flicks as I've seen in just the last couple of days. I can't really make out who it is, and as I stand pondering, I catch a whiff of the burnt hair and flesh. True to form, I spin around and vomit. The old mausoleum in the graveyard smelled like potpourri compared to a burnt human being. I quickly took leave of this place, back out front, where now the police have arrived. Medics started pulling dead, burn victims out of the charred church. At final count, there were seven bodies: two females and five males.

"As best as I can guess, these would be the other seven of our nine." Dugan lowered his head, as if all hope was now gone.

"Guys, what do we do?" I nervously asked, slightly relieved, and hoping that Dugan's' observation was correct. The lesser of two evils would be that at least Ellen was gone when this occured.

"We go find these bastards and do likewise!" Sarge blurted out.

"We'd best get going, before the cops want to question down Ben." Dugan headed back to his still running truck. Sarge and I followed suit. As I climbed back into the cab, I caught a glimpse of Jeff, standing next to his car. His car was running, as the billowing cloud of exhaust, carrying a reddish hue from the taillights, informed me. He stepped in front of his headlights, and put his hand up as a visor, attempting to better assess the situation. Momentarily, he caught my gaze. As I was being shoved in by Sarge, I thought I glimpsed a set of red dots floating over Jeff, I attempted to yell out, but the car door was pulled shut by Sarge, and Dugan wasted no time in heading out.

* * *

I could have very well been seeing something not there. Why would one stick around and risk being caught?

"Guys, I can't believe they're all dead...all dead. Guns alone won't stop these guys..."

"Like hell they won't. Just watch." Sarge snapped.

"No, Ben is correct, we still need the Tome of Uhr, and it'll just be up to us to decipher it. We need to get in, retrieve the tome and get away, so we can learn how to stop these bastards." Dugan added.

"Is it just me, or does it appear that these, 'The Nine' guys, don't let emotion affect them at all?" I mean, Malley and Wang are dead, as well as the others. It doesn't seem real. I can't get my head around it and they seem angry, not sad. I guess I need to keep it there. For no reason what so ever, I reach down and grasp my medallion, I squeeze it, as if in an attempt to crush it. The medallion doesn't give. What happened back there?

As if in answer to my question, a little white Chevette, with some rust on the wheel wells and one head light out, attempts to cut us off and force us off the road. Its little horn is screeching at us. How annoying, I didn't think anyone still owned one of these. What? Like, does this person meet with the Pinto, Gremlin, and Chevette owners' classic car club or something? I mean hey, combined all those cars would bring maybe, I don't know, a hundred bucks or so?

Dugan decided to stop. Why does he always do that? Oh, well, I suppose it isn't as bad to stop, when you and your passenger are packing M16's with RPG's, (Rocket Powered Grenade launcher). After allowing the boys to check out the scene, I bravely leave the cab. Ellen comes running over to me.

"Guys, thank God! Everyone, they're all dead! All of them! I would be too, except for Wang…he…he saved me, I can still picture his face…he wanted me to give this to you…" Ellen handed me Orvin's tome, and immediately dropped her teary face into her hands.

"Ellen, what happened? We were there at the tail end of the fire, we…we saw all the bodies, but we couldn't be sure who they were…oh, man, Ellen…I'm so glad you're ok!" I couldn't stop my self; I immediately reached out and hugged her with all my strength. It felt so right, holding her like this. Her warm breath brushed against my neck and I buried my face in her hair. I felt her shivering. I really wanted to comfort her. I really wanted to keep her safe. If only I could go back to the library, when I first met her, and leave her out of this mess somehow. It seems like everyone I've involved in this has been hurt, lost their life or had it completely screwed up. A small part of me longs for the naiveté of those who are carrying on their normal day-to-day activities, unaware of all that is going on, and a large part of me really wishes that I'd never mixed Ellen up in this.

"Ellen, I'm so sorry you ever met me...I'd give anything to have not involved you in this..." In spite of myself, my eyes welled up with tears and my voice broke. Ellen puts her finger on my lips, as if to hush me. Then, she makes the most incredible move. Her cold, trembling lips press against mine, and I realize that all the emotions that were building were as real as could be. I...I think I'm falling in love. I dare not tell her now...but what if I don't make it on this little journey; she'll never know how I felt. I can't take that chance.

"Ellen..." again I was shushed, this time verbally.

* * *

"You guys need to do something...you need to pay them back! We owe it to Wang and Malley and the others..." Ellen looked around at the three of us...her frozen breath, distorting our view of her.

"How did it happen Ellen? Who set the fire...was it Jeff?" Dugan asked.

"It's a little foggy; it all happened so fast...I was in the kitchen getting a drink of water, when Jeff came down the stairs from the bedrooms. He looked at me and smiled. I said, 'Hi Jeff, you're looking much better.' And I smiled back at him. He...he said in a cool tone 'I look however I want to look.' Then he started walking into the living room, but just before leaving my sight, he cocked his head a little and said 'I can see what Ben sees in you.' Then, he smiled and nodded and entered the living room."

"Wait, I never said anything to Jeff about you...I mean my feelings...I mean...I do...care about you, but I never told..." Oh, look, being shushed again as she puts a finger over my lips and nods her head in understanding.

"After registering what he said, I decided to follow him, perplexed. I swear it couldn't have been three minutes...and when I entered, some guy dressed all in black, with black hair and glowing red eyes, was holding Malley out at arms length, his hand clasped around his throat, and...he was suspending Malley about two feet off the ground. Malley pulled out a little revolver like gun and emptied six shots into this guy's chest. This guy said 'I hate the fighting Irish, Lad!" And...and...he snapped Malley's neck with one hand and bit him in his throat! Oh God, blood squirted out like three mini-geysers, and this...freak reveled in it. He smiled, brandishing blood soaked teeth and fangs...the, the most grotesque thing I'd ever seen...Ben...he...he tossed Malley aside like a...a...couch cushion! Two more guys...Villareal and...that professor guy came at him and started shooting. Ben, he would go from one spot to the next in the blink of an eye. I swear I never saw him move, Villareal started shooting and this guy was standing behind him, he grabbed Villareal and swung him around as a...human shield, the professor put like, I don't know, several shots into Villareal's body, and Ben...Villareal was still standing and by the last shot, Villareal started to fall, before his body hit the floor, the guy in black had moved across the room and had slashed the professor's throat open with his bare hand. The professor grabbed his own throat and attempted to stop the bleeding. It was incredible...the professor dropped to his knees at the same time Villareal's body hit the ground. Then, like ten guys, all dressed like you and Keith, came in through the kitchen, carrying torches and glass containers of...kerosene or gas or something and started igniting the place, they attacked the other folks. The head dude...???"

"His name is Jessup." I interjected.

"Ok...Jessup slowly started walking toward me, I frantically looked for someone to help, then looked frantically for something to hit him with. There was, like nothing, I panicked and ran into the kitchen. Just before I made it, someone grabbed my hair and yanked me back. I...I could feel his hot breath and his heavy breathing, then he...he...Ben, he licked my cheek!

He said 'If you weren't claimed, I'd have dessert right now!" He let go of me and said, "But it looks like I'm having a little Chinese first." Standing in the kitchen in a suit of oriental armor of some sort, was Wang.

He had a thin curved sword drawn and then he yelled out some chant '...apitu, apitu, tiamet,...something. Anyway, Jessup, bent over, grabbing his stomach, and Wang quickly shoved that book at me.

He said 'Run girl, get this to Ben. Go now! I'll end this bastard's life here and now!" Then he raised his sword and leapt out to that Jessup. As he swung down, one of those kids in black threw his body between Jessup and Wang. Wang cleaved him in two, it was horrible. As I looked away, I saw that everyone was down and the fire was in full form, smoke began to sting my eyes... I ran. Through the smoke, I saw three more kids jump on Wang. Wang fought like a warrior born, he'd kicked one across the room, sliced another one, and threw the third onto Jessup. I guess the smoke got to be too much for Wang too, he grabbed me and ushered me out toward the back door. As I went through, he turned me around and said 'It's up to the three now, as it was written, find them!' He shoved me through the door and shut it. Not three seconds later, as I turned to look, he came smashing through the door and landed sprawled eagle on the snow. It took him no time to jump back up to his feet. As he regained his stance, three more of the kids followed...and that...Jessup...stepped out and walked slowly toward him, clearly toying with Wang. I had seen how fast that Jessup could move. I had gotten to my car and started it. Two of the boys jumped toward Wang, Wang cut them down, swinging. The third came after me; I tried to get it in reverse, but not before the boy reached me. He started to pound on my window and cracked it. He stopped suddenly, and slowly dropped to the ground. I looked over to Wang, he was standing there weaponless. He had thrown his only weapon at this boy, to allow me to escape. As I pulled away, I caught Wang's gaze, he brought his legs together, and clasped his hands as if to pray, and closed his eyes. That Jessup smiled, brandishing his hideous fangs, and that's when I tore outta there. Ben, it was like a horror movie, it doesn't seem real...but it is, isn't it?" Ellen's face looked to me, hoping for the answer to be 'no'.

"Yeah, Ellen, they're real enough. I think maybe one of us should stay with you..."

"NO! I mean, no. Ben, Wang gave his life so that you and these two would finish the task. I'll be fine; I'll just go to my mother's up to Carson's Point. I'll leave now." "She drops her voice." Ben, when you're done, I've left a number at the library for when it's safe for you. Go get them and then call me. Only you will know how to find my number. Maybe you could come up when this is over...and, well, there's lot's of 'fish' up there." Ellen planted another one on me, you know the kind, it was the kind that says, there's a lot more where that came from, the kind that almost makes you give up watching football for...almost. Ellen got in her cute little Chevette and sped off. I always did like Chevettes. I turned to the other two, and saw a large amount of question in their faces.

"Guys, see, it's all true, that's what I meant by guns alone not stopping these guys. But apparently the chant did work. I must have said it wrong the first time. Well guys, it looks like we are The Warriors Three."

"Son of a bitch! It looks like we got our work cut out for us. Well, we're not getting anything done standing around here. But, what ever happened to Jeff?" Dugan asked.

"Every kindred's gift is different. Jessup's' gift must be shape-changing." I answered.

A set of headlights approaches us as we start climbing back into Dugan's truck. The vehicle slows and Sarge hops back out and heads back to the car.

Suddenly we hear Sarge's M-16 set of a volley of shots…

Chapter Thirteen
A Sudden Turn of Events

I immediately jump back out of the truck, pulling my pistol out as I do. Dugan does the same. As we reach the back of Dugan's' truck, we see Sarge standing over a man laying face down in the road, next to his still running car.

"Sarge…is he…" I never got to finish my question.

"He's fine…I just wanted to let him know that he needed to do what I asked. Get up boy, slowly, but get up." Sarge kept the nozzle of his M-16 within inches of this guy. I don't think even Jessup could dodge bullets, especially from this distance.

"What do you want Mister…?"

"Kane. Kevin Kane." He shouts shakily, keeping his hands on his head, as he stood up. He drops his voice. "One of you IS Ben Rudin, aren't you?"

"Yeah, one of us is. What do you want?" I bravely offer, feeling pretty much in control of things here.

"Look, I just came to warn you…you're going into a trap. I don't even know how I know that, I just do."

"Kevin Kane? The police psychic from upstate? You wrote a book right?" Dugan looks surprised as he speaks.

"Yeah. Look, I knew of Orvin Stiltwortth. He was a strong telepath...or psychic, if you will. His passing was felt by all who share the psychic plane. He is dead, correct?" Kevin ponders.

"Yes, he was murdered just days ago. Why are you here? We're aware of the dangers we're approaching."

"Look...I'm a trained police psychic, I've even done some work for the FBI, but I'm not able to pick anything up about you guys...however, the most powerful psychic mind I've ever run across sent me to warn you that you're going about this all wrong." Kevin demands.

"Why didn't this guy come himself?" I boldly counter.

"Because...he's eleven years old." Kevin throws back at me and gestures.

"This is a bunch of malarkey! We don't have time to sit here and fart around with this clown!" Sarge spins around and headed back to the truck.

"John Peacock...Jason says that if you pursue this path...you will personally be responsible for your son's death." Kevin shudders before the big man can even react. You could tell Kevin expected the worse.

"What did you just say?" Sarge turns back around and slowly walks back toward Kevin. You could virtually see the damp snow steaming of sarge's forehead, as snowflakes pelt him. Dugan wisely steps in between them.

"Look, I didn't even want to approach you guys, and I can't begin to say that I have even a clue of what's going on here, but I'd highly recommend you come visit Jason. He can probably shed some light on this subject. Remember Ben, Kendall is also a sage...he'll know when you arrive, unless you take certain precautions." Kevin's eyes plead.

"I agree that it sounds like a good idea…except that if we don't go tonight, we may not be able to find Kendall again for a while." I shrug and look for their response.

"Look, just follow me over to where Jason is, if he can't convince you, you'll be an hour later than you originally planned. Oh, yeah, and Ben…Ellen's fine. She's not home yet, but she's doing fine." Kevin turns to get back in his car.

I look over to Dugan, confused. He nods his approval. I look over to Sarge, he just glares at me with that perm-frown.

"Well, I say we go meet this Jason. If it starts getting weird, we bust out." I turn and climb back into the cab of Dugan's 4x4. Dugan and Sarge follow suit. Dugan spins the truck around and after a quick fishtail, he follows this Kevin Kane guy.

"The answer is 'yes' guys, this could very well be a trap. We'll just have to chance it." Of course I've already thought of that, but how did he find us? How'd he know about Ellen? I think it's worth the chance. Without Orvin, we're pretty blind to this.

"It's not a trap." Dugan assures us.

We finally pull into The Castle motel. Kevin parks and motions for us to follow him into a ground floor room. As we approach the motel room door, Kevin swings it open, and allows us entrance. The room is decorated with heavy, harvest gold curtains. They come just short of the air/heat unit under the window. The carpet is a lovely orange and gold shag. Even the bedspreads and picture share in the color scheme. Over on the dark brown dresser under the mirror, is a small TV. There are two double beds, one is neatly made, and the other has an eleven-year-old boy, laying on his belly drawing or coloring or something. He's wearing dark blue jeans, a red paid flannel shirt and has his legs crossed and kicked up behind him. His white socks are dirty on the bottoms, as if he doesn't prefer to wear shoes if he can help it. He is definitely blond, a real toe-head. I didn't think anything short of Santa could have hair that white. I half expected an albino when his little face looked up, but instead of pink eyes, they were crystal blue. When he looked up he smiled. He spun himself around to a sitting position, and handed his pad of paper to me. On the pad was a sketching of a man's face. It was a very sad face.

"That's pretty good Jason..." I attempt to be polite, but it truly was very good. The shadowing and definition was uncanny.

"He needs your help Ben." Jason states in a sweet little eleven-year-hold's voice.

"He does, does he? Well just who..." my words freeze in my throat. Upon a second look; I could tell it was Russ.

* * *

"Jason...this is my brother...Russ. What did you mean he needs my help? Is he ok?" I have a million questions. I kind of sold myself on the fact that Russ was dead.

"Ben...your big brother is not ok. He's alive, sort of...but needs relief. Ben, he wants you." Little Jason stands up and slowly walks over to Sarge. This small four-foot kid looked up at big ol' Sarge. His little voice doesn't match his obviously-superior vocabulary and intellect.

"Wow, you're big John. You're kind of a gentle giant, huh? I mean you're pretty scary, but don't always mean to be. Mister...John, I'm glad you came, Mike will be too." Jason raises his little hand, Sarge responds by reaching out his own hand. Jason's hand is only big enough to cover two of sarges' fingers. When Jason's hand rests in Sarge's' massive mitts, his little body jerks and stiffens. His little voice becomes a little deeper and steadier.

"It was cold…he should've waited for the car to warm up…it was a little hard to see…the front window was only defrosted in two small half circles directly above the vents…it was the kind of frost that a scraper can't really scrape…kind of like hard fog…but he's in a hurry…going to be late…needs the car again…if he's late Dad won't let him use the car again for a while…he needs it Saturday night…big game…hot date…he hopes…it's so cold though…he hopes a 'C+' is good enough in history…Connie's in history class…she's a babe…Dad would like her…Sarah would hate her…she seems smart though…I hope she goes with me…I'll play my best for her…she'll like seeing me kick some ass…how come it's still so cold…Brent's an asshole…he'll get his…maybe washer fluid will clear the windshield, yeah…it steams, but it's working, oh man, it's freezing up again…the roads aren't too bad…a little slippery…was that my name?…who could say my name right now?…Hello?…what are those red dots?…it feels like someone is in here with me…whoa, shit!…that's a funky outfit…cool!…it's a skull with wings?… Like Harley Davidson motorcycles?… Oh…I'm Michael…how'd you get in here?…you're not some freak, are you?…I don't think so, lady!…that's bullshit!…Look, I'm almost home, I'm going to let you out…no, now…what the hell? Back off! Careful! It's hard to drive, no!…I have a family…I don't need a new one…look psycho, get out or…no…no…all of them?…Dad, Sarah, and Mom?…I'd have to ask them…Jeez, what stinks so bad…that's your breath! Look the other way…no…I think you're pretty…you look kind of older…Ha! Yeah, experienced I guess…what are you doing?…wow, I, uh, I…shouldn't we pull over…oh, my God!…I like you, too…sure, lots of times…I guess not…while I'm driving?…it is warm in here now…yeah, who wouldn't like that?…how do you know me?…Chosen?…How many?…Well, that's cool I guess…ouch! Careful…that's good…very good…Shit!…turn into it, Dad said!...Damn!...Dad...I love you guys...help...I can't stop the car...Mom...Dad...please...Daaaad..." Jason rips his little hand away from Sarge's and weakly walks over and sits on the bed, rubbing his temples. It was as if Jason was hearing Mike Peacock's thinking and dialogue during the car crash...that had to be Shanestra in the vehicle with him, Shanestra the great seductress.

Sarge continues to stand motionless, his cheeks and ears beet red. He looks over to Jason, a tear rolls down his cheek. "He...Mike called out for me?"

"Yes sir. That's how I saw it. I can't read him now. I think he's still alive though." Jason looks over to me, and he smiles and says, "Ben, I can read Russ. He's in bad shape, but definitely alive. He's thinking about you. He's not at Kendall's. Only Kendall and Frank are. Jessup is on the grounds, outside of the house with a bunch of big kids. Mike is one of them, I think. They're supposed to take out Dugan and Sarge, and let you get through. Later, in two full cycles, they're all meeting...all the Kindred and their Embraced and their kids, out at Post 555, the old airfield. They're having a huge meeting. There's something wrong...they want to rush...a ritual...they..." Jason gets up and slowly heads toward me. He puts one hand on his forehead and when he finally reaches me, he puts out his hand, and weakly embraces the medallion and drops to his knees. He appears to be on the verge of passing out. Kevin runs over and scoops him up.

"Sorry, this has been a lot for him. His little body can't always keep up with his mind. He'll need to rest now..." Jason weakly lifts his head and through squinted eyes whispers,

"Ben...you...you don't know...only you can save..." he drops into a deep sleep.

Kevin puts him in his bed and covers him up. "You're welcome to wait; he may have more for you later, when he's rested."

"I don't think so, let's head to the base. Hey, thanks. Tell Jason, we'll thank him personally when we're done with this thing." Dugan sincerely states.

Sarge walks over to where Jason sleeps and lays his massive hand on Jason's little lump of a body covered by those gross motel bed spreads, and leans down and kisses Jason on the forehead. He softly speaks, "Thank you Jason, thank you for allowing me to be part of my sons' life again, allowing me to share one final experience with him, even if it ends up being my last. I'll never forget it. You're truly an Angel from Heaven. You have my eternal thanks, and may God protect you." Sarge rises and pats Kevin on the shoulder on his way by and leaves out toward the car. Dugan nods and exits as well.

I ask "Kevin...how'd you know it was us in the truck?"

"Well, I'm not on Jason's level, but my specialty is finding people. Being psychic obviously helps me there. Ben...Jason has been reading you for the past three days now. I'm glad he was able to get most of it out. Thanks for trusting me. Godspeed!"

"Thanks for bringing us. Thank Jason when he wakes up. He's truly a marvel. Take care of him." I head back out into the cold. The truck is running, and Sarge has the perimeter covered. I hop in and Sarge follows.

Dugan looks at us and simply says, "That was wild, huh? Ready to go to a vampire meeting?"

I nod yes, Sarge doesn't do anything, so Dugan wheels his rig around, and we head out toward the old base. A light snow begins to fall, the kind with big fluffy snowflakes. As they hit the windshield, you can make out their unique designs, only to quickly be wiped away, and replaced by a new one.

That Jason was incredible. I pull out my folded drawing of Russ and in the darkness, look down and try to make it out. Sarge lays his large hand

CULT OF THE VAMPYR

on my shoulder and says, "We'll get them both out. I promise." He then turns and looks out the side window. I lay my head back against the seat, and close my eyes. All I can see is the little white hair kid looking at me and smiling. 'He needs your help.' He said. Well Jason, as God is my witness, he'll get it!

Dugan's truck hits a bump, the Tome that Orvin gave to me, plops off the dashboard and lands in my lap open. As I glance down the heading reads: 'THE GATHERING'

155

Chapter Fourteen
The Gathering

The caption was followed by passages written in those funky hieroglyphics. On the opposite pages were handwritten notes by Orvin. Orvin's notes stated:

The Gathering:

THE ANGLO-SAXONIAN 'WICCA' RELIGION, MEANING…TO BEND OR TO SHAPE, IS THE VERY ROOT OF OUR CRAFT. THE BURNING WAS MEANT TO HAVE CLEANSED ALL VIA JUDEO-CHRISTIAN LAW, FAILED. THOUGH DRIVEN AWAY IN DROVES, MOST INTO HIDING, MANY NOT ONLY SURVIVED, YET FLOURISHED, HAIL TO THE GOD AND GODDESS, WHICH TOGETHER CREATE THE BALANCE. WE ARE A BALANCED PEOPLE AND ACT AS THE DEFENDERS OF THE FAITH, ALL WILL COME TO DEPEND ON THE MYTHOS CALLED WITCHCRAFT…'

Holy…witchcraft? Orvin was deciphering some passages of witchcraft?

"Hey…uh…Dugan?" I stammer.

"Yeah, Ben?"

"This here Tome…Orvin's translations are speaking of witchcraft…" I wait for some input.

"Yeah. It's a spell book or a prayer book I guess." He nonchalantly answers.

"Wait…you mean…all we were doing was witchcraft?" I don't know why I am so shocked.

"Well yeah. You mean you didn't know? I would have thought Orvin would have filled you in. I mean he was First Circle of The Nine. He was our caster." Dugan still keeps his eyes on the road; he appears genuinely surprised that I don't know.

"Ok, look, guys! We need to stop somewhere, and figure some things out before continuing on." I virtually demand.

"Yeah, ok, fine." Dugan drives on. I switch my glance over to Sarge. He sits very still, almost like he's in a trance.

"That ok with you Sarge?" I ask, mostly just to see if he is still with us.

"If necessary." Sarge answers.

As we enter the new township limit, there's a motel on the right. It kind of reminds me of Bate's motel, you know: eight rooms and an office, with a big farmhouse behind it. You bet I'll be looking for eyeholes in the wall. It's in pretty good shape, with the exception of needing a fresh coat of paint. The light's on in the office, but a portion of the neon sign out front is burnt out. I'll never understand why some places still use those.

* * *

After we settle in to our room, Sarge volunteers to go get food while Dugan and I talk. I guess Sarge doesn't know or care about this whole new dimension of witches being added to everything else. I, on the other hand, am feeling just a touch overwhelmed.

"So, Dugan, are you a witch?" I decide to get right to the point.

"Yeah. At least that's the religion I was brought up practicing. I guess my dad was a true witch."

"Don't you mean warlock?"

"No, Ben. A male witch is just that, a male witch. Warlock was a term made up some time ago meaning evil spell caster or something to that effect. Look Ben, practicing Witchcraft isn't what you think it is. I mean, you've been dealing with The Nine for days now; they are...or were all, witches. Think back to the ceremony at Wang's restaurant, and the chant you were taught, and all the stuff Orvin did. Ben, what did you think it was?" Dugan looked at me with question in his eyes.

"Well, yeah, I suppose...but I never thought witches really existed...or vampires either for that matter. I mean, what's next? Frankenstein? The Wolfman?"

"Ben, really..."

"All right, but come on! witches and vampires? It seems so unreal."

"Why?"

"Well, it's like myths not reality."

"Look son, a myth only stops being a myth when people start to believe in it. Humans have been deifying things for centuries. Anything they don't understand, they try to explain with a myth or a legend. Historically, Witchcraft and Vampirism pre-date the Judeo-Christian, Moslem, Buddhism, Islamic, and Hinduism religions by centuries. To those of us of the old faith, all these newer faiths are the current mythos. Ben, I'm not a major player in the Witchcraft religion, but I do know that it has far more proof of existence than any of these newer religions."

"So, aren't witches evil, turning people into frogs and stuff?" I felt dumb asking, and Dugan was kind enough to roll his eyes at me, but come on! I've been siding with witches to oppose the vampires. I don't know who to trust now.

"Ben, we don't wear black cone hats and fly around on broomsticks. We are a religion, like any other. We worship the God and Goddess, and realize earth is as much a deity as anyone. We are not Satan worshippers, Satan doesn't exist, that's a Christian invention, and they can have it. We don't require an opposing force of evil for the force of good; our balance comes from the God and the Goddess, the hunter/provider and the nurturer/mother." Dugan looks tired.

"Dugan, so why are you witches fighting the vampires?" I was curious.

"Well Ben, in every town, no matter how small, there is an inner circle of The Nine. Have you ever noticed that no matter how small or large a town is, there are always a handful of people that everyone knows? Business owners, regulars, mayors, police…whoever? Well, they are usually members of The Nine for that town. The Nine was created to protect all the witches from that town from there ever again being THE BURNING. The Burning was at the Salem witch trials and elsewhere throughout history. Understand, the Burning's really did happen; there is historical proof of that. On December 5th, 1494, the persecutions began. These lasted until well into the 18th century. By the late 17th century, most of the Old Religion was forced underground. We slowly had to rebuild, and decided to set up strongholds in every town where witches inhabited. Finally around 1695, Massachusetts law about persecution of witches ended. England continued to be in frenzy over the inaccurate Christian definition of Witchcraft. It was the easiest way for them to punish criminals and place blame on anything they didn't understand. Try as they might, they couldn't destroy every witch, in fact, they ended up killing more humans than witches in these trials."

"You keep referring to witches and humans as being different. Aren't witches just humans following the witchcraft religion?" I thought he'd said that.

"No, not just anyone can be a witch. You must possess the aura. Ben, witches can travel many planes of existence. The powers we are granted are strictly focused prayers that get answered! Turning people into frogs is NOT Witchcraft. Placing up wards to protect you from evil is." Dugan looks at me like, 'get it yet man?'.

"Ok, so, why are you opposing the vampires again?"

"Ben, the Undead Gods the Kindred worship, and the God and Goddess We of the Craft worship, have been at war for centuries. It is an age-old argument between which religion pre-dates the other. Regardless of that, many of the Kindred put themselves in positions of authority, for the sole purpose of being able to find us of the Craft and persecute us. The Kindred believe that we take human sacrifices in some of our rituals, so to them, we are stealing their food."

"Do you? Do you take human life in some of your rituals?" Please answer no.

"Well, in the far gone past,…yes, in the last five hundred years? No."

"So, once a witch is killed, what happens?"

"Well, we come back reincarnated. I know that sounds difficult to understand, but everyone on earth, belonging to the Craft, has already lived many lives here. I am a reincarnation of someone, my former self I suppose, but Ben, I haven't studied the Craft for years, I wish I knew more to tell you, but that's about all my knowledge on the subject. Oh, by the way, Jason is an ancient witch, an inner-circle caster. Kevin was just a human who received a gift of using more than 20% of his brain. Every witch is psychic to some degree. Kendall, the Kindred you told me about, may have been granted the gift of telepathy, but for the most part, Kindred are not psychic."

"And you? Are you psychic?" I inquired.

"I knew you were going to ask me that...just kidding. Yeah, I am, but I must have been a very young witch, because my telepathy is barely developed. I'm at the level of having Deja-vu more often than most. Remember, I really haven't used this stuff much. I believe it from before Dad was killed, and remember what he taught me, but have had little use for it on this cycle. I sort of wish I was well practiced, I'd be of more use then. Look, relax about it, the Kindred are whom we have to concentrate on. You see Ben, Witches will be included in the Final Harvest, just like humans, and one on one, a Kindred will win over a witch every time. We have to cast from afar, and set the guards and wards, and prepare. There are times I wish I could just launch fireballs from my hands, but that isn't realistic."

Realistic? This is all so unbelievable. I guess it makes sense, but...

The door swings open, Sarge is standing there, and he's got three big bags of burgers. Immediately upon catching the scent of them, I make for the toilet and vomit. I guess I'm so distraught, nothing sounds good to me. I come back out and collapse on one of the beds. I drift off before feeling my face hit my pillow.

* * *

I waken slowly, the room is dark, a light fog, or mist appears to be whisping around, and Dugan appears to be in the bed next to mine. I don't see Sarge anywhere. I go to the front door, I unbolt it and swing it open slowly, a small pile of smooth rocks gets knocked over by the door as I open it. I look outside and standing guard, like England's royal guards outside the palace is Sarge. His thoughts are his own as he appears to be staring off into space. I decide not to interrupt him. I slowly close and bolt the door. I turn to head back to my bed, and standing directly behind me is a cloaked figure.

"Shit!" I yell out. I reach for my Barretta and realize that I'm stark naked. I start to back off, toward the door, and then the cloaked figure speaks.

"Ben, they can't hear you." The hooded figure lowers his hood to reveal that he is Barry, the confederate soldier vampire; I met my first night with Pastor Frank.

"Relax Ben. I'm clearly not here to harm you. You merely didn't show up at Kendall's, and we became concerned. This is the best way for me to reach you in private, it is my gift." He awaits a response.

"Can you hear me?" I ask.

"Of course. Now, here. Perhaps you should put something on. You...mortals, always feel vulnerable when you're naked." He tosses me a robe like his.

"Why have you come? And if you can just come at will, how come this is the first time you've come to me like this?"

"Ben...this isn't an easy thing to do. You're making a grievous error throwing your hat in the ring with the Witches. Theirs is a dying breed. The Roman-Catholics saw to that. The Wicca's, the Druids, and all of the old Celtic religions lay on the brink of extinction. Like modern religions, they feud within their own religion as to which interpretation is the true path. Christian's vs. Catholics vs. born-again Christians vs. Baptists vs. Latter-day Saints vs. Lutherans, etc...are all under Christianity, yet all feel the other is wrong. The old Druidic religion, from which the Wicca religion was birthed, believes in different Gods. At least Christians all believe in the same God. The difference, my boy, is that we believe not in true Gods, but ancients who have centuries of experience. We are our own true Gods! Yes, there is a being of immense power that grants us our dark gifts, but it is no God!"

"You came here to preach more Vampire lore to me?" I feel a little out of place here.

"Ben...why are you so against accepting your true destiny?" Barry looks to me as a kind old man would.

"How about...because you guys want to annihilate the human species by tearing out heir throats and drinking down their blood? You see, being one of those humans, that just doesn't sound very appealing to me!"

"Ouch! The boy speaks with a speared tongue! You are more than they are. They are livestock; you are bred to be superior. Their time has come to an end. It is time for Vampire to continue on in our travels to embrace cosmic greatness! We will no longer need the blood-bags for sustenance! This is but one farm of thousands! Think of it boy! All the cosmos can be yours, we will no longer be bound to this mud ball and forced to co-exist with our livestock!" Barry actually looks excited as he is spouting off about this crap.

"So, if you're leaving anyway, why not spare the humans, and leave?" It seems like an obvious answer to me.

"Ha-ha-ha. Well-played boy. We will need the auras of many as we traverse through the Cosmic Gate. We bred these blood-bags for this very purpose! This is their day of reckoning! Their Rapture! This is the ultimate sacrifice for humans to their true Gods, THE VAMPYR!" His enthusiasm is sickening.

"You said yourselves that the humans have grown almost out of control in numbers, perhaps not all humans must suffer this fate…maybe a lot could be spared…" I already didn't like where I was going with this.

"How to choose, hmmm? Well, maybe just all the bad people deserve this fate. Or all the religious people who would see this as their redemption, giving it up to their makers, us. What of the innocence of the children? How do we choose? Would the fact that, we choose for each life or death, not in itself, define us as their Gods? By their own definition?" Barry smiled. Damn him!

"There are going to be those who oppose you! People won't just lie down and bare their throats to you! Something has you guys worried, I don't know who or what, but something is scaring you guys." I look for reaction.

"Son, there will be no opposition. Does the farmer not lead the cattle into the slaughterhouse by merely prodding them along? Humankind is no different. Remember when Frank explained how Judeo/Christianity was created in order to control humans? The Final Harvest IS their redemption! The Second Coming IS the Rapture. Most will come willingly into the slaughterhouse. We have allowed those of the new religion to wipe out those of the old. Our only true opposition is those left of the old religions, and they are few. Their power wanes. It pales beside our own. Our Harbinger will allow us to seek out and destroy all, which are of the old religions." Barry again chortles at his own story.

"Won't you need a lot of vampires to drain all of these humans?" I really don't know what to say.

"My boy, very few are blood drinkers. Mostly, only the footpads feast on the actual raw blood of humans. Those of us in the higher ranks are psychic-vampires. There's a certain…thrill from actually drinking of the blood, even for psychic-vampires, but it is pure necessity of the lower circle of blood vampires. We generally use the blood vampires to do the grunt work. Blood vampires are usually those who've been Embraced, as opposed to those who are pureblood Kindred. A few who have been Embraced, have attained high levels in the hierarchy of the Kindred. We know who those would be by their aura…" He stares at me.

"So, would I be a blood-vampire, or a Psychic-Vampire?" Just curious.

"Psychic." He answers without hesitation.

"So I could read peoples minds like Kendall?" Again, just curious.

"Read…? No, son. Psychic Vampirism is not limited by your definition of being psychic. You see boy, all individuals that are of some import, have an aura. Your aura is larger than the body of flesh it inhabits. Picture a glow or force field around your body of approximately six to eight inches. This field is the outer edge of your aura. Once you come in contact with that aura you can actually drain a portion of it and add it to your own, empowering you. As Vampires, we must always spend our aura to the Great Beast to retain our immortality and dark gifts, and thus must replenish it. Ben, you ever notice how around some people, you are just energized, and how around others, you are completely drained? You are either feeding or spending. Those humans we consider close friends, the ones we're comfortable around, are the ones we feed off of the most. It doesn't hurt the humans, it just drains them. Thus, humans must replenish themselves, by feeding off the animal blood and meat. Or humans can now feed off of plants, and allow the Sun to replenish their aura. It's all a cycle Ben. We're all carnivores, just at different levels. It simply took us this long to perfect the cycle, and become ready for The Final Harvest…"

"Barry…it makes sense, I guess, but seems so amazing…Barry? Barry?…" Barry starts to fade out; he's getting more difficult to see.

"Ben…don't forsake us…go to Kendall's…not base…"

Another hooded figure steps into the place of Barry. "Be gone vile nightmare. Hecatu, Acatu, Vehemus!"

Barry is completely gone. This new hooded figure lowers his hood, to reveal an older man, maybe in his fifty's or sixty's, he has a very sculptured face, almost like it's chiseled out of stone. He has long, white hair pulled back into a ponytail. As dark and misty as it is, I clearly see bright green eyes. He turns and looks at me and says, "Ben, Ben, get up."

I startle to a quick, though foggy consciousness. I see Dugan and Sarge standing over me. "Ben, get up…its dusk and we've got to get a move on."

"Dusk, then didn't I just lay down…"

"No, Ben, dusk the next day, you've been out for a full day."

"A full day…but it all seemed so quick…I talked to Barry and some guy…Dugan! Do you know a guy…uh, clean shaven, maybe fifty, white hair…long, very sculptured face…green eyes?"

"Green eyes? Mason! Ben are you sure he had green eyes?"

"Absolutely! They appeared to pierce the darkness as much as Jessup's red eyes do. He appeared and banished Barry with a chant." Dugan cracked a smile.

"Ben, Mason is the most ancient of any living Druid/Wiccan. He's the Master Caster. He saw the Dream-Walking Barry was doing and Dream-Casted his way into your Dream Walk! He then cast Barry out of it. That must be Barry's dark gift, but he's no match for Mason! Mason is at one with the Lifetree. All of nature is his to command! We have to go to him, he could help us! Oh man! Mason is like the Pope to us Witches, with his help we could actually pull this off!" Dugan seemed energized by this new revelation. I, as usual, was not sure anyone could help us against the up and coming apocalypse.

"Dugan…I'm not sure anymore…I think we need to hand this over to someone else. Dugan, I'm not so sure even this Mason guy can stand up to the Vampires…" My voice shook hesitantly.

"Ok...ok...so who was more powerful during your Dream Walk?" Dugan asked and then smiled.

"Well, yeah, ok. Where is this guy?"

"A couple of hours North. I imagine he'll be expecting us."

"Wait. What about the Vampire meetin' at the old base? We can still make it there!" Sarge added in.

"Um...no, sir. Going there would not be good. I suggest we go see if Mason can help us and then meet Kendal when he is NOT expecting us. I believe this Mason dude can shield us or whatever. Please, Sarge, I have my reasons for taking this tact." I look to him. His grim visage gives way to the kinder gentler Sarge.

"Sure kid, you're the boss." Sarge turns and heads out of the room into the parking lot to secure it.

"Dugan, you really think this guy can help us?"

"Ben, if I'd thought he was still alive after all these centuries, we'd have gone to see him first. Ben, if he can't help us, no one can. Mason IS Witchcraft. He ruled the Celtic islands and single handedly diverted The Burning. Mason influenced the other rulers to put an end to the foolish notion that anyone could cast spells in league with the Devil. This happens to be true, since there is no Satan. Ben, Mason cast from StoneHenge! That was his first Sacred Circle, and indeed the first Cromlech or altar, if you will. Be'Al, 'the source of all beings' was to be worshipped from here. One God, who later took on a bride, became the Wiccan God and Goddess. Celtic Druids still only worship Be'Al, and Wiccans worship both. This is the only true separation of the two religions. The humans Old and New Testaments are fashioned after this."

Wow, now the Witches are taking credit for creating Judeo/Christianity.

"Come Ben, I bet there will be a full Eisteddfod in session upon our arrival!" Dugan hurried out the door.

"Eisteddfod? Dugan, what is that?" I asked hurrying after him.

"Oh sorry, a session of the Bards and minstrels…a party, with music and historical stories!"

"Oh." Whatever, I think.

* * *

We entered the vehicle, and Dugan fired it up. We headed out. The traffic was light, especially for being around dinner time. Dugan pulled into a gas station to fill up the rig. A biker was leaning up against his Harley, boy, talk about being chromed out; it almost looked like it was constructed out of mirrors. The man leaning against the bike was chewing on a cigar. He was dressed in all black leather. He almost looked like he was looking over at us, but it was hard to tell. His black helmet only had enough of the visor open to allow the cigar smoke to escape. I felt very uneasy about him…

"Sarge, that biker, I don't like him. Keep an eye on him will you?" Sarge nodded and turned his full attention on him.

Dugan headed in to pay for the gas. I saw the biker start to head in also. Sarge immediately headed in after the two of them. I heard him cock his gun on the run. I jumped in the rig and headed toward the store. As I pulled up to it, Sarge came crashing through the plate glass window. Shit! That's got to be Denny in there! The smelly, road warrior guy with the pussy name!

Sure enough, Denny saunters out of the store and heads toward Sarge…

Chapter Fifteen
We of the Craft

Denny looked over to me sitting in the truck and smiled, brandishing his fangs. He says something, but over the sound of the running engine, I couldn't quite make it out. It was probably just a smelly grunt anyway. Denny once again turns toward Sarge, and heads toward him. Sarge, recovering faster than I would have expected, swings his large gun around and launches a grenade at Denny. Denny quickly, in a blur actually, sidesteps the projectile, only to step into the second grenade launched by Sarge. The second grenade catches Denny in the right shoulder, removing his arm from the shoulder down. The force of the explosion sends Denny about ten feet straight backward, smashing back through the window and back into the store. Sarge jumps to his feet with speed that belies his bulk, and jumps back through the broken window.

"Kid, Ben, come in here." Sarge yells out to me.

I hop out of the truck and enter the store through…the door, unlike how anyone else around cares to enter places. Upon entering, I see that the store is in a shambles, there was obviously a fight in here as well as outside. The store clerk, a dude about twenty or so, is leaned in the corner, pale as a ghost and stiff as a board. He's obviously been dead for quite a while, and apparently drained as well. Dugan lay over the counter, on his back. Empty shells from fired bullets litter the floor at his feet...his feet are turned facing the counter. That's impossible...oh my God...he's been twisted completely around. His spine must be in splinters. Denny apparently broke him in half and turned his upper body to face the other direction. Oh, man, I was getting to like Dugan too! He was also our witch. Well, shit. I guess its GI JOE and me over here to find the rest of The Craft. Great. Just great.

"Damn, Sarge. Dugan was a good man. I'm going to miss him."

"What about that whole 'Warriors Three' mumbo-jumbo? I thought Dugan was our third." Sarge looked at me with his most confused look since I've known him.

"I really don't know...where's Denny?"

"Den...you mean the biker? He was gone when I got in here. He was a fast one, strong too." Sarge rubbed his own shoulder. He then stripped all the weapons and ammo of Dugan and headed back out toward the truck, carefully of course. I followed suit quickly.

"You drive Ben. I need to be keeping my eye out for...well, you know." Sarge sternly adds.

"Yeah, no problem. Let's go."

I shift and gun it. The great beast moaned then jerked to a forward motion. I felt like I was ten feet in the air, the smell of gas and exhaust permeated my nose. Sarge sat silent and grim. My own mind was racing with thoughts of Orvin, Dugan, Wang...the vampires, the witches, and how many people I've seen dead. I decided that I was actually handling all of this pretty well. I yearn for my life to just get back to normal. I also start to accept the fact that my life may never get back to normal. This, of course, just makes me want my old life back all the more. Sarge mentioned on our long trek, that of all the deaths he had seen in the war, none of it seems as gruesome or real as the last few days.

We mostly drive in silence, both wondering just what we are getting into now. I suppose there are good witches, but I'm just not comfortable with the idea that this guy, Mason, walks into my dream and casts Barry out with a mere sentence. Dugan said, 'Mason Is witchcraft'. So, like, that's a little scary right?

For the first time in days, I am actually beginning to feel hunger pains. Food has mostly made feel sick at the very sight or smell of it, but now I am hungry, nonetheless. Sarge continues to sit in silence. I watch, as he appears to be deep in thought.

"So…Sarge, what do you think we ought to do? Find this Mason guy?" I ask, simply to get a conversation going.

"If that's what you think. If he can help me find those bastards, let's go find him." He never even looked at me.

I can always tell when I'm getting up north; the roads appear to have been cut directly through the forest. There's nothing but the bare trees of winter, and the occasional greenery of the evergreens. We pass an occasional car or truck now and again, but for the most part, traffic appears to be quite light. We finally come upon a sign to the next town. Mason Creek. I suppose that means we're here. I can't tell if that's the town's name, or directions.

The town is quite small, not unlike any small town in the northernmost parts of any given state. You have your general store, your little white church and your two gas stations (both advertising bait for sale), your mechanic's garage(with more cars out front than people living here I'm sure), and of course, the sight of a future Mickey D's. The downtown diner aptly entitled; 'The Downtown Diner', is packed full of five or six men in flannel shirts drinking coffee. I figure, this is as good a spot to stop as any. I wheel into a parking spot and step out to stretch. Sarge and I go into the diner and sit at a table. Sarge puts his back to the wall, apparently so no one can sneak up on him. So, what's he so paranoid about? Just kidding.

A waitress approaches us, chewing gum, (spearmint by the smell of it). She smiles, her face shows of a long, hard life. She appears to be a smoker and a drinker. It's obvious from the smell coming from her. She's only missing one lower tooth, and the rest are stained by tobacco. Her lips sport a dusty-rose colored lipstick, eye shadow appears to be a couple of days old, and bad make up helps to cover the bags under her eyes. She's wearing a white t-shirt, blue jeans (form-fitting), and a stained apron draped over the front of her. Her reddish hair is pulled back into a messy bun.

"So boys, stoppin' in for some of Larry's famous chili ?" She smiles again.

"Well, it's our first time to Mason Creek." I reply.

"Well, then, you are definitely here for a bowl of Larry's chili. It comes with corn chips, shredded cheese, and sour cream. Will that be two?" She winks at us, holding her pencil over her order pad, and manages to smile and chew gum at the same time.

"Um, sure, sounds good." Not really, nothing sounds good.

Sarge kicks me under the table, and motions with his head out the window. The town sheriff and another man are looking over the truck.

"Should I…" I put my hand up to stop Sarge from completing his sentence. I get up and walk out to meet with these guys.

"You own this here vehicle, boy?" The portly little village constable asks.

"Yes, sir…well, actually it's on loan from a friend, he's got my car and I've got his truck. It wouldn't do to come up to the Creek here, and not have the right kind of vehicle." I reply with a smile.

"Nice truck, boy. You here huntin' or fishin'?" He asks, removing his hat and dabbing the sweat off of his forehead. I'll be damned if this isn't Boss Hog from the Dukes of Hazard.

"Actually we're looking for an old acquaintance, maybe you know him? Mason?" I ask.

"I see…afraid not boy. Don't know no Mason around these here parts. You have a nice vacation, ya hear?" He turns and waddles off.

The other fella stays to stare at me for a minute, he appears to start opening his mouth, as if to say something, but stops himself and quickly spins around and follows the sheriff. I hear someone rapping on glass I turn to see Sarge knocking on the diner window, motioning for me to come in. I re-enter to see two large, steaming bowls of chili, heaped with cheddar cheese and sour cream, surrounded by corn chips. Sarge is digging in like he never ate before. The smell alone makes me nauseous; I have to get over this! My body needs food! I head up to the cook's window, and yell through for Larry. A tall, slender man with sandy colored hair and a matching handlebar mustache, decked out in a food stained apron steps through the swinging doors.

"Who wants ta know?" The man asks.

"Hey, me. I'm Ben…Ben Ruden. I was just wondering if I could get a steak from you, rare."

"Sure, no problem kid." He turns and heads back into the kitchen.

"Hey, honey, you don't want to order from me?" Our waitress asks me, sticking her bottom lip out as if to pout.

"Oh, it's not that, I just didn't see you around."

"Ok sugar, I'll get it right out to you."

Within minutes a steak is brought out to me, rare with the cool, pink center. I devour it. The juices explode in my mouth, the salty, beefy juices that make me the beef lover that I am. My body shakes, in excitement, from ingesting the protein. Sarge helps himself to my bowl of chili.

Our waitress comes and sets down the tab. She smiles and tells us to have a great day. She then disappears into the back. I continue to scan the room and realize that everyone is gone, except Sarge and me.

"Sarge, looks like it's just us."

Sarge looks up, wiping his chili soaked moustache.

"Huh." Sarge slowly raises up and pulls out a firearm

We both swing around to the sound of the bells on the diner door ringing, as the door swings open. Entering the diner is three individuals; the sheriff, the townie that was with him earlier, and a women dressed like a schoolteacher. All three have a leather bound tome under their arm...

* * *

"It would appear that apologies are in order." The sheriff stated.

"I do indeed know of a Mason. If you boys would follow us, we'll take you to his place of residence."

We follow the three out to the squad car. The sheriff engages Sarge in a conversation about all his guns, Sarge responds as would be expected. The other fella drops back with me. He's an Up-North, outdoorsman type, the kind who can wear a flannel shirt and no coat, and is warm enough to go snowmobile riding. He wears a seven-o'clock shadow, a hunter's hat, which is green with the earflaps that could be tied down, but never are. His black denim jeans have extra padding in the knees, like maybe Dickie's or something. Upon further investigation, I realize that the jeans are actually overalls, the top of which is covered by his flannel shirt. His breath stinks of smoke. He's probably in his late thirties and probably ways one hundred pounds soaking wet!

"You…you are the one ain'tcha?" He asks, smiling, with his smoke stained teeth glaring at me.

"I don't know what you mean…exactly." I respond.

"The one…the one Mason was talking about." He pulled up a lit cigarette, and sucked it until the bright orange ember grew to about half the size of the cigarette.

"Well, I sort of met Mason, once." I picked up my pace.

"In a Dream Walk, right?"

"Well, I guess. I don't fully understand…" I was cut off.

"You were in a Dream Cast, and DON'T understand? Wow! Jason was right!" He slapped his hand over his own mouth.

"Jason? You mean Mason, right?" I inquired.

"Yeah, yeah, Mason, that's what I said." He quickly moved around to the other side of the squad car and climbed in.

"You boys can follow us. It ain't far." The sheriff climbed in, and the lady got in back.

We hopped up into the truck and took off following the sheriff's car. We continued through town, houses mostly. About half of them had visible addresses, and the other half had none to be seen. I always thought it ought to be a law that everyone should have his or her address visible. I know as an insurance salesman, it isn't easy to find some of these people with no address posted, I don't see how 911 could do it either, but no one thinks of that!

The sheriff turns down a dirt road cutting into the woods, it looks more like a trail really. The branches of the trees are scraping along the sides of Dugan's truck, sorry pal. The squad car comes to a halt. The three get out and turn to us. I look over to Sarge, he shrugs his shoulders and pats his firearms, as if to reassure me. We hop out, and head over to them. They pop the trunk of the cruiser, and hand us robes. They match the ones The Nine wore at Wang's. We don them, as do the others. They start off further down the trail; it starts to get thicker with over-growth. The townie that talked with me earlier starts chanting something under his breath, I can't quite make it out. The over-growth starts to spread and open up, as if alive. As we pass through it, it closes behind us. At this point, we'd need chainsaws to get through these thickets, but even the tree branches yield to the yokels' chants. Finally, we break into a clearing. The clearing is about a four-hundred foot diameter; at the very center is a set of large, rectangular stones, about twelve-foot high, three feet thick, and five-feet wide. They form a circle, and a dais or stone altar is in the middle. Nine stacks of small, smooth oval stones are stacked in a pyramid of nine, in between each of the larger stone rectangles, of which there are ten. Partially melted candles sit atop each of the stone pyramids, unlit at this point.

It is unusually warm in this clearing, the wind is dead silent. The Sheriff and the others all go to a spot and kneel in front of a pile of stones. They are all kneeling in front of a separate pyramid of stones. The piles are at their backs as they face inward, toward the dais. They all pull their hoods over their heads, and bow their heads, revealing none of their face. I look to Sarge, again he shrugs his shoulders. He cocks his gun. As he does this, we feel a slight tremor in the ground; it violently shakes below us, causing us to stumble, forcing us to regain our balance. All at once large, brown tentacles, tree roots actually, burst forth from the ground, like living snakes, they writhe around us. Sarge takes to fighting against them, snapping the first few that reach him, within minutes; however, he is overcome and bound tightly. I'm not nearly as tightly bound as Sarge is, but I'm surrounded none-the-less. I guess I'm not as threatening as Sarge is. The smell of damp wood surrounds me, and as I get ready to ask what in the Hell is going on, a succession of six more robed individuals parade into the middle of the area, and then continue on to, what must be assigned areas, and kneel, looking down. All but one, that is. The one who does not sit, is facing us. The one standing lowers his hood, and sure enough, it's Mason. His piercing green eyes seemed to look right through me. His stone cold, expressionless face, turns from me to Sarge and back again. He slowly strolls toward me. Sarge gets real restless, and begins thrashing. He growls and grunts as he attempts to bust free from his wooden bonds.

"Let me go! You son of a…! I'll get you! Damn!!" Sarge spouted out! The conviction and venom in his voice, did not match that of the man I'd gotten to know over the past week or so. Sarge was a man of few words, and they were carefully chosen.

"Why dost thou travel with yon creature?" Mason asks me, and then cocks his head awaiting my answer.

"Creature? So, like, humans are creatures to you witches as well?" I'm getting a little upset with all of this.

"This creature 'tis not human. He is Vampyr. I asketh thee, for a second and final time, why dost thou travel with him?" Mason folds his arms across his chest.

"Sarge is NOT Vampyr! He's as human as they come!" I turn to look at Sarge, expecting a little reinforcement. Instead of reassurance from Sarge, I see Seth, the surfer dude Vampyr that I met the other night, when I met all of Death breath's friends.

"What in the Hell…where's Sarge? How did this happen? I don't understand…" Oh man, I don't even want to hear this answer! I know I don't!

"Sorry Benster, he never quite made it back out of the party store. But like, we needed you to keep on your way, so I had to use my gift, making you think everything was how you thought it should be. But old man dipshit here, had to go and ruin everything! Thanks pops!" Seth smiled and then hisses, brandishing his fangs at Mason.

"Shit! So Sarge is dead?" I demanded out of Seth.

"Yeah dude. Oh, and Denny is pissed! That blood bag got him good! His arm will never be the same..." Mason makes his presence known.

"Seek ye naught to ignore me creature. Are anymore of your kin nearby, or shalt we destroy thee in peace. Yes or no?" Mason waits for a response.

"You'll never know, tree hugger. So I guess you can move on to the destroying me part, but be careful, because if you do it wrong, I'll be drinking witches' brew for dinner...and I've worked up a killer thirst! So, like, bring it ya old fossil." Seth's eyes start glowing red, and he slowly starts tearing through the thorny branches and roots that held him fast.

Mason's eyes start glowing green, green as emeralds held in front of a flashlight, and the other eight hooded figures of the Craft stand and show their eyes glowing bright white. The wind starts to pick up; all nine candles ignite in unison. Mason raises both arms toward the sky, the large sleeves of his robe slide down toward his shoulders, revealing his muscular arms, they appear to be straining, as if he were lifting something very heavy over his head. His gold bracelets, large enough to cover most of his forearms, and very ornate in detail, appear to be glowing as well. Above Mason, the sky grows dark and very cloudy. The clouds roll in at an unnaturally quick rate. Thunder claps and lightning strikes. Rain lightly pelts me and suddenly, the downpour becomes torrential. The candles still burn. Above all the commotion and noise, I hear Mason's voice cry out.

"By the Mother Goddess! For the Father God! Grant me the divinity to do what must be done to cleanse us of the Evil of the night! Basque me in your power! ANTILLA-APITU-CRESTILIA-LITNI-NIVEE-ASQUATIA!"

Mason raises a dagger into the air; a bolt of lightning strikes the very blade of the dagger, the electricity dances on the blade, Mason swings the dagger downward. The dagger sinks into the chest of Seth, who was getting closer to freeing himself, and as the blade strikes Seth, a bright yellow flash, and the sound of a clap of thunder, causes Mason to be hurled twenty feet back in the air, striking the altar. As my eyes clear, I see Seth, engulfed in flames, burst free from the entanglement, and leap twenty feet through the air and land on top of Mason. He looks like a meteor streaking through the air. The branches around me drop to the ground, releasing me. Seth wrenches the knife out of his chest and flings it to the ground. He then stands still, and stands over Mason as the flames slowly extinguish themselves.

What's left of Seth, the blonde surfer kid, is a hairless, charcoal gray, smoking husk of a body. The stench of burned hair permeates the very air. Seth looks around, as he turns and sees the other seven of the Craft close in on him, their eyes glowing white. I notice several wet, pink spots on his gray hide start to appear, then turn back to gray. Seth turns to me, his burned, eyebrow less face, looks to me as if for compassion, and when he receives none, he turns back and says:

"I…I can't regenerate. I…I'm to stay like this…forever? I'll suck your eyeballs out of your skull witch!!" Seth steps toward Mason as the rest of the Craft cause a single stream of fire from each of their personal candles to form a grid of flame between Mason and Seth. Seth screams at an inhuman, almost beast-like pitch. In the blink of an eye, Seth darts off, passing one of the robed figures on his way. As he passes this robed figure, he reaches out and snaps the neck with a sickening crack. He holds the limp body against his and says to Mason, "You'll not live into the New Year witch, and I'll personally taste of your essence, as bitter as it may be."

Seth turns and darts off into the woods. The storm subsides, the glowing eyes dim, and a unified sigh of relief is released. Mason pulls himself up off the ground, and faces me, his soaked hair only adds to his stoic expression.

He puts his hand on my shoulder and whispers; "I be getting too old for this shit."

The others go over and lift their fallen member; they carry their brother off into the woods.

"Mason, I'm sorry for bringing him here, I thought he was a friend..." I couldn't finish. The tragedy of the Peacocks, losing a son and now a father, a father desperately trying to find his son, is beyond comprehension. Sarge was a kind, gentle, caring, yet strong man. He didn't deserve this. I've reached a decision...

"Mason, tell me what you need me to do. I pledge my very life to the service of the Craft; in order to stop The Final Harvest."

Mason places his hand on my shoulder, and smiles. "Ben, 'tis good to have thee aboard. Come, let's rest and discuss our next move." Mason heads off. I follow.

As I walk, I glance at the ground and notice the dagger which was used against Seth...is missing.

Chapter Sixteen
The Commitment

"Hey Mason!" I yell after him.

Slowly, he turns and again smiles. "Yea Ben, what 'tis it son?"

"The knife...dagger, whatever...did you pick it up? It's gone. Is this ok?" I assumed it was bad, I mean this knife had a lot of power in it obviously.

"The Boleen? The one I used on that base Vampyr? T'was one of The Nine that hath picked it up..." Mason, turned and walked back to where it originally lay.

"Why is it called a Boleen? Does that mean anything?" I inquired.

"Yea, 'tis not here. Someone didst pick it up. 'Tis no big deal Ben, 'tis not like it's an Athame or anything." Mason turns and starts walking again.

"Oh, right, because THAT would be bad! Good thing it wasn't an Athame, because...want to fill me in there Mason?"

"Thy sarcasm's match thy effrontery! I warn thee, take thee care in how thou wouldst speak with me, if indeed, thou dost require information from me." Mason continues down the now much-narrower path.

Although it is obviously a trail, it is one that is quite overgrown, both behind and ahead of me. Although when I reach a spot ahead of me it doesn't appear as overgrown as it did prior to arriving. The night is still quiet; it's also warmer than it should be. I can see my breath fog in front of me, but don't feel as if it is cold enough for that to happen. Mason, by all rights, should be freezing in his dark robe, but I get the feeling he wouldn't let me know if he was cold.

"A thousand pardons sir, but I know, like, zilch about the craft. I can't be any help if I don't know anything."

"I shalt commune with the Goddess and God tonight. They wilt let me know if thee'll be any help at all, and to what degree I must involve mine own Nine and myself. Ben." He turns and meets my eyes, again the depth of the green in his eyes render me motionless, and I stand and listen, unable to break away. "An Athame is one of the most powerful tools of the Craft. 'Tis, in most cases, a black-handled, double-edged knife. It represents both the male aspect and symbolizes fire. In most cases it is used during the Great Rite, it assists in the blessing. We have used it to cut a doorway in the circle to allow one entrance into the circle, or to cut a cord in a passing, or even to cut the handfasting cake. The Athame 'tis NOT to be used as a weapon, due to the fact that we of the Craft art indeed a peaceful lot. Make no mistake about the energies the Athame possesses, but 'tis a mighty and sacred tool, unlike a Boleen. If that night creature took the Boleen, he probably assumes it's our Athame, and wilt be quite disappointed, I assure thee!" Mason releases me, by turning away and once again heading down the path. I follow quietly. Boy, is this guy a killjoy. 'watch how you speak to me' he says, well maybe he ought to watch how he addresses me! Ok, maybe not. That whole lightning on the knife thing was pretty impressive, even to a guy who met with nine vampires.

We finally come to another clearing, I lost track of which direction we were heading, which is odd for me. Normally I can tell which direction I'm facing at any given time, but the trees and clouds are blocking out the moon, and I often use that as a point of focus. This clearing is roughly the size football field. Several, well ten actually, stone buildings are peppered about the field, the tenth and largest building, roughly 30' x 30', centrally located. Mason motions to one of The Nine, and a robed figure approaches me. The robed individual lowers his hood to reveal a young man, maybe twenty-two or twenty-three years old. He has stark black hair, is well kept, and is clean-shaven. Throw a football jersey on him; he'd fit in at a Frat house at any major university.

"Hey, my name's Craig, I've heard a lot about you. Is it true, about you? You've actually met Kendal?" The wonder and excitement in his eyes told me he was probably new to this whole Wicca thing.

"Yeah, it's true. So, Craig, what is this place?"

"It's sort of our get away. So, you're getting Janet's place. She, uh, won't be needing it any more. Come on, it's right over here." Craig led me to the third of the nine smaller stone structures. It appeared to be a pile of stones with a wooden door on it from the outside. Once I stepped in, it was lit, somehow, and was a perfect 10'x10' square room. A cot and trunk were the only items in here.

"Do you guys, like, live here all the time?"

"No, we live in town, but if our Caster needs us out here for an extended period of time, we have this little camp. You'll find the staff, boleen, robes, wand, thurable, and chalice in the trunk. Mason is communing tonight, so you might as well get some sleep, and we'll see you in the morning." Craig stood there a minute more; I could tell he had as many questions about me as I did about Craft. He quickly turned and left, the door shutting tightly behind him.

A knock came at my door within minutes of Craig's departure. I opened the door and Craig handed me a tomb. "This is some basic history and stuff; it should answer some of your questions. The rest will be answered after you've done the Great Rite. The Goddess and God will answer your questions after that. It was kind of my journal, as I did stuff I wrote it down. It should be some good reading."

"Thanks Craig, and yes, Kendal is everything you've heard. I am here to help you guys take him down. I just hope we can do it."

"Ok. Thanks. May the Goddess and God watch over us all." Again Craig took his leave.

I decided to skim this new book by the artificial light, illuminating this hooch. Some of the headings were; THE LAW OF THREE, TOOLS OF THE CRAFT, LAWS OF THE NINE,

CEREMONIES, THE BURNING TIMES, THE CHARGE OF THE GODDESS,

THE CHARGE OF THE GOD, SUMMIS DESIDERANTES DEC. 5TH,

1484, THE DRUIDS IONA, WICCA AND WICCE.

There were more, and the information was interesting, but the bottom line was that witchcraft was forbidden to be used offensively or for revenge, and that the Craft, not unlike Christianity, Judaism and the Islamic religion, etc., was just that: a religion. With all of this going through my mind, like how can they battle the Vampyr without going against their own by-laws, I drifted off.

* * *

As I roll over, and slowly opened my eyes, again, I see the artificial glow illuminating my stone shelter. I feel as if I'd slept. However, it doesn't appear to have been very long, it's still dark out. I sit up, and rub my stiff neck. Craig steps in through the door; "Hey, Ben, you're awake. It's good to see you up and around."

"Yeah, what's it been, two or three hours?" I smiled sarcastically.

"Ben, it's been three days. Mason thought you were in a Dream Walk. He checked and said you probably weren't, but he was worried none-the-less. Then he said you probably needed the rest. He said this is probably the first safe place you've been in a while." Craig continued to look at me, as if requesting answers to questions he hasn't asked yet. It's like when a kid says, 'Gosh, I sure wish I could get this toy, but I probably can't.' Then they look at you hoping for a yes.

"Look, Craig…I can tell you're very curious as to what's going on, but Mason is really the one who should fill you in on what he thinks is best."

"Oh, I know Ben; he is the High Priest of The Nine. He knows what's best." Still he looks at me.

"So, do you do whatever the high priest tells you to?"

"Within reason. Look, Mason is THE High Priest of all circles of The Nine. Every circle has its own High Priestess or Priest. Like, Orvin was Havenhill's. You knew him, right?"

"Yeah, since childhood. But they all called him their Caster."

"Right. Group ceremonies require a High One or an Elder to cast. Otherwise, individuals can cast. A High Priest can focus the energies of an entire covenant into a single, powerful spell. You know…Orvin was a good one. Everybody respected him. I'm sorry you lost him, but the Goddess and God must have had bigger plans for him, they will balance the scales. Look, if not for the passing over of Master Stiltworth, you may never of met Mason or…me." Craig looks off to the corner, as if embarrassed.

"I think you're right Craig. Look, could you take me to some food?" Craig eagerly motions for me to follow.

As we step out of my little hovel, I note several people milling about, more than just The Nine. Craig leads me over to a bonfire; it's in the twilight hours now. Everyone milling around is in burgundy or black robes. The Nine are in the black and everyone else is in the burgundy, almost like a caste thing or rank, like belts in martial arts. Only one other of The Nine is at this particular fire pit. There is a female, one of Asian decent I believe. She smiles as I approach, and motions for me to sit down on a log. They are roasting a pig, or wild boar. The entire area is busy with chatter and laughter, not sacrifices and cackling, like you'd expect at a witches' camp. With all the eating and drinking, the fellowship and laughter, you'd think you were at a church picnic, not Wiccan ceremonial grounds.

"Welcome Ben, sit, are you hungry?" She asked me?

"Yes, thank you, Miss..."

"My names Tioli, just Ti for short." She reaches out to the blackened carcass and slices a chunk of white meat off the pig, all the while muttering 'Blessed be the creatures of the forest, the sustenance of The Nine, blessed be the Goddess and God, with the passing of this creature, so has the balance been attained.'

Ti hands the chunk of pork, the other white meat, to me (still steaming) on the end of a small knife. The fatty juices sweat off the chunk of meat. I bite into it, it tastes like charred paper, but I decide not to let on. I smile and nod, continuing to pretend to enjoy my chunk of meat. Craig sets next to me and starts in on his chunk of pig.

"Is there any wine?" I inquire.

"No, nothing alcoholic. But I'm sure we could get you some berry juice or fresh stream water." Ti responds with a smile.

"Um, sure, water would be fine." I finish my meat and feel a little ill, and completely unsatisfied. I feel queasy…but hungry. Ti comes back with water. So far, Ti and Craig are NOT what I'd expect witches to be like, in fact with the exception of Mason, none of them seem like witches. They seem like ordinary people who love to commune with nature.

Suddenly, they all stand up and don their hoods. I decide to follow suit. Mason approaches and all the others move to form a circle. Mason moves to the middle, he lowers his hood to reveal a golden mask. The only way I can tell that it's Mason, is due to his robes, his stature, and his piercing green eyes. All the witches drop to one knee and bow their heads, I quickly follow suit. The emerald glow from his eyes shine like tiny, twin flashlights spilling over each member of the covenant. I feel sudden warmth, and then it quickly fades. I can only guess that Mason's stare struck me during the time I felt the warming sensation. I decide to look up, finding that all the others had the same idea. Mason pulls out a large, bladed knife that fits his earlier description of an Athame. A black handled, double-edged knife, the blade is about eleven inches long. Mason starts to swing the knife in mid air as if slicing at an invisible foe, but as we watch his movements become much more orderly, as if this were a dance with the knife. He manages to get it going faster and faster, so fast that he eventually seems to swinging as fast as a ceiling fan on high speed. Just to glance at him, you can almost see through where his arms are swinging, but to stop and focus on just one arm, you can start to follow it, but it gives you a headache. Eldritch energies start to burn in the very air around Mason, you can hear the crackling of energies, as a trail of energy follows the Athame as it swings through the air, eventually the trails of energy start to solidify into glowing bands of crimson light. The whole time Mason is swinging both arms and the Athame at a startling speed in a semi-circular motion. Craig, Ti, and the rest of The Nine hold wide their arms, still kneeling, and looking skyward, slowly raising their arms toward the sky. As their hands meet above their heads, a thin, almost foggy stream of pure white energy darts into the sky, followed by a much broader stream of crimson energy. The energy streams meet far overhead, as they meet they explode into a misty cloud, and through the mist you can almost make out two large faces. The features are dulled and obscure at best, almost like a bank robber with dark panty-hose over his head. Within seconds the forms fade and the energy stops firing into the sky. Mason starts to speak in a loud voice, still looking skyward, and holding his Athame with both hands, straight above him, with the blade pointed skyward.

"Goddess, hear your people,
Mother and provider,
God above, we cry out to you,
Father and protector,
Aid us, though we be few,
We seek council with you the wise,
We the humbled beg of thee,
Cast your wisdom before our eyes.
We desire naught but balance,
We ask for guidance and justice,
Naught otherwise.
Council us against this nightmare,
That threatens all of life,
Cast your guidance and power alike,
Into this Athame, most mystical
Knife."

With this said all is quiet and still. Mason slowly appears to be struggling against an invisible opponent; his Athame rips itself out of his grasp, and rockets through the air directly at me, frozen in my kneeling position, I attempt to dodge it. The Athame drops to the ground in front of me. Mason slowly starts toward me. As he reaches me, he motions for me to rise. I do so, and Mason puts his strong, yet still-tremoring hand on my shoulder.

"Thou, Ben Ruden, thou who be a warrior true, must take this Athame, and against all of our laws, against all of our virtues, for the first time in known history, thou art to use the mystical Athame as a weapon. Blessed be the Goddess and God."

The entire covenant gasps for air, as if shocked by this announcement. A barely audible murmur breaks out amongst the thirty or so individuals of The Craft.

"So, on whom do I use this Athame."

"'Tis the will of the Goddess and God that thou useth it to slay the Harbinger. No spell, Wicca or Vampyr, canst halt the arrival of the Harbinger now. The Athame is charged with the full power of the Wiccan Nation; including The Craft entire, The Nine, and the Celtic Druids. Be thee forewarned, thou canst use this but once. Be thee certain whom or what the Harbinger 'tis before expending its astronomical power."

"Wait, so I just head out, find this Harbinger creature and stab it and win?" It probably sounds easier than I bet it is.

"Ben, dost thou remember not pledging thy life entire to the Craft?" Mason asks.

"Yeah, like three days ago, I sort of thought I'd learn a little more...hey, why me and not a member of The Nine?"

"'Tis Their will."

"Right, so like, what makes them think I'll get anywhere near this Harbinger, or even be able to identify it?"

"Deep down thou dost already know the Harbinger. Search the deepest recess of thy memory and thou shalt know."

"Is this guaranteed to work and will I survive this encounter?" Sorry to be selfish, but come on.

"There 'tis no guarantee, but please know thee this, 'tis our last defense against total

Genocide. Wouldst thou do the Goddess and God's will?" Mason looks at me, for the first time since I've met him, "Well, I guess." Images of all the people I've seen massacred flash through my mind, "Yes! Let's do it!"

"Praised be the Goddess and God!" Mason bellows out, and the covenant entire yell it out in unison immediately following.

"How about a 'Praise Ben' or something." I whisper under my voice, I mean I'm the one going back in the vampires' den. When will I learn to back out of stuff?

The covenant quickly disbands and drops their hoods, going back to their earlier festivities. Mason picks up the Athame and hands it to me. It feels warm in my grasp; it pulsates in my hand as if it's breathing. I tuck it in the rope belt that holds my robe closed.

"Mason, how can I be sure I even make it close? I mean, the Vampyr have been very open to me up until now, but if Kendal reads my mind...won't he know about the Athame?" I guess I'm just looking for a little reassurance here.

"Ben, for reasons un beknownst to me, the Kindred want thee in particular to join their ranks. Understand Ben, they need every Vampyr at their disposal in order for the Final Harvest to be successful. The more Kindred, Embraced, Thralls, and Vampyr auras gathered in one place, the greater the power of the Harbinger. 'Tis similar to a Mass Casting ceremony for we of the Craft, the more energy available to harness, the more powerful the spell, and grander the results." Mason appears fatigued, but I'm just not satisfied.

"So I suppose its best that I go alone...not like with...you or anything?" Having a Wiccan High Priest would sure make me feel more comfortable.

"No son, 'Tis not *their* will. And quite frankly, I'll aid thee all the better here than in hand-to-hand combat. It falls upon me to keep your Athame charged, no matter how far away thou dost travel. This 'tis my charge, just as striking down the Harbinger dost fall to thee."

"I don't mean to sound negative Mason," Even though, if anyone has earned that right, I feel like I have. "but isn't the Harbinger like some sort of *Super Vampire*? I'm hardly strong or fast enough to hit Jessup with bullets, let alone the Harbinger with a glowing, witch knife."

"Granted, 'tis not an easy task you are charged with young Ben, but a necessary one. Without the Harbinger, the Vampyr cannot usher in the Final Harvest. I've not a simple answer for thee. Just know, that thou art indeed humankind's last chance. Sleep well young Ben, I shalt work on a masking spell for you come the 'morrow." With that Mason took his leave.

* * *

I awaken to the scraping noise of my door being slowly pushed open. By instinct I pull out my gun, to see that its Craig creeping in to my humble abode.

"Ben, it's me, Craig." I lower my gun.

"Yeah, what is it Craig." I've never been much for conversation when being awakened pre-maturely.

"Look, I want to go with you. Mason probably wouldn't agree, but I really want to help. I have my reasons."

"Craig, we all do. But mason says you'll be more help here than face to face. I think we need to go with Mason's knowledge on this one."

"I know, but there is a way we can guarantee Kendall and the others won't find out about the Athame."

"Yeah, Mason said like a masking spell or something."

"No, that won't be good enough. That may or may not work. However, if I carried the Athame, and Mason masked me as having a Vampyr aura, instead of that of a Wicce, I could carry it. You could have recruited me, and I could refresh Mason's spell as necessary, and also concentrate on masking the Athame. They would never pick up anything weird on you."

"Craig, that sounds like a good plan. However, please understand, I will not take anyone else into the Kindred's den. I've lost too many good people to these bloodthirsty bastards. We're just a bunch of walking Twinkies to these guys, defenseless and delicious. I'm sorry; I couldn't handle something like that happening to you as well."

"I understand. Just think about it increasing your chance for success, and know that I *want* to go. Also, I'm pretty adept at my craft, and could come in handy. See you in the morning." Craig exits, and my mind is racing. I finally drift off again.

* * *

I hear muffled shouts and conversation. I roll off my cot and don my robes. As I push the old door open, I see a majority, if not all of the members of the covenant standing in a circle. Their conversation is rushed, and they're all trying to talk over one another.

I approach and the crowd immediately grows silent. Lying in the center of the circle of witches is another member of the Nine. This is a blonde gentleman, I never met him personally, but he had a kind face. He lay on his side, with a large, ivory handled spear stuck through him. There was a word, or actually a name carved in the handle. It read *ZEPHYR*. There was a note also, rolled like a scroll, and hidden in a carved wooden tube, with a lid on it. The tube was tied onto the spear handle. Mason arrives. The group splits to allow him easy access. He leans over, picks up the tube, pops the top and unrolls the letter;

MY DEAREST NINE,

YOU HAVE BY NOW COME UP WITH, WHAT I'M SURE IS A MAGNIFICANT PLAN. MY SINCEREST HOPES GO WITH YOU ON YOUR LONG, ARDUOUS, ALBEIT DOOMED TO FAILURE QUEST. TO THIS POINT, THE GAME HAS BEEN...ENJOYABLE TO SAY THE LEAST. HOWEVER, AS YOU KNOW THE TIME GROWS SHORT. YOU HAVE STRUCK ADMIRABLE BLOWS TO MY COHORTS, AND WE'VE ONLY RETALIATED ONE FOR ONE. I WARN YOU NOT TO FORCE ME TO PERSONALLY MAKE YOUR OWN 'LAW OF THREE' COME TRUE. YOUR GUARDS AND WARDS ARE QUITE EFFEC-TIVE ON MOST OF US, BUT NOT ZEPHYR. HE COULD SLOWLY KILL YOU ALL, ONE BY ONE, WERE I TO WISH IT SO. MY TERMS ARE QUITE SIMPLE REALLY. RELEASE BEN RUDEN, AND I'LL CLEAR ZEPHYR FROM THE HUNTING GROUNDS. IF BEN IS NOT BACK IN HAVENHILL,

AT MY RESIDENCE BY MIDNIGHT TOMMOROW, MY MESSAGE TO ZEPHYR WILL SIMPLY BE; HAPPY HUNTING. OH, A ND DO BE CAREFUL LEAVING YOUR LITTLE HAVEN. YOU MAY WISH TO SEND BEN ALONE. I CAN'T REALLY VOUCH FOR ANYONE ELSE'S SAFETY, ONCE OUTSIDE OF YOUR PROTECTED AREA. AS ALWAYS MY REGARDS TO YOU AND YOUR LITTLE GODS, SEE YOU AT THE HARVEST.

SINCERELY,
KENDAL ONTOLLI

Mason turns a little red in the face, and orders the covenant over to a specific bond fire area. Mason chants as he walks and as we all reach the specified area, Mason stops chanting, and walks over to me.

"Zephyr's a big, African vampire. He still looks like he's from a lost tribe in deepest Africa." I assumed I was answering a question before it was asked.

"Ben, 'tis now or never. We can't afford to lose too many more, or I'll be unable to maintain the charge of the Athame."

"I agree. I'm out of here." Before I can leave though, Mason places his hand on my shoulder. His green eyes glow, almost blinding me.

"Good fortune young Ben, may the Goddess and the God smile upon thee." Mason turns away.

I head out, but before leaving the area, I turn to wave good-bye, only to find the place deserted. I shrug my shoulders and head back the way I think was the way where Dugan's truck is parked. I find the overgrowth much more difficult to get through without Mason leading the way. Behind me a twig snaps, and I hear leaves crunching, as if under footsteps. Having little choice, I swing around to see who is following me...

Chapter Seventeen
...And the Next Victim Is...

I swing around just in time to notice a robed figure standing behind me.

"Craig…" before I can finish, he interrupts me.

"Look, I know what you're going to say. But come on, you need the help and you know it. I truly feel it is the will of the Goddess and God that I come along, as a distraction if nothing else!" His eyes are that of a man ready to lay his life down for his beliefs.

"Look, I can't stop you, but as I told you before, everyone that get's involved in my end of this thing, ends up dead. The Vampyr feel that you guys kidnapped me, and will kill you without provocation." I had sincerely hoped this would sway him.

"Great! Let's move on then." Craig smiled and led the way, the trees parted for him, just like Mason.

"Ok…well I'm glad you listened so well. By the way, remember that the note said that Zephyr was around here somewhere. He's a big; mean mother…" the hairs on the back of my neck stood on end. A chill went down my spine. Out of pure reflex I raised my right arm. In doing so, I smacked the shaft of a hurling spear. My interference sent the projectile spinning off into the trees, far from its intended target. I immediately spin around, the stench of dried, aged human blood mixed with teeth that have gone without any sort of dental hygiene, almost overwhelms me. I'm standing face to…well, chest I guess, to a large, black man. His body looks as if it were chiseled out of ebony marble. His physique obviously created by being a hunter in Africa and running and wrestling large animals, looks almost fake. Kind of like a cartoon super-hero, if you will. With his oversized muscles flexed, Zephyr breathes at me, and through the putrid odor, I hear him say;

"Why did you do dat Ben? I had him, an' now he's gone again!" Zephyr doesn't seem mad, more like, hurt and confused.

"Did it ever occur to you, Zephyr, that I was letting him follow me on purpose? Huh?" I was rolling the dice, hoping his years as a vampire didn't increase his wit at all.

"Oh, Kendall wouldn' like dat Ben!"

"Like what zephyr? Kendall wouldn't like that I recruited a new thrall to the ranks? Look at his aura! Is Kendal into killing thralls now?"

"Oh, I get id. Sorry. I'm not so good at reading aura's Ben, I tought he was a witch! I tought he was followin' you." Zephyr lowers his head and steps off the path and literally fades into the surrounding greenery. I was lucky that Zephyr wasn't the sharpest spear in the tribe. I almost felt sorry for the big lug…almost.

* * *

Craig and I made it back out to Dugans' truck without any more incident. Craig was grateful that I had knocked the spear out of the way. I explained that I'd like to say it was on purpose, but it was obviously just reflex and luck! Craig thanked me anyway.

As I revved up the truck Craig and I breathed a sigh of relief. I backed out of the field and headed back South toward Havenhill, and Kendall's place. I whispered a short prayer under my breath, and Craig continued to study his Tome. We drove silently for about an hour when Craig discovered my Tome, well, Orvin's old Tome.

"Hey look, is this yours?" Craig asked.

"Well, yeah. It is now. It was Orvin's. I sort of...inherited it. You're welcome to look at it."

"Wow! No wonder Mason had such respect for Orvin. Look at all of these Slavic writings!"

"Yeah, we were going to try and decipher them, but never got around to it..."

"Well, that's only because the Havenhill Nine didn't need to practice writing spells. I could cast a decipher spell and read it to you." Craig asked that I pull the truck over, I refused. I told him if he can't cast in a moving truck, then not to worry about it.

Craig started chanting and pulled a twig out of his robe. He set it on a blank page of his journal. The twig jerked twice and then stood on end. The twig started to dance on the page. As the twig moved, letters and then words started to take form as if the twig had a pencil lead in it. And Craig began to read as the twig wrote:

WHAT HAS GONE BEFORE

IN THE BEGINNING WE WERE FEW, WE WERE KEPT IN CHECK BY THE SPARSE HERDS OF HUMANKIND. IN ORDER TO EXPAND OUR CONQUEST AND GOALS TO THAT OF THE ASTRAL AND PRIMATERIAL GATEWAY, WE WERE

IN NEED OF MORE CONCENTRATED EFFORTS. WE NEEDED TO MAKE THE QUALITY OF LIFE FOR HUMANKIND FAR BETTER.

THE HERDS WOULD DIE OFF AT THE AGE OF 30 OR 40. DISEASE, PESTILENCE, FAMINE AND WAR, THE FOUR HORSEMEN OF APPOCALYPSE, DECREASED THE HUMAN HERDS BY LARGE NUMBERS.

WE WERE FORCED TO SHARE MANY OF OUR MAGICKS WITH THE LOWER LIFE FORMS. WE WENT OUT AMONGST THE HERDS AND BECAME THEIR LEADERS.

WE INTRODUCED FIRE, THE WHEEL, WEAPONS FOR HUNTING, AND SLOWLY

WE WERE ABLE TO KEEP THE FOUR HORSEMEN AWAY FROM OUR HERDS.

SOME OF OUR NUMBER FOUND SOME OF HUMANKIND CUMLY, AND SLOWLY, AS FORETOLD, WOULD A NEW BREED OF BEINGS BE BROUGHT INTO EXISTENCE. THE VAMPYR ARE THOSE WHO HAVE THE AURA TO JOIN THOSE WHO HAVE RISEN, AND COULD JOIN THE ASTRAL PLANE TO BECOME FULL VAMPIRE. AS HUMANKIND CONTINUES TO PROSPER AND TAKE BETTER CARE OF THEIR HERDS, SO MUST WE. AS HUMANKIND MIXED WITH THE KINDRED, MANY OF OUR NUMBER LIKED THIS NOT!!

THOSE IN RESENTMENT WERE THE YOUNGER UNDEAD ELDERS. THEY WANTED THE VAMPYR

DESTROYED, NOT FOSTERED AND EVENTU-
ALLY EMBRACED.

BEING OF THIS DECISION DID THEY START
THE INNER WAR OF EKTAR, NAMED AFTER THE
ELDEST OF THE YOUNG UNDEAD ELDERS. THE
WAR OF EKTAR LASTED FOR FOUR CENTURIES.
DURING THIS TIME, THE VAMPYR GREW IN
NUMBER AND EVEN ORGANIZED SOME OF
HUMANKIND TO FOLLOW THEM. THE ELDERS,
BEING MADE AWARE OF THIS, DEEMED IT
NECESARRY TO KEEP HUMANKIND AND EVEN
SOME VAMPYR UNDER SLAVE MENTALITY. IN
ORDER TO DO THIS, ORGANIZED RELIGIONS
WERE FORMED. KINDRED WERE PLACED IN
CHARGE OF FORMING GROUPS AND HAVENS
FOR THE HOPEFULS OF HUMANKIND TO COME
TO.

THESE KINDRED TOOK HISTORY AND ADDED
FIGUREHEADS FOR PEOPLE TO LOOK TO IN
TIMES OF NEED. BEFORE FINISHING THE
WORKS, THE KINDRED WERE CALLED BACK IN
ORDER TO JOIN THE WAR OF ECTAR. VAMPYR
WERE LEFT IN PLACE TO TAKE UP THE
LEADERSHIP. OF TIME. THE VAMPYR THEN
AGREED ON GRANTING THE RELIGIOUS FIG-
UREHEADS SOME OF THE MAGICKS KNOWN TO
ONLY THE VAMPYR.

THIS ALLOWED BLIND FAITH TO BE THE
EXPLANATION FOR THE MISSING TIME BLOCKS

IN THE TOME WRITTEN FOR HUMANKIND ENTITLED THE TORAH AND EVENTUALLY THE BIBLE. UPON THE ENDING OF THE WAR OF ECTAR, WERE THE KINDRED ALLOWED TO RE-ENTER THE PRIMATERIAL PLANE. UPON ARRIVAL, WE FOUND THE ENTIRE WORLD SET UP IN WARRING FACTIONS. THE VAMPYR TOOK THEIR FOLLOWERS AND TAUGHT THEM THE DARK MAGICKS, WHICH ALMOST LED TO GENOCIDE OF HUMANKIND. THE KINDRED WERE CHARGED WITH RETURNING THE HERDS BACK TO OBEDIENCE, AND THAT THE GATEWAY OFF OF THE PRIMATERIAL PLANE WOULD BE CLOSED UNTIL THIS WAS DONE.

THE KINDRED ATTEMPTED TO UNITE THE WORLD THROUGH RELIGIONS AND POLITICS, BUT HAVE FAILED. THE ONLY ALTERNATIVE LEFT, IS TO USHER IN THE FINAL HARVEST. A FEAST SO GRAND, THAT ALL VAMPYR WILL WISH TO BE EMBRACED AND THE ELDER UNDEAD WILL BE FORCED TO OPEN THE GATES, AND BE TEMPTED TO ENTER BACK INTO THE PRIMATERIAL PLANE. ONCE THOSE WHO WALK THE DARKSIDE HAVE ARRIVED, ORDER WILL BE RESTORED, AND WE KINDRED CAN ONCE AGAIN LEAVE THIS LITTLE PRISON, AND TRAVEL INTO OUR COSMIC AWARENESS. THE KINDRED HAVE NOT THE POWER TO USHER IN THE FINAL HARVEST ON THEIR OWN, THUS SHALL A

HARBINGER BE SENT BY THE ELDERS, TO LEAD THEM INTO THE FINAL FEAST. UPON THE KINDREDS COMPLETION OF THE INNER CIRCLE, THEN WILL THE HARBINGER BE REVEALED. THE HERDS, UNDER FALSE PRETENSES OF BLIND FAITH WILL ENTER THE FIELDS OF HARVEST-ING, FOLLOWING THE HARBINGER TO THEIR SUPPOSED SALVATION, AND OUR HOUR OF THE RE-OPENING OF THE COSMIC GATES WILL BE AT HAND.

"What a bunch of malarkey Ben. The Goddess and God have written against this! This can't be true, right Ben?"

"Craig, I don't know. But if it isn't true, then why did the Goddess and God send me to kill the Harbinger? Is there any more?" I feel so cold. The trucks heater isn't even affecting me.

"Yeah, but it's something different. It goes on to say…"

THE BYLAWS VAMPYR

IT IS WRITTEN THAT HUMAN LIFE IS SACRED AND MUST BE PRESERVED. LET US NOT LOSE OUR WAY AND WASTE THAT WHICH GIVES US LIFE. IT IS EASY TO DRAIN A HUMAN'S LIFE ESSENCE AND MOVE ON TO THE NEXT ONE. REMEMBER THAT HUMANKIND FEEDS US. NEITHER ANIMAL NOR PLANT CAN WE LONG SUSTAIN US. NOT UNLIKE HOW HUMANS RAISE, FOSTER AND CARE FOR CATTLE FOR THE SOLE

PURPOSE OF MILKING, IS HOW WE MUST RAISE, FOSTER AND CARE FOR HUMANKIND. WE CAN FEED OFF HUMANS WITHOUT ENDING THEIR EXISTENCE.

WE ARE MASTERS OF THE UNIVERSE; WE EXIST TO RULE THE PRIMATERIAL PLANE OF EXISTENCE AND BEYOND. OUR EARTHLY PRISON AND FLESHY SHELLS ARE BUT A MEAGER STOP OVER, ON OUR WAY TO THE BLISS OF THE ASTRAL WHOLENESS, WHICH HAS SO LONG BEEN DENIED US.

WE MUST EMBRACE CUNCTATOLANY. FEED BUT DO NOT WASTE. LET NOT THOSE WHO HAVE RISEN FIND YOU FOOTPADDING OR WASTING THAT WHICH PROVIDES OUR LIFE ESSENCE. THE PUNISHMENT IS SEVERE. THE PUNISHMENT IS TO REVERT TO THE LOWLY STATE OF MORTALITY AGAIN, AND EXIST TO FEED THOSE WHO HAVE BEEN EMBRACED.

LET THIS BE **THE BYLAWS VAMPYR,** AND IF DONE SO CORRECTLY, THOSE WHO HAVE RISEN WILL REWARD US BY SENDING US OUR HARBINGER AND USHERING IN THE FINAL HARVEST.

LET IT BE COMMON KNOWLEDGE TO ALL VAMPYR AND VAMPIRE ALIKE THAT THE HARBINGER SHALL BE IDENTIFIED AS THE ONE WHOM...

"That's it. That's as far as Orvin got. Crap!" Craig slams the Tome shut. The twig drops to the floor of the truck.

* * *

I look over to Craig, I can tell he's stewing, his face is red, and he's ready to get real defensive about how the Wiccan religion is right, and all the others are not. I'll tell you what; religion seems to cause more division than anything else.

"Look Craig, I can't tell you what's right or wrong, all I know is, all of a sudden there are witches and vampires running around, when just a week ago or so, I wasn't aware of either. All because it's written down doesn't make it real. There's no proof of Elder Gods or anything other 'Gods' for that matter, it's all based on belief. You believe in the Goddess and God, so that's what's real to you. That's good enough for me."

"Yeah, but Ben, why would Orvin, an Elder of The Nine, the Havenhill Caster no less, write out such things?"

"Craig, he was only deciphering what he was reading, it doesn't mean he believed in it."

"I suppose you're right. Alright, I'm going to start on the masking spell to hide myself, and the mind shield to protect you from Kendall."

Good luck, it had better be pretty effective to fool Kendall. I couldn't tell Craig that after all my experiences; I tend to feel that Vampyr Lore appeared to be the story that made the most sense.

Damn if this truck won't warm up, twice I hit the window washer fluid and all it does is clear the window, steam and then freeze on the window itself.

The drive is surprisingly quiet, Craig appears to be in some trance, and I've only seen one other vehicle so far, a semi. It's too quiet; my mind begins to think back to all of the recent events, how unbelievable it's all been. Yet, I've seen more proof of vampirism and witchcraft in one week, than proof of other religions in my whole life. All the people I've gotten to know who are now dead and gone. It almost doesn't seem real.

As I cross Havenhill city limits, I pull over and shake Craig out of his four-hour trance. He looks over to me, shaking and looking as if he just finished running a marathon.

"Look Craig, I can't do it, you can't..."

Before I can finish a car comes screeching to a halt right in front of the truck. It's definitely on purpose; he was heading toward us and crossed both lanes to stop in front of us, as if he was looking for us. I pull out my gun and lay it on my lap, I hand the Athame over to Craig, through the exhaust, looking thicker than normal, exaggerated by the cold, and the headlights casting an eerie glow from the other vehicle facing us, only allowing us to see the silhouette of a person approaching us...

* * *

The individual approaching us doesn't expect me to jump out of the truck, gun in hand.

"Ben, oh man, finally...I found you!" I'll be, it's Jeff. He's strapping a piece to his side as well.

"Jeez Jeff, I didn't know it was you..." quickly I leap at him and punch him in the face. The punch turns his head and forces him to his knees. I examine my fist and see blood on it. Shit! It really is Jeff.

"Hey, sorry buddy. I wanted to make sure you weren't Jessup." I could never have hit Jessup, and if I did, I certainly couldn't have hurt him, and he wouldn't have bled.

"Oh no problem, just punch first...hell, you should have just shot me to be real sure…asshole…" I help him up while he tends to his face, continuing to mumble obscenities.

"Look, Ben, they're looking for you, the police are, everyone. They couldn't identify you out of all the bodies from the fire. Where have you been, and who's the geek?" Craig makes his way over to us.

"He's ok Ben, he's definitely…human. No aura to speak of."

"Oh, this is Craig, he's a witch, and Craig this is Jeff, he's…a human, for lack of better…"

"A witch, huh? And I'm just a human? A boy witch is like a male nurse… Where's your broomstick…oh, never mind…look Ben, you're driving a stolen truck, get in, I'll get us somewhere, and you and…witchy-poo here, can fill me in on the way. Nice robes fellas." We all get in Jeff's car and he heads off toward the outskirts of town. Jeff's never been one to mince words, we might as well be wearing dresses for all he's concerned. This could be a tough sell.

"Look Jeff, I appreciate the help, but you need to let us out over by the boat launch, and then move on."

"Nope. Look man, I started this thing with you and now I want in. A bunch of weird shit is going on around this town. In fact, did you know that there used to be a cult and…of course you did, the medallion. Ok, look, I ain't good at this weird stuff, but I want in!"

"Listen Jeff, you hang with me right now, and you'll end up like the guys in my house. You still want in?" Gods above, I can still smell the burnt flesh and hair.

"Yeah, I do Ruden! I'm in this…now fill me in."

"Ben…he could be our third. WE are the Warriors Three minus one. Two witches, one human and one Vampyr comprise the warriors three as was predicted. This…Jeff could be that human." Craig interjected.

"What is it with you two idiots that you're so willing to throw your lives away? You will NOT live through this! You won't, and I probably won't! Forget this...this Warriors Three crap, we aren't warriors! We're more like a joke...So this insurance salesman, this gym teacher, and this witch walk into a bar...don't you chumps get it? This isn't some grand adventure, or game...fellas...look...these are guys that are vampires. They move faster than you can follow, a gun doesn't hurt them, and they feed off guys like us. We're a freaking food source to them. We're three walking doughnuts to these guys. We can't beat them, they...they practically created us...I'm sorry Craig...Jeff...but I need to do this on my own. I couldn't take it if you two died too..."

"Touching speech boy-o, but no can do. Endora? What do you think?"

"Other than you being a Neanderthal Jeff, I already told you Ben, I'm going after Ontolli, either way."

"Ontolli? Kendal Ontolli? Wait...he's one of these vampires Ben? Come on."

"Not a vampire Jeff, but the head honcho...in fact I still think he's the Harbinger, and they're trying to protect him until it's time. Craig give Jeff Orvin's tome, I'll drive us there. That tomb should explain most of it Jeff."

"You know Ben...I didn't want to bring this up, but I once heard my grandfather in a conversation with Kendall. He told me he knows all about the Ontolli legacy. You know, them being so rich and foreign and shit. Maybe we ought to go see him for a minute."

Craig grabs Jeff's hand and spits in his palm. He then starts pushing his spit around with his finger and says "Aha! Just as I thought."

Jeff jerks his hand back and says, "What the hell was that?"

"Yeah, what did it tell you?" I asked.

"Well, nothing really, just that Jeff is an idiot." Craig and I start cracking up. Jeff doesn't find it so funny.

"Touch me again Hilda and we're gonna be the Warriors Two. Jackass." We head toward Jeff's grandfather's house, Old Man Tical. Under his breath, Jeff curses most of the way.

Chapter Eighteen

Who's the Fourth Warrior of the Warriors Three?

The walkway up to old man Tical's was cracked and even missing in places. I stumble more than once trying to avoid the snow and attempting to stay on the cement. The yard was severely overgrown, and although the weight of the snow hid most of the tall weeds that were once grass, in some areas they poked through. This led you to believe that once the snow was gone, you'd find a veritable jungle of overgrown grass and weeds. Apparently I wasn't the only one to notice.

"So, Jeff, you don't help your papa out with the yard work? What, are you too busy NOT finding a girl friend?" Craig sarcastically stated. It definitely brought a smile to my face. I'm shocked at how Craig and Jeff get along after very little time together. Interesting chemistry.

"Feel free to help out Sabrina, just don't include me. "Papa" and me don't see eye to eye really. But you'd probably get along with him fine, seeing as to how you're both freaks." Jeff smiles quite pleased with himself.

"Hey guys, if I may interrupt, Jeff could you go first? It is your Grandpa."

"Sure...ladies, welcome to the Chateau Tical."

We go up some old steps, soft with age, if you really tried, you could probably stomp through them. The whole porch appears to have been painted white at one time, but for now, more old wood shows than white paint. The wood is probably too spongy at this point to hold any kind of paint. This is a small Cape Cod style home, a large swing sits at one corner of the porch, one end is held up by a chain, the other sits in a pile of snow, its chain snapped. Jeff opens the screaming screen door, which of course has no screen in the bottom half, and only a partial, rusted screen in the top. The hurricane arm is snapped, so the door swings open, and smashes into the wall. This creates loud creaking, followed by aluminum smacking into wood.

Jeff opens the main door and yells out "Gramps", it's me, Jeff. You here?"

An older fella comes walking up to us; he's very thin due to old age. His skin looks as if it were stretched tight over his bones and veins. His skin almost seems transparent. He's bald except a little white patch of hair stretches around from one ear to the other, covering only the back and sides of his head. He's wearing an old, tattered blue robe, and those slip on vinyl slippers. He smiles to proudly show off his four remaining teeth. As he prepares to talk, he appears to be chewing his own mouth, he then blurts out, in a very old man voice "'Course I can hear boy! C'mon then."

He leads us deeper into his abode. I get overpowered by that...I can only describe it as...old people smell. You know what I mean? Very stale, and I don't know, Geritol or Formaldehyde? I don't know. Anyway, as I sit on a plastic covered paisley, gold and green couch, I can't help but wonder, at what age is it, do you suppose, you decide to just quit updating your décor, and decide to wrap everything in plastic for posterity? Old man Tical sits in his easy chair, and kicks up his footrest. He then decides to club Jeff with his cane and say, "See boy, I told ya they was lookin fer ya." He smiles, again showing pitch blackness, blocked only by his four yellowed teeth.

"Grandpa, these guys want to know the Ontolli Legend. It's very important." He winces as if papa was going to smack him again.

"Well, first off it's 'The Legend Ontolli' and second off, it ain't for kids like you to be worryin' about. Lessin' one a you boys is Ben." He squints one eye and widens the other, as if allowing him to see better.

"That would be me sir, Ben Ruden."

"Well, I'll be hornswoggled, it shore is! Alrighty then…"

* * *

Approximately an hour later, the tale of Kendall's venture to America with Bill and his ascension to vampirism is explained quite clearly to us. I'm a little uncomfortable, but Jeff and Craig appear horrified, as if for the first time realizing how real this whole vampire hunt has become. We thank old man Tical, and head out meeting in the car, no one speaks a word, the fog from our frozen breath makes it near impossible to see through the frosted windows, Jeff starts the car and cold air blows up against the windshield, as it warms, the frost begins to fade.

"So, Craig…Who's the fourth member of the Warriors Three? You said one Vampyr, one human, and two witches, right?" Jeff inquires to break the silence.

"Well, I think Dugan may have been the fourth, but he's no longer with us…so, I guess it's just we three." Craig states in an unsure tone. He then turns to face me.

"I don't know Craig, doesn't Orvin's tome say?".

"No, not really. It describes the Warriors, but doesn't name them. It states, 'the Vampyr will be trusted by both, but truly belong to neither, the Human will be affiliated with the Vampyr though not be aware of the Vampyr's true aura, Witch number one will be a young witch, eager to serve, and Witch number two will be an ancient witch, and though appearing harmless, shall be incremental to the success of the Harbingers downfall and thus disrupting the Final Harvest.' I didn't really want to read that part to you, since Dugan isn't here anymore; I still think we can do it, just the three of us!" Craig's enthusiasm obviously outweighs his confidence.

Suddenly, it hits me…it wasn't Dugan at all.

"Jeff, turn left here, and get us to the Castle Motel."

A look of recognition hits Craig's face, it turns to unbridled enthusiasm, and he blurts out "Jason! Of course, he's our fourth! It makes perfect sense!"

* * *

After a long drive, made longer by listening to Craig carry on about Jason's age and ranking within the Wiccan Caste, we finally arrive at the Castle Motel. Jason is so young, and vulnerable. I almost feel bad about approaching him on this.

As our headlights hit the room he was previously staying in, the light flicks on and the door swings open. Kevin steps out of the room and leans against the doorframe with crossed arms. He raises one of his hands and motions us in. We step in to see Jason fully dressed and ready to go, tying his second tennis shoe. He looks up and smiles and simply states. "Show me that which will bring the downfall to the Harbinger, most mystical knife."

Craig pulls out the Athame, and hands it to little Jason. The knife is pulsating with power and glowing with energies. It looks more like a sword in the hands of little Jason.

"We should consider going, Ben. Craig, nice to see you again, and yes, Mason is going to have words with you upon your return. And, this guy…is this to be our human then?"

"Yeah, my names Jeff, junior, I'll be your little human for the duration of our Vampire hunt."

"Very well then, Jeff Junior, welcome aboard. Let's be off shall we?"

"Not Jeff Jr., Jeff…junior, I was calling you…oh never mind. Sheesh. Punk." Jason goes over and gives Kevin a hug, says something in that witch talk, and we all load up in the car. Kevin stays back in the motel room. We head off toward Ontolli mansion.

We've a full crew; I just pray that we can pull this off.

Chapter Nineteen
Three (or Four) Against the Darkness

As we pack into the still running vehicle, well warmed by now, I watch in amazement as young Jason climbs in, with no hesitation. He truly is an old soul. He looks over to me and smiles…yet, something in his eyes…an uncomfortable shiver goes down my very spine. My first reaction is wondering if this really is Jason. My suspicions are put to rest rather quickly, as Craig and Jason start bantering back and forth in their own Wicca tongue. Jason picks up Orvin's tomb, and starts leafing through it as a child would, just receiving a new storybook about their favorite subject.

Jeff points out that we are nearing the lake, which is closing in on our destination. I realize that, even with all I've been through, I'm quite nervous about entering the nest. I can't help worrying about Jeff, Jason and Craig. I happen to know who we're going up against, but these three don't, and they still are brave enough to risk it. That alone helps to feed my conviction if not my courage.

Jeff brings the car to a halt, and kills the headlights. We are about thirty feet from the iron gate that opens to an extremely long driveway. It leads to the Ontolli mansion's front door.

"Ok, Craig, cast that hide spell or whatever, we can't have these Vamps knowing you three are with me."

"Already done Ben, Jason backed it. We should be hidden from the most sensitive of vampires, even Zephyr." Craig smiles, obviously very proud of himself.

We exit the car and start walking along the tall stone wall leading to the cast iron gates. Dropping down in front of me, forcing me to back peddle and almost fall on my ass, is the big guy, Zephyr.

"Ben! Dis is a good ting! Kendall wants to see you! Come on!" The ebony giant swings around and heads for the gate. As we reach the gate, Zephyr raises both of his massive arms and belts out some loud incantation, and the gates slowly heed the words and grind into an open position. Standing on the other side is Denny, still messed up, and looking uglier than ever. Behind him are about twenty or so thralls, bouncing around, howling and just plain acting like animals.

The drive itself is old cobblestone. The shrubs and trees are neatly trimmed, and follow the drive to the mansion. Denny approaches me and sniffs me. Please, if either of us smells, it's the road warrior here. Apparently, even a Saturday night bath is out of the question for the undead. I continue past Denny, ignoring him. I mustn't act even remotely suspicious.

"Hey, boy toy, who's your friends?" There's that, I-want-to-lick-whipped-cream-off-of-you, voice again. I spin around to see Shanestra standing behind me. The lights from the gate glow from behind her, outlining her exceptional form. Damn, she can't be on to me, can she?

"Just Zephyr and Denny. Why, are you unfamiliar with these guys?" Roll the dice Ben, playing stupid has always been a strength of yours.

"Ooooh, I'm familiar with them stud, but I'd like to become more familiar with you." Damn, but her voice is entrancing.

I immediately spin back around and say over my shoulder; "Sorry, Shan, but the boss is waiting, and you wouldn't want to be the reason I'm tardy, now would you?" There is no answer, as I suspected.

As I continue to follow Zephyr, Craig gives me the thumbs up. All the Thralls, stop and stand almost at attention, allowing Zephyr and I through, lining up on either side of the drive. Zephyr must have more clout than I thought.

As we round the bend, we finally can se the mansion. It is enormous; the lights from it glow, and cast a shimmering reflection on the lake. It is almost castle like. No, not like Dracula's castle or anything, but more of a modern day castle. It's difficult to describe from just walking up to it, but this palace has two large spires on either end, and a stairway in the middle that has to be thirty feet wide, leading up to two grand wood doors. The doors are open, and servants (thralls most likely), are walking around serving refreshments to guests. Everyone is dressed for this black tie affair, except me. Shanestra approaches and takes me by my arm; and in the light I can see that she's wearing a gorgeous evening gown. We head up the steps, arm in arm, like a couple on a date. The front porch matches the entire width of the house. On the porch, enormous columns support the porch roof, and in between each set of columns is either a statue or sculpture of some sort. On either side of the entrance are suits of armor, holding battle-axes. The porch floor is covered in red carpet, trimmed in gold. As I can finally see into the mansion, I gasp at the size of the foyer, highly polished marble floors and pillars, the double stair way even appears to be carved of this marble. Suits of armor, shields, swords, maces, morning stars, and axes are displayed everywhere. The chandelier alone dwarfs most people's living rooms. I'd assumed that the lights were electric, but upon closer inspection, every sconce, lamp, and even the chandelier is candles or torches. A classic sound of...Beethoven...I think, plays in the back ground. Shanestra leads away from the main foyer, and to a room, she opens the door and laying there is a tuxedo.

"Why don't you put this on, sugarplum, and we'll worry about getting you out of it later." She licks her lips again and closes the door.

"Ok, Ben, so far so good, put on the tux, and we'll go see if the Harbinger is here yet." Craig whispers.

After I don the perfectly sized tuxedo, I wonder, how they knew my size and everything. Admittedly, even tuxes that fit right are extremely uncomfortable, and hate the shoes.

I open the door to exit back to the main hall, and standing there waiting is, you guessed it, my friend and yours, Jessup.

"Benny boy, how's it hangin'?" Jessup smiles at me with his…smile. Lord, how I despise this creep.

"So, Kendall got even you to dress up, huh?" I walked as I talked, hoping to escape much of a conversation with this creature.

"Oh, this old thing? I just threw it on. Do you like it? I borrowed it from my last victim. It's not like he'll be needing it. So, this is your big night, huh? Catching up with the in-crowd? Your un-holy communion, so to speak?" I swear he doesn't even realize how evil he sounds, even trying to carry on a pleasant conversation.

Finally, I make it back to the main hall. Surprisingly enough, it's empty. I look to Craig and Jeff, they both shrug their shoulders. Jason stares at Jessup, as if trying to see right through him. Jason is concentrating on something. Probably a spell or something.

"Ok, Benny, let's head on down to meet Kendall, and do this wacky thing." Jessup happily glides across the marble foyer.

"Jessup, I have to ask, why are you so happy tonight? I mean let's face it; normally you're an asshole, even when you're happy." In a flash, he zips around to face me, I hardly see him move, and in his own distinctive way, with that all too familiar death breath stench, he states; "It's not every night that the Final Harvest starts. I've waited centuries for this!" In a blur, he heads back across the foyer.

I look to Craig, Jeff, and Jason...they look as bewildered as I feel. I had no clue the Final Harvest was beginning tonight. The end of human kind, the final life drain of all living mortals, starts in two hours...

* * *

"Ben, my boy. I am extremely happy to see you. Why, this makes tonight perfect." A familiar voice states. I swing around to see Kendall standing there. Craig, Jeff, and Jason, all seem to hold their breath at the same time. I have to be careful of my thoughts, even with the spells cast. Time to fake it until I make it.

"Kendall...the pleasure is mine, sir." I attempt my best fake smile.

"Come, lad, there are some very important people, I'd like to introduce you to." Kendall places his hand on my shoulder, and starts leading me out of the main hall. Kendall appears to be genuinely happy, and I suppose, why not? We all are at our happiest, right as the meal is getting served.

He leads me down several, winding hallways. He doesn't speak...I wonder if he's trying to read me? So, I attempt to get his mind off of that, and onto a conversation.

"So, Jessup says, this is the big night, huh?" Again with a nervous, fake smile.

"Yes, Ben, indeed. We can go to the main meeting of the elders, directly after turning you." He seems lost in thought.

"So, you're not upset with me?"

"Ben, I understand being hesitant about being re-born. I know I was.

Besides, no permanent damage was done. Oh, except for some physical scaring on a couple of my brood." He smiles with that Don Johnson like smile.

We finally arrive at another set of doors. Two very dark, foreboding figures open the door for us. A chill goes through me just walking past them. I catch one of them staring at me…they appear to be almost a light shade of green. I sense that they are bald under that hood. Their eyes look like a cats eyes, only sideways. Veins run through their face, up their forehead, and on their baldheads. Their ears appear to be non-existent. As awful and scary as these guys look, they refuse any kind of eye contact. Kendal simply mutters a few words. "We're not to be disturbed." Both, almost in stereo utter, "Yes master."

The doors open into a large room. I get the feeling every room in this place is large. Craig and Jason don't enter with me. They stop at the threshold, as if some unseen wall is blocking them. Jeff looks to me, worried. I motion for him to stay with them. The two creatures, in tandem, close the heavy wood doors. Kendall looks at me smiling. He says, "Well, now that we are finally *alone* Ben, you can drop the act."

"Act? Kendall, you invited me here…no…in fact you threatened everyone else, if I didn't show up. What *act* are you talking about?" Alone? Did he find out about Craig and everyone?

"Your mind is…clouded. Perhaps you *are* still confused. Well, no matter, once we bring you through, all will be made clear."

"Alright, so you've made your demands, now I have one of my own." I blurted out with surprising conviction.

"A…demand, Ben? *You* have a demand? Well, let's hear it then. And please, don't allow the fact that you are residing in my Haven, of which I am the master, influence your conviction." Again, with that damned smile.

"It's really very simple. Kendall, you've wanted me to join you for some time now. And, admittedly, I've fought you every bit of the way. So, here is my demand. If you introduce me to the Harbinger first, I will willingly convert." I held my breath. This was the only way I could think of, to get close enough to the Harbinger, without being a vampire first.

"Ben," Kendall appeared to be thinking before responding this time; "Were I to grant this boon, I fear that the Harbinger would drink your life force, before you could say HI."

"I'm willing to risk it!"

"Oh, well, in that case...no. Ben you will become Kindred tonight, one way or another." His smile was no longer present.

"And if I say no, Kendall, what then?"

"Then you will become Kindred the hard way."

"Why? Why me? There has to be a million guys that would make a way better Vampire than me!!"

"I would imagine so, Ben, however you have been chosen by those who have risen before. So it falls to me to fulfill the prophecy, and Ben?"

"Yeah?"

"Ben, I don't fail...at anything...ever." Of course, there's no smile here.

"Well, then, that's how it's going to be! You will have to turn me against my will! And IF I become Kindred, I will make it my life's goal to hunt you down and make you pay!!!" I surprised even myself with this brash outburst. So, I figured I needed to play it out.

"Ben, Ben, Ben...relax son. There is no need for such a violent reaction. I guarantee you will have a change of heart, once you join we that have risen."

"Kendall, Kendall, Kendall...fuck you!"

I turn and start walking toward the doors, I figured turning my back on an Elder Vampire, would be certain suicide, but I did it anyway. Before I reached the massive doors, I turn back around. Kendall is standing there, where he was before, lighting a cigarette.

"Yes, Ben?" He says while exhaling a trail of smoke.

"Tell me this, Kendall. Are YOU the Harbinger? Be honest, are you?"

"Ben, this I will say. I am not HE. But you have known HIM."

Oh, goody, riddle time. "I have known him." Huh? Well, he's gotta be a Vampire, so if Kendall is not him, I only *know* 8 others. But all eight of them are Kendall's Brood. It must be someone else I know...someone I never realized were Kindred. But who???

I turn to pull open the doors. They are too heavy. I hear Kendall chuckling behind me, through his smoke. If only Vampires died of cancer!!! I spin back around. I reach for the Athame, remembering that little Jason has it. Kendall cocks his head, as if hearing something...or reading something from me...oh, crap...ummmm...gotta think about my gun...I was reaching for my gun...I remember it doesn't hurt these guys.... Kendall's face returns to normal, his head back to its proper position.

"Well, then, are we done throwing our little tantrum, Ben?" The tip of his cigarette burns orange, illuminating his facial features from the bottom up." Enter." Kendall calmly states.

The doors creak open. The two creatures that were there before step through. Craig and Jason are clearly attempting some spell or something. The guards and wards are holding them fast. Jeff looks to me, placing his hand on the butt of his gun. I nod 'No.' He stays put. The doors are slammed shut. The creatures de-robe. As they drop their robes, I see that their whole body is a light, greenish hue, with white veins covering their entire bodies. They both open their mouths brandishing a full set of Vampiric chompers. They bend forward, sniffing, like some kind of a dog, perched, ready to spring. They dart off in different directions, bounded more like animals than men. They reach opposite walls, and push aside large tapestries. I hear grinding, like stone against stone. The oriental throw rug in the center of the room starts to rise off the floor. No wait, something is pushing up from underneath it...a round cylinder...very similar to the one I saw at the last haven I was at with Pastor Frank. One of the creatures springs over and rips the rug off of the, now, fully raised, cylindrical pedestal. The other creature approaches us handing both Kendall and I folded robes. Kendall retrieves them, and the creature backs way, with his head still bowed to Kendall. Kendall tosses one of the robes to me, and almost as if sighing while speaking he says;

"It's quite a shame really...I was so hoping we could enjoy the party first, but you had to go and make it difficult, Ben."

"I...I am making this difficult? Do you know how many people you have senselessly slaughtered, just to get me to do something; I have no desire to do? Do you? Well?"

"Yes. However, they could all have been spared, had you complied with my wishes initially..." He appears lost in thought.

"Kendall!" I blurt out his name, hoping to distract him from whatever he is attempting to do.

"Put the robe on, Ben."

"I just put the tux on...I don't want to put on the damn robe!"

"Defiant to the end, eh? Well, unless you are an exhibitionist, and wish to get Shanestra all hot and bothered...I'd recommend the robe over a polyester Tux..." Kendall starts to don his robe.

"Why? What's the difference?"

"The tux will not endure the communion, and at the end, you'll be standing there, naked as a newborn babe..."

As I finish donning my robe, some sort of silk, near as I can tell, and believe me, you can tell when you're going commando! The large wooden doors fly off their hinges, splintering, and sending out chunks of wooden shrapnel in various directions. As the smoke clears, a man is standing in the doorway, fists clenched, and a scowl on his face. He's a slender man, probably in his late twenties, wearing an all white tux, with white shoes. He appears paler than the rest, with white hair pulled back into a ponytail, and blank white eyes, with no pupils, kind of like an albino.

In unison, Kendalls' two…things…leap at this guy, emitting deep, gurgling growls. The man in white simply raises his hands, and both creatures are stopped in mid air, and then flung backward, smashing full speed, into separate walls. They don't get up.

Chapter Twenty
The Harbinger Cometh

"Lumus…was all this necessary? You know how sensitive Vamptures can be…" Kendall doesn't seem worried in the least.

"Kendall…this is it!!! It is now!!! The Final Harvest approaches and the Harbinger is arriving!!!"

With speed defying description, this…Lumus…guy, sails across the room, embracing Kendall. Kendall embraces him back, and then pushes him to arms length.

"Welcome old friend, I am as excited as you, but might I recommend that you don your robe, we, none of us, desire to see your lily white ass again." Kendall and Lumus both laugh, as if remembering a bachelor party or something.

"Oh, but how my manners escape me, Lumus…this is Ben…Ben…this is Lumus, he sires a clan from New Orleans."

Lumus reaches out and takes my hand, he then bows slightly.

"So, you are Ben…my pleasure, young sire, I'm sure." He pulls back and stands next to Kendall. Both are smiling, like two old army buddies getting together for the first time in ten years.

"Um…yeah…nice to meet you…I guess."

"Ben is communionizing tonight, Lumus, just in time for the Harbinger to arrive, and usher in our finest hour."

"Come Lumus, knowing you, you came unprepared, let's get you a robe. It appears my Vamptures, aren't up to the task." They both head toward the other side of the room, I turn to look to my companions, and they have all stepped through and are in the room.

"Ben…now is our chance to make a run for it. We can hide and wait for the Harbinger." Craig whispers to me.

"No." Jason states. "Ben needs to stick with these elders, it is the only way **we** can get close enough to the Harbinger."

"That's bullshit little dude, you heard the man, Ben could get turned or whatever, it isn't worth the risk!" said Jeff, throwing in his own two cents worth.

"I'm sticking it out guys, right or wrong, I gotta take a shot at this, and since I can't carry the Athame without Kendall noticing, you guys have to stick right with me!"

"Benny, who you talking at bud? Your invisible fan club?" Jessup says, causing me to jump a little, he is entering through the shattered remains of the doors.

"Hey boss, everyone's waiting…well, hey there Vanilla puss, long time, no getting blinded by the reflection off your white ass." His standard cocky smile, followed by the licking of his teeth, rears its ugly head.

"Kendall, have your pet clean up this mess, and then get me a drink, won't you, I think it's trying to communicate with me." Lumus walks right by Jessup, Jessup hisses as he walks by, Lumus motions with his left hand, and an invisible force pushes Jessup about five feet away. Jessup remains on his feet, even though he is forced to stumble backwards.

"One side, Footpadder, I'd hate to get your stench on this fine robe. Be seeing you Ben."

"Bite me snow cone!" Jessup yells after him.

You faintly hear, "Like I'd ever get *that* taste out of my mouth..."

"I take it you two aren't friends, better watch yourself, he seems pretty high up..."

"Yes, Ben, like myself, Lumus is an elder..." Kendall is interrupted.

"That's it, Ben, he's just old! He's not even upper caste! He's a wanna-be!!!"

"Don't forget yourself, Jessup." Kendall gently states. Kendall then turns face to face with Jessup; his eyes begin to glow and his voice lowers, almost to a growling sound.

"You're not to interrupt me again, and you *will* respect your elders. Are we clear?" Jessup surprisingly nods yes, and backs away. As soon as he reaches the hall he sprints away, leaving behind one of his famous smart-ass remarks;

"Clear as Vanilla Ice, boss! Ice, Ice, Baby..." Kendall looks at the ground, and shakes his head back and forth.

"He's over excited about tonight. Well, then, shall we Ben?" Kendall smiles, raising his arm, pointing down the hall, with an open hand.

I obediently walk next to Kendall, heading down a dimly lit hallway. The various art works and tapestries smell as old as they look, I half expect a tapestry to move and someone to emerge from a hidden passage way. As we continue, I feel a tug on my robe, I turn my head and see little Jason, holding my robe and looking up at me with his pupils fully enlarged, his eyes are almost all pupil.

"The psychic energy is...overwhelming...Ben...it's too dangerous...you can't go...our mission is lost if you..."

Jason drops to the floor, unconscious.

"Hey, Kendall, can I rest a second...I'm a little nervous...please?" I'm attempting to buy time for Craig and Jeff to help Jason.

"Ben, you must go ahead of us, with Jason out, I'm not sure how stable our spell will remain, and we should be ok, except for Kendall. Go ahead, we'll be right behind you. We need to stay out of Kendall's immediate range. We've got Jason." Craig looks to me, pleading, but with definite conviction in what he's saying.

I rush to Kendall, pleasantly stating; "Well, come on then..." He looks down the hallway behind us, toward the guys. I place my hand on his shoulder and try to move him along, all the while, trying to get his attention.

"So, does it hurt?" I ask.

"I'm sorry? Does what hurt Ben?"

"Communion...you know...turning?"

"Ben, you are potentially, the craziest human I've ever met. You go from abhorring your true destiny, to embracing it, and back again...by the minute!!!"

"Ok, so does it? Does it hurt?" Yeah, I'm the crazy one here. Right.

"It's nothing you can't handle, Ben, come now, we've many waiting for us." We continue down he hallway for what feels like an eternity. It seems impossible that any hallway could possibly be this long...I mean, I know it's a mansion, but it seems like I've walked miles!!

"Two point three miles to be exact Ben...it's nice to see you have a clear head again...I was beginning to think you would remain foggy to me forever." As we continue...I notice it gets damper...mustier maybe. I can smell mold. We must be on a decline, however slight.

I see the end of the hallway now; it's a dead end. A dead end? How can that be?

"Kendall..."

"You worry too much, young Benjamin. Fear not, all is not as it seems." Kendall places his hand on my back, and steps through the masonry and stone. We enter into what appears to be a large open courtyard. Almost like a stone quarry, where all the water has been drained. The sheer stonewalls must go up at least a thousand feet. The area appears to be about the size of eight or nine football fields. As I continue in, I see hundreds of people...or...eh...Vampires? I would probably go with my second guess. All of them in robes, each clan with a different color robe, one robe in each group has trimmed out sleeves, like Kendall's. I suppose that means that these are the masters of the clan. I see Craig and Jeff make their way through the illusionary wall, Jeff is carrying Jason. Poor little guy, he's so young to be involved in this.

Craig nods to me, as if assuring me that all is well, and to carry on.

The various faces that peer at me from under hooded visages look at me like a biker would peer at a waitress from Hooter's. You know like, I want her, but can't have her, so I'll pretend like I come here for the food... Others look at me like I'm a free buffet at a weight watchers convention. Luckily, even as some are bold enough to motion like they are approaching me, one look from Kendall forces them to back down, lowering their heads. Almost slightly bowing.

I have to say, vampires know the pecking order, no matter which clan they are from.

We finally reach Kendall's clan; here are all the familiar faces. I actually breathe a sigh of relief when reaching this group. I would never guess that I'd be glad to see ol' death breath and his cronies, but even Jessup was a sight for sore eyes. As I arrive, a couple of them, Frank, Barry, and Jessup smile. Shanestra licks her lips and blows me a kiss.

"So, Benny, how's it hangin', bud?" Jessup is giddy as a schoolgirl, who just got noticed by the high school quarter back.

"Fine." I look away, still amazed at the size of this place. Upon further inspection, I see the stone walls aren't straight up and down at all, but rather like a reverse pyramid, with ledges carved right into the stone, like giant steps going all the way around. I'd guess that the ledges protrude about a dozen feet out, then the wall is like twenty five or thirty feet tall, and the next level goes back, maybe fifteen feet and so on. Every so often, you see what appears to be a narrow stairway carved of stone, leading up to the next level.

I stop suddenly; a chill goes down my spine. I realize it's because the entire place went silent.

A succession of robed, hooded figures, carrying lit candelabras, enter the field below...at first count I'd say sixty-ish. They each take a spot in front of one of the stair cases. Then, I hear mumbling, excited, but mumbling none the less. Each clan makes their way up to a spot on the ledge. The vampires all stand in a specific spot. They are side by side, about ten feet back from the ledge, and a couple o feet apart, shoulder to shoulder. They all move as one, like soldiers doing a march, and getting into position. It's like they've trained for this for years...yet, I was told this was the first time they were brought together.

I decide to go to the edge, to look down on the open field. A murmur goes silent, as more robed figures make their way onto the field. They are followed by people...so many people...if there are forty-five hundred vampires here...that's based on nine vampires per clan, times fifty clans per ledge, times ten levels...at least that's the best I can figure...then there are at least five times that many people pouring into the field.

I want to yell, what is wrong with you people? Why are you here?

The answer comes before I can ask the question. I quickly deduce that some of the people are here wearing their favorite pro or college sports team fan wear, others rock band t-shirts, some wearing rap artists concert things, yet others are carrying bibles and singing hymns. It's as if they've all been hypnotized into thinking they are coming to a game, a concert, or a religious revival! Clever.

The people start up the stairs, taking their places on the ledges in front of the vampires. About five or six people crowd in front of each vampire, all the time hooting and hollering; "Praise the Lord", "Go State", and "B-Dizzle", whatever that means. They act like they are actually seeing something. I have to try something, It's certain suicide, but all these people will be killed...I can't live with that!

I go to the nearest person, "Sir, sir..."No response. I nudge him, no response. He's deeply in a trance.

"Ben, they can't hear or see anything now, except that which they desire to see." Kendall calmly exclaims.

"Prepare, Ben, your time and that of the Harbinger is upon us. The Final Harvest will begin!"

I spin to look at Kendall. His outstretched arms, his head tilted back. I can see the veins in his neck attempting to burst through his skin, which is barely burying them below the surface. Kendall starts to lift off the ground and as I watch him levitate slowly into the air, I hear a hushed cheer escape from the vampires (hissing and growling mostly). I look to either side and the leader of each clan is mimicking Kendall. They all slowly float off the ledges toward the center of the field in mid-air. All have arched backs, heads thrown back and arms outstretched.

As they reach the center, they all form a circle, their hands may be touching or may be inches apart, it's hard to tell. They quickly spin around to face outward, toward us. They come to a halt, forming a circle. An exact number of robed figures quickly make their way to just below the floating sires. They flip back their hoods. The one under Kendall is Pastor Frank. I can only assume that each has one from their own clan below them like

Kendall. Frank and the others disrobe. They are standing now, in nothing but bare skin and what looks like cloth diapers. Well, at least this isn't an x-rated Final Harvest, death of all mankind. We wouldn't want to offend the church goers....before eating their life essence.

I see three more figures carrying a round object, blanketed in a large burgundy tapestry. They set it in the center of the circle. And hurry away. Thousands of thralls pour into the field. The vampires with Frank all step toward the object. They yank the blanket off, revealing a large silver, mirrored sphere, kind of like a giant garden ball. Never understood what those were for...

All the vampires on the ground place their hands on the sphere. The sphere jumps to life, emitting a blinding flash of light, and as my vision clears, I see Frank and the others stand as their very flesh appears to burn off of them, starting from the hands and quickly eating its way up their arse...eventually consuming them completely. Nothing but ashes is left in their place. It's gut wrenching. I turn to Jessup.

"That's what the priests do bub." Jessup smiles.

Frank was a priest? A Vampire Priest? That's wrong on so many levels. I almost feel sorry for those vampires...almost.

I turn to Jeff and Craig and Jason, they look horrified. I shrug my shoulders; they nod, as if knowing there's nothing any of us can do yet.

I turn back. The large silver ball starts to shudder. Then cracks start to form, emitting light from them, like a giant egg cracking open. As the cracks enlarge beams of light fire into the sky. Dark clouds immediately roll in. Shadows overtake the entire area. The only light we notice, is that coming from the orb. Thunderous booms shake the very area, making it difficult to keep our footing. A dense fog rolls down from the skies. The fog breaks into four different wisps. The wisps, smoky-thick, start to take form, like that of ghost? Like, torsos and heads followed by a trail of smoke where their legs would be. Mostly, they're transparent at first, but then you start to see veins and bone. The wisps or phantoms if you will, zip back and forth, all over the place. They dive and fly and whiz all over. They then dive and smash into the Thralls. As they make contact, the Thralls almost instantly turn into dust. Aw, these were just kids! The Thralls worshipped the vampires! And Casper and his unfriendly buddies are vaporizing them! Enough!

I step through the people to the edge, the wisps now have some muscle and tissue forming. They're still incomplete, but they are taking on human form. Crap, are there four Harbingers? We only have one Athame. Out of pure anger, I yell to Kendall. "Stop this! I'll do whatever you want! Stop all this killing!"

A hand is set on my shoulder. I am spun around facing Jessup.

"Kendall can't help ya kid, those guys are the Elders. The Undead Gods. They've come to start the Final Harvest, but until the Harbinger arrives, they can't take full form. So guess what kid, you're up, as they say." Jessup steps back.

"Ben!" Jeff yells out.

I spin back around to see four partially formed creatures floating behind me. Staring intently at me, they start to reach out...

Chapter Twenty-One
Decisions

I immediately step back. These are ugly and scary to say the least. Before I can make another move. I feel my body being ripped from the ground. I get yanked upward, into the sky. One must be holding me up. Suddenly, I feel a steely jab, as one of them flies through me. It feels like I was just stabbed, the wind's knocked out of me. They all take turns and I call for help. The vampires erupt in cheers! My clothes are being shredded. My skin is in turn being lacerated. I see my own blood squirt out, as each passing creates more gashes. I barely remain conscious, the pain is so unbearable. I start to black out.

But wait, I feel the pain is easing. I look down at myself. I'm not cut at all; not a single bruise, not a single injury. I am still naked though, that's a little uncomfortable, but I feel great. I feel, I don't know, like I am weightless, like I can fly? The Undead Gods have backed off of me. I will myself back to the ledge from where I came. As I arrive, Jessup and Denny drape a robe over me, bow and back away. They drop to one knee, and lower their heads. I turn and see every vampire doing the same thing.

Kendall and all the Masters are now on the ground maintain the same position. They're all bowing to me? Why?

Wait...my family was killed in a car crash! Ellen was right! I remember now. I was lying there dying, someone lifted me from the wreckage, I was saved. I was turned already? My benefactor, I don't know who he or she was, but my mission is now becoming clear. I was returned to my human state, to stop the Wiccans from figuring out that I am...the Harbinger. Those who Walked Before, saved me, turned me, and made me human again until, today!

I am the Harbinger! I am destined to usher in the Final Harvest! Finally, it is time for my kind to triumph!

I will myself to once again take to the air. I float out to the very center of the field. I slowly turn, and let all see that their savior has arrived. I raise my arms. All of the vampires stand to position. A stone pedestal bursts out of the ground raising itself, as a stone column, stopping just below my feet.

I lower myself to the pedestal. The Four come and land next to me, nearly formed now. I...am the final piece to the puzzle. At my word, all of my minions will drain the humans. Not just the ones here, for you see, I have this same set up happening all around the world. Nearly every human being is at one Harvest Sight or another. How glorious for us complete that of which we have been depraved for centuries!

I hear a small voice, its Craig...and Jeff.

"Ben, what are you doing? What's happening?" they yell out to me. They are my friends. They came with me. They risked their lives. I remember now...so many have died trying to help me accomplish this task.

Stopping the Harbinger, the ultimate harvester. All of those humans…all will die. The Human race will face Genocide; the planet will be rid of all human life. That can't be right!

Can it? I mean, I was human, wasn't I?

"Ben, stop this now! They will obey you!" Craig pleads out.

Is this any worse than they want of my kind? Would the humans not just as well be rid of us? Monsters, they call us, when we are truly their masters! We created them for food for us! They treat us like creatures, not as their superior race at all!

I will not let MY kind go extinct! I raise both of my arms, lurching Craig and Jeff off their feet. Jeff pulls out his gun and I laugh as his man made metal slugs strike me.

"Start with these two!" I scream. While moving at a speed still surprising to me, the Four Elders fly over and rip them apart. Their screams affect me not.

They were mere cattle to the Kings. I announce in a voice that carries to every Harvest Site around the globe. "Let the Harvest Begin!" I summon the Gods back to me. All the Vampires stand ready, when I lower my arms, we shall be raised to the level of existence we deserve! We shall achieve pure astral form and be free of this earth, and take our place along side the Undead Elders!!!! We Shall….

Wait…my back…a burning sensation, I can't catch my breath…my limbs grow weak, I can't stop shaking… There, behind me, Jason…he stands, staring. I reach around to my back…I feel the hot, metallic handle of…the ATHAME!!! Jason, that child, stabbed me with the ATHAME!!!

Am I lost then? I find that I've dropped to my knees…Damn him! Damn him! I swat him off my pedestal and watch as the little witch boy falls into the grasp of some of my minions, and I smile as he is devoured!

I reach around…and rip the Athame out of my body! I stand once again, holding this damned instrument. Why? Why would so many of our cattle sacrifice themselves to stop me? Even I did willingly risk my life, when I was one of them. Didn't I?

Are we so different then? Have they not achieved an equal right to live? If

I order in the Harvest, the totality of human spirit will be forever vanquished. Who am I to make that decision?

Damn them all to Hell!

The Gods only await the final order, for I am their vessel. I speak for them until the Harvest is completed. Mason and the others entrusted me to finish this task...to be savior of the human race entire!

Who am I?

Whom do I serve...to whom do I owe my allegiance?

Whom do I lead?

I remember parents, friends...and I sacrificed them all. All of them, dead, because of me. And Ellen...oh my God! Ellen!

Except, they are but livestock, are they not? Humans eat animals, and we eat humans. With little or no remorse, we all do what we must to survive. I am confused. I have been given the power to do this thing. Yet, I WILL not be responsible for the death of so many. I remain unconvinced.

With nary a thought I plunge the dagger deep into my own chest. The ember flames of the Athame wash over me, scorching and paralyzing me. I don't even feel it, when in slow motion I hit the ground. With what little strength I have left, I open my eyes and see the Elder Gods, hearing their silent screams as their solid bodies begin to peel off. In a fit of anger and retribution, the Elder Undead Gods release a form of energy that blasts from their solidified bodies in waves, and as the waves strike the Thralls and lower caste of vampires, this invisible energy shreds each underling. The true vampires and Masters are knocked off their feet.

The humans apparently take advantage of this bedlam and flee in a panic. Through slitted eyelids, I see Kendall and Jessup approach. They gaze down at me, unaware that I am semi-conscious still.

"Stupid kid, he had it all, we almost did it. I told ya he was good for nothin'!" Jessup says. I hear the people-panicking, running and screaming, vampires attacking and fleeing, total chaos.

"Well, Jessup, I suppose that just means someone else is up for promotion." Kendall calmly states.

"So who will the Elders pick?" Jessup questions.

"Well, my friend, whomever they pick, I'm sure I'll need a right hand man."

Jessup blurts out… "You mean…"

"Yes, Jessup, the Final Harvest will happen again, only this time with a new Harbinger".

A sly smile creeps across the lips of Kendall Ontolli.

The End?

BEHIND THE SHADOWS
by Susan C. Finelli

Born into squalor, Raymond Nasco's quest for wealth and power shrouds two generations with deceit, murder, rape and illicit love. Setting his sights above and beyond the family's two-room apartment in a New York City lower eastside tenement, Raymond befriends Guy Straga, the son of a wealthy business tycoon, and they develop a lifelong friendship and bond. Caught in Raymond's powerful grip, his wife, Adele, commits the ultimate sin; and his son, Spencer, betrays himself and the woman he loves and finally becomes his father's son. Years later Kay Straga stumbles upon the secret that has been lurking in the shadows of the Straga and Nasco families for two generations, a secret that tempts her with forbidden love, a secret that once uncovered will keep her in its clutches from which there is no escape.

Paperback, 292 pages
6" x 9"
ISBN 1-4241-8974-8

About the author:

Susan C. Finelli has lived in New York all of her life and has been a Manhattanite for over thirty years. She, her husband John, and Riley Rian, their beloved cavalier King Charles spaniel, currently reside in Manhattan, and together they enjoy exploring the sights, sounds and vibrancy of the Big Apple.